Beads of Doubt

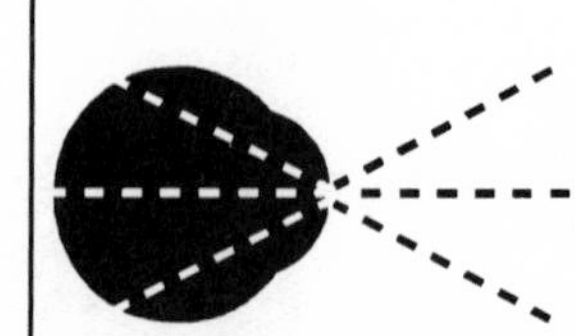

This Large Print Book carries the Seal of Approval of N.A.V.H.

Beads of Doubt

Barbara Burnett Smith

with Karen MacInerney

WHEELER PUBLISHING

An imprint of Thomson Gale, a part of The Thomson Corporation

Detroit • New York • San Francisco • New Haven, Conn. • Waterville, Maine • London

A Kitzi Camden Mystery.
Wheeler, an imprint of The Gale Group.
Thomson and Star Logo and Wheeler are trademarks and Gale is a registered trademark used herein under license.

Wheeler Publishing Large Print Cozy Mystery.
The text of this Large Print edition is unabridged.
Other aspects of the book may vary from the original edition.
Set in 16 pt. Plantin.

LIBRARY OF CONGRESS CATALOGING-IN-PUBLICATION DATA

Smith, Barbara Burnett.
Beads of doubt / by Barbara Burnett Smith with Karen MacInerney.
p. cm. — (Wheeler publishing large print cozy mystery)
"A Kitzi Camden Mystery" — T.p. verso.
ISBN-13: 978-1-59722-646-2 (softcover : alk. paper)
ISBN-10: 1-59722-646-7 (softcover : alk. paper)
1. Mothers and daughters — Fiction. 2. Inheritance and succession — Fiction. 3. Southern States — Fiction. 4. Large type books. I. MacInerney, Karen, 1970– II. Title.
PS3569.M483B43 2007
813'.54—dc22 2007029989

Published in 2007 by arrangement with The Berkley Publishing Group, a member of Penguin Group (USA) Inc.

Printed in the United States of America on permanent paper
10 9 8 7 6 5 4 3 2 1

Beads of Doubt

One

"Ms. Camden, the letter was sent to you two weeks ago, and you signed for it. It is vital that you . . ."

Outside my second-story window a teal and white tent was being erected on the west lawn. The tent was sixty by eighty feet with the hugest stripes I had ever seen in my life. It was also being dragged perilously close, I mean within inches, of my begonia bed.

"Excuse me, Mr. Warrington —"

"Harrington."

"Mr. Harrington. I have a situation here that I need to handle, and I would be happy to call you back in a few days." I was fumbling with the window, which was refusing to move.

I love my house, all eight thousand square feet of it, and I even love most of its idiosyncrasies. The same kind you'll find in every old house. At that particular moment, however, I was not particularly in love with this particular stuck window.

"Go up," I commanded under my breath, but the window didn't budge.

The Camden Manse, as it's known, was built by my grandfather back in the twenties when he was governor. When I was a child, over fifty years ago, I thought if heaven was all it was cracked up to be, then it must be just like this house. With the wisdom of age I now think that if the house and heaven are alike, God must have an easier time keeping his place in good repair than I do mine, although I try my best.

I jerked at the window again and it flew up so unexpectedly I almost fell out. "Hello — hello!" I shouted at the truck driver, but he wasn't hearing me.

On the telephone Mr. Harrington sounded exasperated. "Ms. Camden, you must read the letter today."

Patience has never been my strong suit. In fact, I'm not sure I even have that suit. "Mr. Harrington, tomorrow we are having the Bead Tea for ovarian cancer on my grounds. There will be thirty-four vendors and artisans, tea for hundreds being served in the conservatory, and right now, even as I speak to you" — I looked out the window and yelped — "a truck is backing toward my begonia bed."

"That is not really important. This letter is about your future."

I turned away from the window. "Fine. Mr. Harrington, what is in this letter that is so terribly important it can't wait for three days?"

"You need to read the letter."

I huffed. "So you've said, but at the moment I can't read the letter. I don't even remember signing for it. That may have been my mother." Who, at seventy-nine years old, is as elegant and charming as she ever was. She still has a great memory, too; it's just short. She could have signed for the letter, then sent it off to her cousin, or thrown it out.

I knew for sure she hadn't given it to me. "Mr. Harrington, you are going to have to tell me —"

"I'll fax you a copy."

"I don't have a fax. Sinatra, my cat, ate the rubber and I haven't replaced it. If you want some action, then you'd better explain the urgency." I used the same firm tone I used to use on lobbyists when I was in the Texas Senate. "I have three minutes to spare, but that's all."

"All right, if this is the way it has to be." He sounded testy.

"It is."

"The letter states that you are, at this time, in possession of the Camden Manse and are occupying both the main house and the gatehouse."

Since I was standing in one of the upstairs guest rooms of the main house, it seemed to me the letter wasn't terribly informative, and he was using up his allotted time pretty quickly with this statement of the obvious. "My mother lives in the gatehouse, but that's close. And I knew that all along."

His tone got a little snippier. "The letter also states that there have been some changes in the corporation that controls the Camden Manse —"

"There have been no changes to the corporation."

"The changes are in the way the shares are being voted."

That got my full attention as every drop of blood in my body sank to someplace below my knees. "What voting changes?"

"You no longer have sufficient votes to maintain occupancy. Therefore, you need to move out within thirty days. Actually, that would be about fourteen days now. If you had only read the letter, this would not be coming as a shock to you."

I thought I might fall over.

"That's not possible," I said. This was my home. I loved this house as much as anything in the world. My grandfather had built it, and when I was just six he had promised me that I would someday live here. Many years later, after he died and my grandmother had no longer wanted the burden of the Manse, she moved into the gatehouse and my parents and I had moved into the main house.

When I got married I lived elsewhere, but the house has a way of choosing its own, and after the divorce and my father's death, my mother needed help. In fact, just six years ago nobody in the family would take the place. Of course, that was before I'd inspected every inch of it and spent all the income from my trust to restore it.

Mr. Harrington was going on, ". . . therefore, a meeting of the corporation board has been called, but that is just a —"

"Mr. Harrington, I want two answers. And I'll bet you I already know what they are. Number one, who are you representing?"

"Mr. Houston David Webber."

"No surprise." Whenever there was a problem in the family, you could bet that my cousin Houston had something to do with it. It had been that way since we'd been kids. "And, who," I went on, "is changing the way they vote?"

"I'm not at liberty —"

"Fax that letter to my attorney." I snapped out the name.

"Certainly," he said. "I'm pleased that I have finally convinced you of the gravity of my call."

"I assure you, Mr. Harrington, I am suitably grave." I looked out the window and saw that the truck was now in the begonias. "Get out of there!" I yelled, but of course, he couldn't hear me.

Mr. Harrington went on, "Ms. Camden, please. We need to discuss some things. There are some arrangements that —"

"Mr. Harrington, at this minute I don't have time to discuss anything with you. I have to get that damn truck out of my begonias, and I've got to have a very intense talk with Houston." I took a breath and said, "Have a nice day."

Then I hung up and stuck my head out the window. The truck was now *parked* in the begonias.

I grabbed something off the night stand, took aim, and threw. A solid and very satisfying smack let me know I'd hit the hood of the truck. I looked to see what I'd thrown and realized that I had pitched the one thing that might have helped. It was

The Little Book of Calm.

Oh, well, I wouldn't have read it anyway.

Two

The shortest distance between two points is a straight line, so I went flying down the back staircase, the faster to get to my car and to my cousin Houston. While he has every right in the world to try and take the Manse away from me, I have every right to fight him right down to the door of the moving vans. That's what I intended to do, although this little bombshell, coming out of the blue, or the Ethernet, is pretty typical of Houston.

In Apollo 13 when the space mission went awry they created that famous line, "Houston, we have a problem." My brother and I have always said it a little differently: We have a problem; it's Houston.

I was halfway down the stairs, traveling at about the same speed as the Apollo, when my cat came flying down behind me. He miscalculated, passed me up, and landed under my right foot. I grabbed the banister to avoid stepping on him, and Sinatra did a tuck and roll that would have impressed Nadia Comaneci.

"Sinatra!" I shouted, doing a pretty good midair gyration myself. "Cat, you cannot do that. You are going to kill someone."

He stretched out and rolled over on his stomach, the better to have his fawn-colored belly petted.

A voice came up the staircase. "Nice to see Sinatra hasn't changed his ways." I looked down to find my friend Beth Fairfield watching us.

"He's as charming as ever," I said, patting Sinatra briefly. Sinatra originally belonged to Beth, but before he was four months old she knew he'd never work in their family. At least not with her husband Ron around. Then we caught the philandering Ron in the midst of a philander, and a month ago the two separated. It's just a trial separation. I hope the jury makes it permanent, but I don't say that. I also don't let Beth hear me call Ron "Mo-Ron," which is my very apt nickname for him. "Let me guess, you're here early because Ron has changed his mind and wants you back. And Sinatra," I said, making my way more carefully down the last of the stairs. Sinatra was now purring so loudly that the sound echoed all through the hall and the kitchen.

"Wrong on both counts." I heard the little catch in her voice and it worried me. Beth and I have been friends since we were eight and met at summer camp. I may not think much of Ron, but she loved him enough to marry him and have two children, Shannan and Brian, who are now almost completely grown.

"Are you okay? I thought you weren't coming over until the reception. What's up?" I picked up my purse off the dining room table.

"Long story." She sighed and I stopped to give her my full attention. "The short version is that Ron sailed in last night and announced to Shannan that they needed some time together, so he was taking her to San Francisco for a week. Starting Saturday."

Tightwad Mo-Ron, Mr. Ultraconservative, was doing something on the spur of the moment. He should have started that habit years ago. "And what did you say?" I asked.

"You'd be proud of me. I said, 'Oh, Ron, isn't that sweet of you, but I wish you'd given me some notice. The Bead Tea is this weekend, and I promised Kitzi I'd stay at the Manse and help her. The two of you will have to go without me.' Like he'd bothered to invite me."

"Way to go, Beth." We did a high five.

"Yes, but then I had to pack and get out of there. You don't mind, do you?"

"Absolutely not; I'm delighted. You can have any room in the house, including mine, but I'm on a mission now, so we'll have to bring your things in later."

"No problem. Where are we going?" She straightened the runner on the table, which I'd mussed, and followed me into the kitchen. "What happened in here?"

The kitchen is long and wide and vanilla. The only things not antique white are the natural wood counters and the sinks, which are metal. It needs color and some pizzazz, but pizzazz takes energy and time, and after all the other work I've done on the house, I've run out of both. Today the place was particularly drab because the counters were absolutely barren. Not a piece of paper, not a dirty dish or a canister in sight.

I glanced around at the newly empty counters. "For the caterers. They'll need every inch of counter space and more."

During parties this is the staging area and it buzzes with activity. Caterers putting last minute touches on trays and plates of food so delicious looking they would tempt Gandhi on a hunger strike. Waiters whizzing in and out of doors, and the organizers, overseeing, double-checking, and making sure that everything runs smoothly.

Our family has always believed in not only sharing the Manse with organizations, but also helping out when someone is shorthanded. My grandparents started that tradition, and my parents and I have carried it on. As a child I liked the time before and after a party best. Before is when you can sneak a taste of one of the ripest strawberries and the most scrumptious desserts. Afterward always seemed fun to me, too, because that's when the stories start getting told. As a child I used to beg my grandparents to let me stay here during a party. When they said yes, I'd get paid a quarter to help with the cleanup, only it wasn't the money I was after. I loved to hear the adults talking. *"Did you see that woman in red? I heard that she . . ."* I learned pretty fast that as long as I kept my mouth shut and kept working, no one paid any attention to me. The minute I stopped to look at whomever was talking I got sent to my room.

Even now, there are times when the cleanup is as much fun as the event itself.

Beth opened the door and we stepped outside into as beautiful a clear June day as you could ask for. The tent was repositioned and apparently about to be raised. The big pecan trees fluttered above it, and the begonias in the bed to the right of it were blooming a clear pink except where they'd been run over.

My mother stood by, still with her clipboard. She looked as regal and lovely as she ever had, if a bit more worn from her seventy-some years. Think of Pat Nixon in her seventies, only more petite.

Today she was wearing tan slacks and a mint green sweater. From the back you might mistake her slender figure for that of a teenager, except she was too well dressed and her peachy blonde hair isn't a shade or style seen on today's youth. She turned and caught sight of us.

She and I have the same light coloring, although I'm four inches taller and outweigh her by a good twenty-five pounds. I don't have my hair done as often, either, so mine is more blonde with what I like to call silver highlights.

"Beth, I've been meaning to tell you how good you're looking," she said as we neared her.

"Thank you, Mrs. Camden."

My mother was right. Since the first revelation of Ron's extramarital activities, Beth has lost twenty-one pounds with only forty-five to go. By her count. She has cut her hair in a style that looks like a modern version of the old shag, and she's started spending money on a new wardrobe for herself. A first. Used to be that Beth spent money on everyone but herself. Today she was in beige crop pants with a sage green T-shirt. In her hand were sunglasses that looked like something purchased from the estate of Jacqueline Kennedy.

"How are you doing?"

"I'm lovely, thank you. We are having a few problems getting ready for tonight, though." The paper-thin wrinkle on her forehead creased a tad further. "Kitzi, I've asked the driver to keep the tent six feet from the flower beds. That way people won't be forced into them if they walk around the tent."

"Excellent idea."

She looked down at the paper on her clipboard. "I have also told him that I expect someone to replace the damaged plants by two this afternoon." She dropped her voice and leaned closer to us. "It's early enough that if the plants don't arrive, we can do the replacing before the opening cocktail party this evening."

My mother is half terrier and half Dresden doll. She can be so precious and petite,

I can't help feeling protective. And I've seen her terrify a whole crew of burly workmen. Come to think of it, she's done that to me, too. It's when she wants everything to be "nice." Her *nice* stands for absolutely-no-kidding-downright perfect. An impossible standard she demands of herself and the rest of us. I try to disappear when she's in one of those moods — not to protect myself, but to keep family harmony.

"I'll pick up some flowers while I'm out," I said.

She noticed the keys dangling from my fingers and frowned. "You can't possibly think of leaving right now. The caterers will be arriving, and the chairs and tables are going to be delivered. There are a thousand things to be done."

For the moment, everything we could do was already taken care of, but apparently she was in one of her moods. I should have been tipped off by the clipboard. "Mother, don't worry. Several of the women from the OCO will be here shortly. Plus the volunteers from the Bead Society. They're in charge of this." OCO is the Ovarian Cancer Organization, the official sponsors of the Bead Tea.

"Kitzi, it is our responsibility to be here and help."

"I won't be gone long; I just need to run out and see a lawyer."

"What lawyer? And why in the world would you schedule an appointment today?"

"Something just came up. It's for Houston." My mother is a sucker for Houston, as are most older women. Especially his mother, my aunt Miranda, who always says that he is the light of her existence. When we were kids and she said it, I always thought he was a pretty dim bulb and she must live in a cave, but I never said it out loud. Well, maybe once or twice to Houston, but never to her.

"Is he all right?" my mother asked. "He's not hurt —"

"Nothing like that. Just some legal thing with some silly deadline." I was not going to let my mother worry about Houston taking over the Manse. If I loved the Manse, she obsessed over it. Six years ago, when the doctor told her that she needed to turn it over to someone else because it was killing her, she was devastated. As tough as it was on her, though, she did it all in her own inimitable style.

The Manse is actually owned by a family corporation created by my grandfather. Every member of the family is a stockholder, and provisions were made for new members who joined the clan either by birth or marriage. Divorce is figured in, too. I don't understand the numbers of voting shares or the percentages, but that's never been an issue. It certainly wasn't the day my mother gave up residency.

She'd had her lawyer send out meeting notices to all the family members, and everyone showed up as if it were a funeral. There were canapés and drinks for all, until it was time to call the gathering to order. Mother did that, proud and as tall as she could stand at the head of the table. She explained that she could no longer care for the house and she was ready to turn it over to someone else. There was no self-pity; I was the one feeling teary eyed. As I looked around the room, several others seemed sad, too, although one or two seemed eager.

Then Mother pulled out a stack of bound presentation folders and passed them around for all of us to see. It was an inventory of the contents of the house, and the results of an inspection. I skimmed through the papers, as did the others. Muttering started and expressions turned to surprise. Even I was stunned.

Oh, I knew the house needed a coat of paint and some other things, but I was so used to seeing it that I just didn't notice.

That inspection brought reality crashing down on all our heads.

According to the report there was a serious foundation problem that had caused cracks in the walls and had jammed many of the windows. The plumbing was rotting. The water was not up to drinkable standards, and there were leaks inside some walls. The leaks had caused mold, and the old aluminum wiring was considered a fire hazard.

Those were just the major problems.

All in all, the cost for repairs was so high that the corporation didn't have the funds to cover it. People started muttering. Uncle Larry, the senator, said, "How reliable is the company that did the inspection?"

"Very reliable," my mother responded. She sighed but her head remained unbowed. "I've been fighting these problems for years, but there's never been enough time or money to get it all done. I'm afraid one of you has some work in your future."

Except one by one they all declined. No one wanted to spend that much of their own funds on the Manse. Some didn't have the money, and others didn't want to part with it. Some lived away from Austin, and the remaining few didn't want the responsibility. In the end it came down to my brother and me. Stephen was rubbing his forehead, thinking hard. At that point in his life he was going through a divorce, his second, and I knew that money was tight.

He dropped his shoulders in defeat. "I decline." He looked at my mother. "I'm sorry, Mom, I just can't."

She nodded, then turned to me. A quote, I think from Dale Carnegie, kept running through my head: "If it's to be done, you are the one."

I loved the Manse, but I had my own house that I'd recently remodeled after my kids had gone off to college. It was fresh and sparkling, with the peace and tranquility that comes when the workmen finally leave.

I had looked at my mother and seen the hopeful expression on her face.

"Lillian," my uncle asked, "where will you go if you leave the Manse?"

She hesitated and finally said, "I've been looking at houses, but I've finally come to the conclusion that an apartment might be best. Or a duplex."

That had been the deciding factor. My mother had dedicated her entire life to others, and I was not going to let her spend her senior years in an apartment with a sea of asphalt parking lot around her and some rapper upstairs blowing out his speakers.

"I'll take over the Manse," I said, stepping toward the conference table. "You can move into the gatehouse, Mother. We'll remodel it first, so you have somewhere nice to live."

Everyone cheered, grateful that they hadn't gotten stuck with the job. Or the Manse. The bar was reopened, and I was toasted repeatedly.

Within days I was hard at work, selling my house, finding a contractor, making up plans for modernizing, all the while letting my training business slip because of all the time it took.

I wrangled with carpenters, plumbers, and electricians to keep it architecturally authentic, while making sure it was sound and functioning smoothly. I fought off termites, black mold, and the city council that wanted to "annex" half the grounds for some electrical substation. I even cleaned almost every inch of it on my hands and knees.

In the end it was all worth it. The Manse is now beautifully restored, and I've added modern conveniences to boot. The kitchen isn't up to par appearancewise yet, but it will be eventually. We've turned the gatehouse into a little charmer. Before it had been nothing more than a large toolshed with a small mudroom. Some of the walls hadn't even been finished. Now it is elegant and charming. There are pegged hardwood floors, a fireplace, a small but colorful kitchen, a spa bath, and a brick patio out back. We've put up window boxes and added a flower-bordered walkway from the front gate. Mother and I did much of the planting and decorating together. She calls it her nest, and I couldn't stand the thought of her losing it.

Which is why I had to get moving. I'd bet my hormone pills that if Houston got the Manse my mother would be out of the gatehouse and looking for a place to live before her next phone bill was due. "I'll be back as soon as possible."

"Who is this lawyer?" Mother asked.

"His name was Warrington, I think. No, it's Harrington."

"Not Edward Harrington?" She suddenly looked wary.

"I don't think so," I said, only because it seemed important to reassure her. "Why? Do you know an Edward Harrington?"

"A little. From years ago when your father was in office. But how can you go see the man if you can't remember his name?"

"I have his address written down," I said, waving my purse. "Mother, don't worry.

Everything is under control. Really. Tell her, Beth."

Before Beth could speak my mother said, "Beth, maybe you can talk some sense into Kitzi."

"It would be a first," Beth said. "I could chauffeur her, though, which might get her back faster."

"Is that fast?" My mother looked at Beth's red PT Cruiser and shook her head. "I would think it's a little young for you, but you're going through a trying time."

"We'll hurry," I called over my shoulder as I moved toward the driveway. "I have my cell phone if you need me."

"Guess she didn't like my car," Beth said, popping on the oversized glasses and climbing into the Cruiser.

"As we've noted before, she's a tad more conservative than we are. Don't take it personally."

"I don't. So where am I taking you?"

"We're going to see Houston and wreak some havoc."

"My kind of day."

Three

I spent most of the trip to Houston's office trying to explain to Beth the shares and how they are voted in the corporation that actually owns the Manse.

"You don't really understand yourself, do you?" Beth asked when we pulled into the parking lot.

"No. But I can explain the Electoral College and how that came into being."

"Thanks, but I'll pass."

"Well . . ." I said, looking up at the plain-Jane, white building. It's on a hillside across from Pease Park in what used to be near the center of Austin. "Here's the deal. If I'm not back in thirty minutes, come in and get me."

"Why? Will Houston be holding you captive?"

"No, but I could be seriously hurting him."

"Then I'm coming in." Beth got out

of the car.

"Okay, but if I start throwing things, you better duck. My aim isn't what it used to be."

We went up the cracked concrete staircase, then through the doors into his office, where things were dramatically different. The receptionist's desk was made of polished mahogany, dark and rich looking, like the office of someone important. Behind her was a panel of the same wood with an inset of etched glass, but the kicker was the rug. It was a hand-knotted Mashad, a good ten feet by twelve in a shimmering cranberry red with a design of cream and faded turquoise. I'm not an expert on oriental rugs, but the Mashad had been in the front hall of the Manse when I was a kid and my mother was big on having us appreciate the beautiful things around us. When it was decided that my parents would take over the house, they had insisted that Aunt Miranda take the Mashad and some of her other favorite furnishings.

Ridiculous though it might be, it still galled me that some of them had made their way here.

"Can I help you?" the young woman at the front desk asked. She was not anyone I'd seen before, nor was she dressed like anyone I'd seen around here before.

Austin is casual; you can wear jeans to everything including your own funeral. This woman was not in jeans. She was wearing an ivory crepe pantsuit with a string of small creamy pearls at her throat. Her dark hair was down and straight. The Mashad of receptionists.

"Yes, you can help me," I said. "I need to see Houston Webber."

"Certainly. Do you have an appointment?"

"No, I don't. I'm Kitzi Camden and I'll bet you a hundred dollars that he's expecting me."

Not only did she not recognize my last name, which in Texas is in every history textbook, but she also didn't get my joke. "He's very busy today; may I make an appointment for tomorrow?"

"Won't be convenient," I said.

"Perhaps next week?"

"Not to worry, I'll just pop in on him." I stepped around the panel behind her and saw four doors.

"You can't go back there!"

"Of course I can. I just did." I heard voices behind the door on my right and started in that direction.

"There's a meeting — you can't —"

I stopped and asked quite reasonably, "Then where is Houston?"

A door that had been ajar opened and Houston stepped through. "Kitzi Camden. My favorite cousin!" He was tallish and slim, with sleek, prematurely gray hair. His smile showed off his teeth, and he had his arms open as if he were going to hug me.

"Houston," I said, keeping well back from him, "we need to talk."

He looked at the young woman. "Lauren, I'd like to introduce you to my cousin." He stepped forward and tried to put an arm around me, but I dodged. He went on, "I'm sure you've heard me mention her, the infamous Katherine Camden. She was senator here in Texas."

"Yes, of course." Lauren's annoyance fell away and she smiled, back to lovely and gracious. Houston has a lot of flaws, but he somehow has the smarts to surround himself with exceptional women. "How do you do, Ms. Camden?" she said.

"Fine, and thank you for asking," I said. "This is my friend, Beth Fairfield. Houston, I'm sure you remember Beth."

"Of course." He shook her hand, looking happy, maybe because someone was willing to touch him. "So, Kitzi, shall you and I go into my office? This won't take but a moment, Lauren."

"Glad to hear it," I said. "Beth, you come along, too."

"Maybe we should —" Houston began.

"Have a witness," I finished for him. "I couldn't agree more."

He didn't take us back to the room he'd been in, but to the one next door, obviously his office, since there were pictures of him and his wife, Rebecca, on the carved credenza behind the desk. Rebecca is the primary exceptional woman in his life.

Now, I'm not an expert on offices. However, my own, which I call the epicenter of my empire, was originally designed to be British Colonial, but it has evolved into a hard-work area with too many papers, too many cords, and too many files.

Houston's space doesn't appear to have evolved at all. It was still an elegant Ralph Lauren gentlemen's office in mahogany, hunter green, and navy blue. There were no papers, although he did have a computer. One of those slick little silver models often compared to executive jewelry.

Once Beth and I were seated in the client chairs, Houston took his rightful spot behind the massive desk and leaned forward. "Miss Kitzi, what brings you to my humble offices?"

"Well, Houston, why do you think I came here?"

He smiled. "Now, Kitzi, the last thing I want to do is rile you," he said with a smile. "It's about the Manse, isn't it? I'm so sorry that we didn't get to talk before Edward called you. It's just been chaotic."

A phone call would have taken five minutes, and he'd had a fair amount of time to do it, since Edward Harrington claimed he'd sent me the letter two weeks ago. I wasn't buying it.

"Bottom line," I said, "is that you want me out of the Manse, and you've got the votes to make it happen."

"Oh, Kitzi, you're my favorite cousin," he said like he really meant it. "And I've hurt your feelings. That was the last thing I wanted to do."

My daughter used to make gagging sounds when I said things she wasn't buying, and I thought now was an appropriate time to make one myself, but I held back.

"My feelings are just fine, thank you," I said.

"Now, Kitz," Houston went on, "you know that Grandfather was a man who believed in fairness, and he loved his family. All of us. Your side of the family has enjoyed living in the Manse ever since he passed away —"

"At the request of your side of the family. And we've paid all the taxes and all the upkeep and improvements."

"You've been wonderful caretakers of the family tradition."

Beth was watching us patiently waiting for something to happen, but I kept my composure.

"Thank you," I said, more politely than I wanted to. "However, you make us sound like pirates, or squatters, which we both know isn't so. When my mother begged for someone to take over the place, I noticed that you didn't jump up and volunteer."

"And you were glad I didn't."

"Wrong. I didn't want to leave my house, which if you'll remember, I had just finished remodeling. My business suffered a huge setback because I had to plunk a whole lot of time into the Manse."

"So now I'm ready to step up and take my turn at the Manse," Houston said. This man went in more circles than a merry-go-round. "I'll take the burden off of you —"

"Don't give me bullshit, Houston."

Out of the corner of my eye I saw Beth grinning.

Houston leaned forward earnestly. "Kitzi, it's really for Rebecca. You know the statistics on ovarian cancer." I surely did: three to five hard years and no cure. Ever. "I'm doing this for Rebecca."

"Houston, if I believed that I'd start packing tomorrow."

When Rebecca and Houston married, they moved into his house, which we all called Tudor Hacienda. Nice neighborhood, ugly house. Rebecca had turned it into a Mediterranean showplace, with an enclosed courtyard, fountains, and lush gardens. She loved that house with well-earned pride, and I'd never heard her say a word that made me think she'd want to leave it.

"It's true," Houston said.

"I thought Rebecca just finished chemo? How can you saddle her with an eight-thousand-square-foot house? You don't have any idea how much work that is."

"Staff, Kitzi," he said as if I weren't bright.

"This isn't the Victorian era and you aren't king. Who's going to manage the staff?"

"I am, of course."

I snorted, which wasn't ladylike, but was quite appropriate. "Oh, right. That's a full-time job, too, and you can't do that and still run a business full-time. Believe me, I know because I've tried to do both." My voice was getting louder, but I didn't care. This man made no sense. "I had to let my trainers go and now it's just me, coaching and training people. And the Manse isn't just time consuming, it's expensive. You don't have that kind of money, Houston Webber, and I can assure you that I am *not* going to bail you out when you get into trouble." Which to my shame I'd done twice before. "And one more thing: all you had to do was call me! You didn't need some lawyer to phone me or start sending letters."

The door swung open. "Excuse me!" A man stepped in and closed the door. He was a Houston clone, except ten years younger and a few inches shorter. He was dressed like Houston in dark slacks with a light blue, French-cuffed shirt, and his dark hair, sleekly cut like Houston's, was even beginning to gray.

"Andrew," Houston said, welcoming him with relief. "Is the meeting over?"

"No." Andrew jerked his head indicating the room next door. "Our new clients were a little concerned about all the noise." Then he looked at me. The irritation disappeared as he suddenly smiled. "Ms. Camden. How are you? I didn't know you were here."

"Yes, I'm afraid she was getting a little excited," Houston said.

Andrew held out his hand to me. "You

probably don't remember me. I'm Andrew Lynch," he said with a smile.

"Of course I do, Andrew," I said, trying not to sound annoyed. False modesty was one of Houston's ploys, as well. "This is my friend, Beth Fairfield." I shook his hand, then returned my attention to Houston. "So, you're sticking to this?"

"I think we ought to talk about this later," Houston said. He smiled, making his eyes warm and sweet. That look hadn't charmed me since I was seven and he'd used it to con me out of all my birthday money.

I was about to ask one more question when Andrew sat down on the front of the desk and leaned toward me, earnestly. Very Houston-like. "It's serendipitous that I walked in here and found you. We were talking about you just the other day."

"Oh, really? You and Houston?"

"Yes. And I couldn't figure out why he hadn't told you about all the wonderful investment opportunities that we've uncovered. I'm meeting with a few of our clients in the conference room right now and I'd love to have both you ladies join us."

Beth leaned forward. "Why, Andrew, that's very generous of you. So if we attended the meeting, something wonderful would happen?" She made it sound like group sex would be taking place. Or more to her liking, Andrew would be serving hot fudge sundaes.

He laughed. "We are returning between a hundred and twenty and a hundred and eighty percent on our client's money. Now that's the way to build a retirement —"

"Andrew," Houston cut in. "I don't think now is the time."

"Too bad," I said. "But I do have one simple question."

"Of course," Andrew said.

"Thank you, Andrew, but this one is for Houston. Who in the family has changed their vote?" Because that's what had to have happened. Someone was going to vote with Houston.

"I can't really discuss that before the corporation meeting."

I stood up. "Houston. Gird your loins, honey, because we're about to have one hell of a fight."

Beth smiled as she said good-bye to everyone, and we walked toward the front.

"Very restrained," she said to me as we neared the front desk.

"Why, thank you." I nodded toward Lauren to indicate we were leaving, then said to Beth, "You know, I'd love to pinch his head off and throw him in the Dumpster. Or maybe I'll just shoot the sumbitch."

Lauren heard and raised an eyebrow. Beth said to her, "Don't worry, I'll take away her guns. Or maybe just her bullets."

As I walked down the steps, crunching acorns from the tree overhead, I realized I had done it again — shot from the mouth, forewarning Houston. I'd have felt bad, except I knew it didn't much matter — he'd known all along he was going to get a fight.

"So, where are we going now?" Beth asked.

"To get a couple of attorneys."

"Ah," she said with a nod, unlocking the Cruiser. "I thought you already had one."

"He's not the right kind."

We both climbed inside the car. "What kind do you need?"

"The kind that are bigger and meaner than Houston's."

Four

"Oblong tables go in the tent, the round ones in the house," I said, pointing. "Someone inside will point you to the conservatory."

A massive truck from the rental company was unloading and I was directing traffic. There were several people from the caterers in the kitchen, and volunteers from OCO and the Bead Society were swirling around everywhere in a happy, hurried state. Some were marking booth spaces in the tent. Several others were putting up decorations in the conservatory, and others were working on placement of the signage. It was like watching children prepare for Christmas, there was that much anticipation. And all I could think of was that damn Houston.

"White chairs in the house," I said to a young female volunteer who had pitched in to unload the truck. "The metal chairs go in the tent. Two per table."

"Thank you."

"Did you see Mr. Harrington?" my mother asked, joining me near the driveway. "What was it about?"

"I think it was a misunderstanding," I said, keeping my focus on the items coming out of the truck. "Some confusion about when we had to have a meeting about the house."

"The house?" Her tone was alarmed, and when I looked at her I saw that her delicately penciled eyebrows showed worry. "The Manse?"

"No, no, of course not. I'm sorry, I wasn't paying attention," I said, keeping my face turned away from her. She can often catch me when I'm prevaricating. "Houston's house. He wanted to talk about Houston's house."

"Oh, Kitzi, you're not harassing poor Houston for the money you loaned him, are you? What with Rebecca sick and all, I'm sure their medical expenses are very high. Besides, it was only a few thousand dollars."

It was seven thousand dollars, which I don't consider a few, and he has never even offered to pay back a pittance, but I suppose that's my fault. I should have made him sign a legal document saying if I wasn't paid back within two years he would jump off the planet. My mistake.

"I'm not harassing him," I said. "I've never asked him for a thing. He has years before he has to give me any money."

"Oh, that's good. I've always felt that you have such an advantage over him. And your brother. Your grandfather really taught you about money. The boys didn't get that tutoring, which is probably why they've drained their trusts."

Or it could be that they're never been profitably employed, they've lived high, and they've pissed away every dime. They also never listened when our grandfather tried to advise them. "The coffeepots go in the house," I said to a young man who was carrying two of the large silver ones.

"I didn't actually come to talk to you about the lawyer," my mother said. "It seems that we have a problem. The Dumpster is still in the parking lot. I thought you had taken care of that?"

"Rats. I thought so, too. Let me go talk with Bruce —"

"I'll take over your job here." My mother was in her element, making sure everything ran smoothly. Only I knew that by Monday she would be exhausted and pay for all the time she spent working.

"I won't be long." I went marching off

toward the back of the property, muttering to myself. It was a nonprofit kind of day. The visit to Houston had been of no value whatsoever, since he was not willing to back down. Then I'd gone to my lawyer, who has about as much killer instinct as a morning glory. He'd given me a copy of the letter from Harrington and the original incorporation papers on the Manse, suggesting that I might like to look them over. Which is kind of like "looking over" *The Iliad* in the original Greek, only less fun.

We'd eaten lunch in the car, and Beth had made me look bad by nibbling on a junior-size burger. She had eaten two of my French fries. That forced me to throw the rest of them away, although I did finish off my double cheeseburger.

Since I had eaten a lot more than Beth had, she had spent the rest of our lunchtime creating a beaded necklace of cranberry-colored freshwater pearls interspersed with Swarovski crystals. It was absolutely stunning in its simplicity, so typical of Beth, who can bead anywhere, and often does. She claims it's more effective than Valium. To add insult to injury she gave me the necklace, so I couldn't even be annoyed with her.

I still had no idea who had changed their

vote, which would take the Manse away from us, and I still didn't have a team of lawyers who would eat Houston's lawyers. My attorney went so far as to say there was nothing legal that could be done, but I was betting he was wrong. If I could just find a legal rattlesnake . . .

I cut through the hedges behind the private drive, then went across the parking area. Because the Manse is on a private street, there just isn't sufficient parking for a large to-do. There never had been, which is why my grandfather came up with the idea of a private parking lot. It works fine some of the time, and when the event is really large, like the Bead Tea, we borrow the church lot from two blocks down the street and run shuttles from North Austin.

It didn't help that there was an industrial Dumpster half blocking the entry.

The house behind us was being remodeled from top to bottom, and since the house was almost as big as their lot, I'd told the contractor he could put the Dumpster on our property. I'd made him promise to get it moved by yesterday. Apparently that hadn't happened, and there was construction material overflowing everywhere.

I went around it and along their driveway. Two men were taking down a scaffold. "Can you tell me where Bruce is?" I asked.

"Que?"

"Donde esta Señor Bruce?" Bruce Burnett is the owner of Accurate Construction, and the general contractor on the house.

The man answered me, but I realized one more time that I have a major flaw with my ability to speak Spanish — I can ask for something, but I have no idea what people are saying when they answer me. I did catch a few words, one being *camioneta,* which means "pickup."

"Gracias," I said, about to turn away when a large white pickup with Accurate Construction printed on the side drove up. For once timing was on my side.

The truck stopped and a big man with light brown hair and a beard came over to me. "Hey, Miss Kitzi, what are you up to?"

"Bruce, we have a problem."

"Not me, maybe you do." He stroked his beard.

"You promised that you would move the Dumpster —"

"That's not a problem. I promised you I would have it out of here by next Thursday, and I will."

"Next Thursday! It's not next Thursday, it's today —"

He started laughing. "I know."

"You rat. You almost gave me a heart attack. That was mean."

"Yeah, but it was fun, too." His teeth showed through his beard as he grinned. "Don't worry, the guy is on his way here now. Should be gone in half an hour."

"That's good, but I still owe you one."

"There is nothing anyone can do to me that would be any worse than the nightmares I've already been dealing with on this house. Oh, and by the way, I got rid of most of the bat colony, so you'll have more mosquitoes this summer."

"You know," I said, looking him square in the eye, "this conversation has gone from bat to worse. I'm out of here."

"Thanks for stopping by."

I was shaking my head as I walked past the offending Dumpster and back to the Manse. If Houston really did succeed in taking the house away from me, maybe I'd just have Bruce build a kind of super duplex for my mother and me. With separate entrances, but a connecting door.

"Kitzi," my mother said as I made it to the driveway. She was checking something off her clipboard. "I'm so glad you're back. Would you find the president of OCO, Judy, and ask her to call the rental company? It appears they shorted us a few chairs. Then someone from catering said the ice machine was making a funny sound. Would you look at it?" The ice machine has been around since my dad's administration and it's always making odd sounds. Usually I just unplug it, wait a minute, and plug it back in again. Kind of like rebooting a computer.

"Be happy to," I said.

When I had accomplished those tasks and half a dozen more, including making several phone calls looking for a badass lawyer, hours had passed and the sun was beginning to lower. My mother was still walking around with her clipboard.

"Mom, you need to go and rest up before tonight," I said. "No need to tire yourself out." She already looked pale to me. "Did you eat?"

"I had some snacks that the caterers gave me to nibble on. Have you tried the salmon puffs? They are excellent."

"I'll be sure and eat some at the party," I said, gently turning and moving her toward the gatehouse. "You might even have time to sleep. I could call you —"

"I forgot. There are some things in the conservatory that need to be moved." She started in that direction. "Candlesticks. And they want one of us to decide where to put them."

"I'll do it," I said, turning her around again. "But only if you promise to put your feet up and relax for an hour."

"Kitzi, you are the bossiest child in the state, even as an adult," she said. "I was planning on resting anyway, so go help in the conservatory."

"I'm on my way," I said, giving her a salute.

I picked up some carrot sticks in the kitchen and munched my way to the conservatory.

I love that room whether it's in party dress or everyday casual mode. The ceiling is high with thousands of panes of beveled glass. The floor is tile, better to have all the beautiful plants that my grandfather cultivated. There are gardenias in tall pots, and two palm trees are in the actual earth, where the tiles are cut out. There is a towering fountain in the middle with blue tiles in the pool around it.

Normally I have furniture in here, too. About four seating areas, but all of that was in the storage building behind the garage to make way for tables to seat the guests. The small, round rented tables were covered in teal tablecloths and decorated with white flower arrangements of carnations, roses, and mums. Each held a sparkling teal ribbon and bead ties. Teal is the color used for ovarian cancer awareness.

Tomorrow there would be teacups and saucers on the tables, along with some luscious cookies, candies, and scones, but tonight, all the drinks would be coming from the three bars set up around the room. Hors d'oeuvres would be on the elegantly decorated banquet tables. I sighed with pleasure just looking at the room. Like most of us, I love beautiful things, and I like them even better when they serve a useful purpose. Like Miss America raising money for hungry children, the Manse was doing what it was created to do: help all kinds of charities, which in turn helps people in need.

Beth touched me on the arm. "No time for daydreaming, we have work to do."

"Between you and my mother I'm working my tail off today."

"Not yet," she said, looking at my rear end. Then she pointed to the fireplace.

It's another of the house's architectural focal points of native limestone, called Austin stone by some. It's a pale cream color with orange marbling. The firebox itself is black from the soot of years of use. A massive fern sat in front of it. Above the fireplace the mantel is wide. Today it was covered in a teal runner with gold threads. Someone had created sparkling bead tassels that hung off both ends.

"Nice," I said.

"They'd like to display the tourmaline necklace up there and some other things. Where do you want to move your stuff?"

On the floor were two heavy brass candlesticks and some plaques given to my father and grandfather in gratitude for something or other that they had done. "Why don't you put the plaques in that glass cabinet upstairs, and I'll put these things in the living room." I made an *ugh* sound as I picked up the candlesticks. "These could be part of my exercise program." I lifted one high, then the other. "One, two, three, four. One, two —"

"You don't have an exercise program."

"I do now." I made my way to the living room. "One, two three, four. One, two, three, four." The table behind the sofa was the perfect spot, and it was close so I didn't have to go very far. I put them there and rearranged a few other things to make space. What I know is that when people come to the Manse they like to look around. I don't blame them; I'm exactly the same way when I go to a home that someone has worked hard on. I knew that at this event there would be people who would peek cautiously into every room, and others who would make themselves at home, bringing their drinks in here to find a soft chair. I like that guests feel comfortable enough to enjoy the Manse. It let's me know I did my job right.

I turned on a few lights and went back to the conservatory, where Beth was waiting for me. "Next," she said, "I could really use some help setting up the booth. Do you mind?"

"I'm there." There is nothing I like better than running my fingers along beads, and since I was actually donating some of the items to be sold, it was my duty to help. "My phone charms are in the pantry; let me grab them." She gave me a funny look. "I wanted them handy. Where are your things?"

"In the back of the Cruiser. Come on."

The pace of everyone working to get ready for the party had picked up. The caterers were slapping intricate-looking hors d'oeuvres together at an amazing speed, and a young woman ahead of us was practically running toward the tent. I glanced at my watch. No wonder. It was getting on toward six o'clock. Who knew so much time had passed?

I noticed a pickup with a large camper on it pulling into the parking lot, claiming a space very near the walkway. There were other vehicles there, too. And now I saw two women pushing dollies and carrying large cases toward the tent. The beads had arrived.

I hailed several of them as Beth handed me two large plastic boxes to carry. I put my things on top.

"Are people mostly selling beads or finished jewelry?" I asked.

"Both. Roberta Wills will have her Swarovski crystals and Pam and Doug will be bringing beads, but I'm guessing the rest of us have jewelry for this show."

"What kind?" Beth is not only a dear friend but also one of those incredibly creative women who can take a handful of leftover beads and turn them into a piece of jewelry that the czar of Russia would have fought for.

She glanced at her watch. "Pearls, lots of earrings — oh, you'll see. I'm hoping I can get everything set up before the party. I already put my clothes in the house."

Once inside the tent I nearly dropped the boxes I was carrying. A few of the booths were already set up, and one had strings and strings of beads hanging from a black wire rack.

I moved closer. There were lemony-colored quartz chunks next to soft orange citrine and then brilliant green malachite. A woman was digging strands out of a box and adding them to the display. Faceted garnets and tiny chips. Something pink, maybe rose quartz, or rhodonite. I was being hypnotized.

"Kitzi," Beth called. "You want to bring that box over here."

"Oh, right."

She already had a tablecloth down and her other boxes open. As we talked she unloaded and set up several displays. "Here's a new piece." She held up a necklace.

"That is gorgeous!" It was made of freshwater pearls in every color. Not just the usual creams to pinks, there were also shades from purple to cranberry to green, blue, and bronze. In between the pearls were tiny seed beads in shiny gold and mauve. "Beth, you are flat unbelievable."

"Ron was saying that just the other day." There was such sarcasm and self-deprecation in her tone I wanted to cry. Beth was one of the finest people I knew and one of the best friends. Why hadn't she married a nice man?

I touched her arm. "That man can be a real jackass when he tries and you know it."

"He can be a jackass without trying."

"Yes he can, and I'm glad you finally realized it."

She sighed and plopped down in a chair behind the table, still bringing things out of boxes and placing jewelry on stands. "Did I tell you that I called Shannan? She can't decide what to pack for San Francisco. I told her it gets cold at night, and they wear a lot of black, but she doesn't think she has anything that's right."

"Then Ron can buy her some clothes in San Francisco."

"Maybe I should go home and help her —"

"Is Ron at the house?" I asked. She nodded and I said, "Then it's not happening. He'll just say something nasty to make you feel bad, and they'll whisk off in a whirlwind leaving you to feel terrible."

"I already feel terrible."

"But here we have a better class of terrible." I handed her my own contribution to the booth: phone dangles. I had chosen some really beautiful beads, about seven or eight on each side, and put them on waxed linen, leaving a three-inch gap in the middle. Most cell phones have a tiny hole somewhere that looks like it was made for a phone dangle. A friend just got back from

Taiwan and said that everyone had jewelry on their cell phones, and some had dozens of strings of cartoon figures hanging off. I used beads because I like beads.

We had a papier-mâché mannequin and I was hanging the phone dangles on that. We had an instruction card on how to attach them that would accompany each purchase. They were very basic, but they were pretty, and I was donating all the money they made to the Ovarian Cancer Organization.

I had most of them attached when I said, "Beth, I think it would be smart of you to just let go of everything to do with Shannan and Ron. Tomorrow afternoon, if you still want to talk with them, then I'll man your booth for you."

"They'll be long gone by then."

"Excellent. Perfect timing on my part, again."

Under other circumstances she might have laughed, or at least smiled, but today I got a sad look. "I hate this divorce. I feel like someone has taken my heart out." She touched her chest. "There's nothing left but a hole, and it hurts."

I could almost feel the ache for her. "I'm so sorry," I said, putting an arm around her. "I know it's awful. Even though I wanted my divorce, it still hurt." Just saying it made me remember what a terrible time it had been. I'd been much younger with two kids and no job. It was one of those step-up-to-the-plate times in my life. I had surprised myself with how efficient I could be when circumstances demanded it.

And it had hurt like hell. I remember dropping my kids off here at the Manse for my mother to babysit and then driving down to Zilker Park where I could cry until I didn't have tears left. My divorce had not only ripped my family apart, but it had also squashed every ounce of my self-esteem. I went through all the steps of grieving, and during the anger phase I changed my last name, and the kids', back to Camden. If he had given me even a few dollars of child support that might not have been possible, but he had never gotten around to helping out in any way. As he so graciously pointed out, I was the dead horse, and he wasn't going to keep feeding me. He didn't care if his children suffered, either, although that was because at some point, after several of his infidelities, he decided I should forgive him and let him come back. Not only should I keep the home fires burning and care for the kids, I should also put on a happy public front so he could continue to trade on my family's name. What a son of a bitch and how lucky I was that I had the strength to continue with the divorce.

I looked at Beth, who was wiping away a stray tear. "Beth, I know how much it hurts, but there is one thing you have to remember: it gets better. Honestly, much better. And at some point you're going to feel like you're eighteen again with a whole big world out there, and you can do whatever you want in it."

"I don't want the whole big world. I want to go home. I want my husband back and my plain life. It was a nice life and I hate this one."

I remembered feeling just that way. But like it or not, life is always changing. It's the one constant. Children grow up, friends move away, parents get old and die. Even young friends get sick. And husbands sometimes want divorces. Life is like a river: you can't stop it no matter how much you want to or how hard you try.

"I have a new saying you'll like," I said.

Beth looked up and I could see the tears still in her eyes. "Are you going to try and be funny?"

"No."

"Okay, then I'll listen." She sniffed. "I'll listen even if you are trying."

"Oh, well then, maybe I am. Here goes.

'Everything turns out okay in the end. If it isn't okay, then it isn't the end.' Well?"

"Did you make that up?"

"No, I didn't, but I can't remember who said it. Oh, and I have another one. This I did make up, but it's true. Men always come back. Always. The trick is that if you're smart, you won't want them by the time they do." This time I sighed. "I especially learned that at the craft retreat when Jeb showed up." Jeb Wright was an old flame who disappeared into the wilds of New York with promises that he'd return, only he never did. Amazing that I still had a crush on that man years after he'd left. Luckily the crush disappeared after I saw him again.

Beth's eyes went wide. "I almost forgot! We've got a cocktail party in" — she looked at her watch — "just over an hour. I'll finish this. You get ready."

"I'm just going to throw on something. It won't take long."

"No. You've worked too hard today. Go take a bath, and wear something wonderful. Oh, I know, that blue dress with the beads on the front." Back around Easter I bought the dress, which was pretty plain, and Beth sewed beads on the bodice. Not too many, just enough to add some sparkle. "You need to be stunning," she added.

"And why would that be?" I hadn't had a date in months. Three to be exact. I had been rather attracted to Nate Wright, who happened to be Jeb's brother, but we had one dinner before he had to leave for a buying trip that took him practically around the world. I hadn't heard a word from him since.

It was a disappointment, too, since I'd liked that man.

"It's because the party is at your house and you are Kitzi Camden. Do you want people to show up and see you the way you are now? No makeup, your hair needs combing, and your clothes . . ." She stopped as if my clothes were too tacky for description.

I was tired. "Okay. See you in the conservatory."

"With beads on."

FIVE

The party was in full swing, although *swing* might be the wrong word since the quartet in the corner was playing something so dreary it could have been used to cure insomnia.

Beth had turned herself out in a sleek navy sheath dress that accentuated her new curves, accessorizing it with a beaded necklace and earrings in lapis and pearl. "I love your necklace, Beth."

"Thanks. I was working on a bracelet, too, but I ran out of time." She reached out to touch my bracelet, which I'd made with amber and green crystals, interspersed with leaves. "This is beautiful."

"One of these days, I'm planning on making earrings. But lately, I've spent all my time on the phone dangles."

"Tell me about it," she said. I knew Beth had been spending most of her time lately getting ready for the Bead Tea. "It's a good thing I like my work; there's been a lot of it lately."

At that moment, one member of the band hit a particularly sour note.

"Now there's music you can really tap your toe to," I said to Beth.

She nodded. "You can't complain, though. They're volunteers." Almost everyone who was working the party, from the caterers to the bartenders, was donating their time.

"Which says a lot for —" I came to a full stop.

Framed perfectly in the entryway was none other than Houston Webber. On his arm was a blonde. A tall, very slender, elegant blonde, which stunned me since his wife Rebecca has curly auburn hair and this woman obviously did not.

Houston paused, the light glinting off his silver hair. He'd have been exceedingly distinguished, except for the furtive look on his face. I could understand why he was looking furtive. These were Rebecca's friends and he ought to be real damn nervous about escorting another woman. My blood pressure shot up and I charged in that direction.

Luckily by the time I got there the blonde was speaking. "Doesn't everything look pretty?" She saw me. "Kitzi!" Both her arms went out.

"Rebecca?" I hugged her. "I was about to give Houston hell — I didn't even recognize you."

She grinned. "When I started losing my hair I was going to get an auburn wig, but I've always heard that blondes have more fun. You don't see people racing out to get their hair dyed reddish brown. So, here I am." She did a small curtsey. "Well?"

I stepped back to look at her. With her green eyes she was as stunning as always — they mirrored the dark green Swarovski crystals against her elegant neck. "You look wonderful as a blonde. An Irish bombshell."

"That's a new one. It's fun, though, because no one recognizes me at first. In the grocery store I was in line behind two women from my bead class and they didn't even give me a second glance." She twitched at the wig, which was short and wavy. "Sometimes I think I look like a demented secretary, like in the old fifties movies."

"Not a chance. How are you feeling?"

"Not too hot — surgery and chemo aren't fun, but they say it seems to be working. And at least I get to experiment with new hair styles," she said.

I smiled with relief. They'd caught Rebecca at stage II, and after her diagnosis she'd gone through an extensive surgery. According to her they'd taken out everything below the waist that wasn't keeping her alive or holding her up. A few weeks later she started on chemo. Fortunately, it sounded like the treatments were working.

"But how about you?" she asked. "How are you doing?"

"I'm doing fine," I said.

"You've lost some weight."

"I have a new exercise program."

Houston was looking nervous again, glancing at the door and around the room. I started to ask why when he said, "Rebecca, isn't that Jill from your bead group?" He pointed to a woman across the room. "Didn't you want to talk to her?"

He moved Rebecca in that direction and she only had time to say, "Talk with you later, Kitzi," before they were out of sight.

I took a few steps and out of the crowd appeared Andrew, Houston's faithful factotem. "How are you doing tonight?" I asked, wondering where in the world he'd come from.

"I'm fine." He was gazing around the conservatory, not so much at the crowd but at the room itself. "This is some house."

"Thank you. My grandfather had it built when he was governor. During that time the governor's mansion was badly in need of renovation, so he used this as the official residence while they raised the money for the work."

It was the standard spiel, but I'd forgotten who I was talking to when I went into it. Since Andrew worked so closely with Houston, he probably had architectural blueprints of the Manse in his coat pocket. Along with Houston's plans for the place. Condos or some such terrible thing.

"I didn't know your grandfather built this," he said.

"I thought you lived in Houston's hip pocket and knew everything he did."

"Not lately." He leaned forward, shaking his head sadly. "We used to work pretty closely, but when Rebecca got sick Houston wasn't around much and I ended up running the whole company. Houston was trying, but his attention wasn't on business, if you know what I mean."

"I do." And I liked Houston better for it.

"It was a tough time, but what came out of it was good: I started developing some of my own investment strategies. I don't want to brag, but I've put together the best deals we've got."

"Good for you."

He looked around. "I get the impression

that you and Houston aren't tight. Is that right? Seems like you've had some, well, shall we say, differences?"

"You can say it if you want." Free world, free speech. Doesn't mean I like it, or him.

"Like the way he's working to take over the Manse." He shook his head. "That's a damn shame. I hope you can stop it."

"Thank you." In that moment he reminded me of Eddie Haskell from *Leave It to Beaver.* Maybe not as smarmy, but there was something . . .

"Can I trust you to keep something confidential?" he asked.

"If you're asking me to keep sacred the sanctity of the confessional, I'm not a priest."

He blinked, trying to figure out what I'd said. "No, I know that." He blinked a couple more times and apparently wrongly assumed I'd said yes. He dropped his voice. "Here's the thing: I'm going out on my own. Not that Houston hasn't been a great mentor, but he's not doing everything he could be doing to make money. You know . . ."

"For his clients?"

"Right." Andrew smiled. "I've found some ways to increase the income, which in turn increases the capital. People are looking for that. After the downturn in the high-tech market, most people want the maximum return they can get. It only makes sense."

I didn't remind him that most people always want the maximum return. "I see."

"And I've got some great investments I'd like to talk to you about. I could make you a lot of money."

I know people think that money will get them anything, but I don't like messing with it. I don't want to have to watch the markets, or real estate, or anything else. I just want to have enough whenever I need it. Like everyone else. "Most of my money is tied up," I said.

"Well, whatever is loose could be working for you. Let me give you a call next week, okay? I'll be looking for new offices. Then it will be official and I can tell Houston."

Now that was an interesting piece of news. "And Houston didn't have you sign a noncompete?"

He shook his head. "Nope. And why bother? This is a right-to-work state, so any judge would throw a suit like that out of court. I have to make a living. They're not going to make me work at McDonald's."

I wasn't too sure about that; however, it seemed Houston wasn't as smart as I'd thought. A basic noncompete would at least prevent Andrew from taking Houston's clients. I was thoroughly disgusted at Andrew's duplicity and annoyed that he was confiding in me. I also didn't like that I was feeling protective of Houston.

"Well, I wish you luck," I said. It's a favorite phrase of mine because I don't specify which kind of luck. "I'm going to get something to drink."

"I see a couple of my clients — think I'll go visit with them. Afterward do you mind if I wander around and look at the Manse?"

Even though he wouldn't be taking measurements of closets or walls for Houston, I still didn't like it. Andrew was not the fine, upstanding young man I'd thought. I hoped the caterers would protect the silver. "Sure. Enjoy looking," I said, with stress on the word *looking.*

I watched him awhile then lost him in the milling crowd. That left me with a moral dilemma. Did I tell Houston about Andrew's intent to defect or did I say to hell with all of them? Except, of course, Rebecca. I don't like it when life gets complicated.

I decided to locate Tess Lewis, my former assistant. When I was in the Texas Senate she was my version of Condoleezza Rice; she knew everything there was to know about Texas Senate protocol, and a whole lot about Texas law. She also knew where all the bodies were buried, as they say. That came in handy when we needed to strong-arm someone to get support for a bill.

Besides being bright as sunshine, Tess loved life. She could have fun at a turtle race. I knew she'd be at the reception because Tess was very active with the Ovarian Cancer Organization and had been ever since she was diagnosed with ovarian cancer almost three years earlier. It hadn't slowed her down any. When I fussed over her, she kept telling me they'd caught her cancer in the early stages and if anyone could beat it, she could. I believed her, because I found it hard to doubt anything Tess said.

I went through the crowd twice, visiting with half a dozen people, but I never found Tess. I did run into Bruce, the contractor from next door. His sister died of ovarian cancer. Once you hear about this disease it's like a new word — it crops up everywhere.

"You clean up real nice," I said to him.

"I try."

"Where is Delphine?" She is his wife.

"She went to talk with someone; she's thinking of joining the Bead Society."

"Oh. Did you get the Dumpster picked

up and moved?"

He took half a step back. "I meant to talk to you about that. We couldn't get the company out here, so we pushed it out of the way."

A Dumpster that size must weigh tons. "Really? Just where did you push it to?"

"Not very far."

"Where very far?" I asked.

"Your backyard —"

"Bruce!" He started laughing and I realized that once again I'd fallen for one of his tricks. "You have to stop doing that," I said.

"I would if you weren't so gullible."

"Go find your wife and be grateful that someone will have you."

I moved off and ended up at the fireplace near the raffle table. My father always said that most people have good hearts and are willing to contribute money to a worthy cause, but they like it better and have more fun when they get something for their money. In this case, they had a chance of winning a necklace that was worth almost seventeen thousand dollars.

"Would you like to buy some raffle tickets?" the woman taking money asked in a high, just short of piercing, voice. She appeared to be in her late sixties, with salt-

and-pepper hair. The kind of woman who was going into old age without caring who knew it.

She held out a picture of the necklace. In the center was a large, square-cut gem of a clear and rich teal. More teal for ovarian cancer awareness. The central stone was held in place by delicate gold leaves, and the rest of the necklace was formed by three strands of gold links, interspersed with smaller stones. The colors reminded me of water rippling through a mountain stream. There was teal, green, pink, and even a dark dusky color just this side of black. All were tourmaline and all set by hand.

"I think I've already stuffed the ballot box," I said. I had a raft of tickets upstairs. "And I don't have my purse on me, or I would buy a few more. I will before Sunday."

"You're Kitzi Camden," she said.

"I am." I held out my hand. "We haven't met."

"Donna Silbert." We shook hands, and she said, "You be sure and come by our booth tomorrow. I'm with the Ovarian Cancer Organization, and I'll be handing out information. All the details on how you can protect yourself, at least as much as you can."

"I'll be there."

I looked up and realized that the mantel was pretty bare. "I thought the necklace was going to be on display tonight."

She glanced up automatically. "It will be later. Cordelia Wright, do you know her? She owns Green Clover Camp."

"I do," I said.

"Well, she came down with something, so someone else is bringing the necklace in. Should be here soon."

My heart did a little hop and spin, which is a completely ridiculous thing for it to do. However, there was cause. Cordy, Cordelia, has three brothers. One is a minister, whom I hardly know, and one is a bounder, a rat, and I used to know him all too well. Neither were the cause of my heart palpitations. Her third brother, Nathaniel Wright, was the cause. I would like to get to know that man a whole lot better, and I intended to if he ever got back into the country.

Nate owns Tivolini, a catalog of wonderful objets d'art, and he was the one who donated the necklace. I sure hoped he'd be the one bringing it to town.

Except he lived in Dallas, not Austin, and he'd have called me if he was back. At least I hoped he'd have called since we had a serious flirtation going. And if he was back and hadn't called, well, it didn't bear thinking about. One more complication to add to the list.

This time I set out to find Beth, since she'd met Nate and even she had to agree he was above average — and way above the average of men I'd dated previously. There must have been a secret trapdoor I didn't know about because I couldn't find Beth either. I did spot my brother, Stephen, lurking near one of the food tables.

Stephen is five years younger than I am and very handsome, but he's never quite grown up. Doesn't particularly bother me, because I don't expect anything from him, but it's played hell with most of his other relationships.

"Hey, Stevie," I called, using my childhood name for him.

"Hey, Kitz." The music changed to something more upbeat and jazzy. "That's a little more like it," he said. "I thought I'd accidentally wandered into a funeral." It was too close to the truth to be clever, and he said quickly, "I went over to the quartet and made a request. Looks like they added a guitar player, too."

"That's nice," I said. "Have you heard the latest about what Houston's done?"

"Our cousin Houston or the city?" He

seemed more interested in the musicians across the room than our conversation.

"Our cousin Houston, of course. That man is not to be trusted —"

"That's nothing new. I was just about to get a drink; can I get you something?"

"No, I've got to eat first," I said. "Anyway, I was telling you about Houston. I think I'm going to need your help on this one. I got a call from some lawyer that Houston hired —"

Stephen let out this long heartrending sigh. "Can we talk later?"

"Why? This is important."

"I'm sorry, life is just a little complicated right now."

"Now that's a first." Stephen has been married three times, has one daughter, and is perpetually involved in something that isn't working. "Look, I need —"

"I'm going to grab that drink; I'll talk to you later." And he was gone.

"Great idea," I said to his back. Like a drink was going to make a difference in whatever complication he was facing this time. "And thanks for your support and concern."

I went for the hors d'oeuvres table and selected a small shish kebab with meatballs and green peppers. I was so hungry I thought about just gnawing the meat off the stick, but the last time I did that, I almost pierced my tongue.

I gathered up a fork and a plate and sat at an empty table. Holding the stick tightly, I used the fork to push the meat. It didn't budge. I gripped both fork and stick even tighter and tried again.

A deep voice whispered in my ear, "Hello, Miss Kitz. I've missed you." His lips grazed my ear. A shudder of ecstasy shot through me, my hand jerked, and the meatball flew into the air.

The very handsome Nate Wright was standing above me. We both watched as the meatball glanced off the chandelier and headed for Earth. I stood up. "We'd better get out of here."

He grabbed my hand and we ran to the foyer. "I had no idea you were interested in the space program," he said.

"Who knew I'd be that good at it?"

Behind us the party went on, and no one screamed about falling meatballs.

Nate was grinning. "Is life always this much fun around you?"

I thought about Houston's bid for the house, Beth's divorce, and my mother's failing memory. "I don't think so."

"I'll bet you're wrong about that. At least

you're speaking to me."

"And why wouldn't I be?"

"Well, you haven't returned my calls. After the third nonresponse I started to think you were sending a not-so-subtle message that I was too persistent to see."

"You called me?" I said. "Here?"

"Are you surprised?"

"Well, I haven't heard about any calls, and if I had, I promise you, I'd have phoned you back. I may be of another generation, but I don't buy that girls can't call boys." I looked at him. "Wait, who did you talk to?"

"Your mother. At least she said she was your mother."

We have one phone line that can be picked up at the Manse or the gatehouse. We arranged that when my mom moved down there so she wouldn't miss her calls. I hadn't bothered to change it, since there hadn't been a need, but now it appeared there was one. "I'm sorry about that. My mother forgets things. And she obviously didn't give you my cell number."

"She gave me three different ones, and none of them were answered by you. Unless you sometimes go by Chenille."

"Nope, that's a bedspread, not an alias." I went on with my explanation. "We have everything programmed into speed dial on my mother's phone, which is why she doesn't know the numbers." It's pretty bad when the man of your dreams has been trying to get a hold of you and you didn't get the message. "How about if I buy you a drink in the other room?" I asked. "I'll even offer you some pretty terrific hors d'eouvres — but I can't recommend the meatballs."

"I can understand that. I mean, who could top your expertise with them?"

"Pun intended?"

He grinned again. "Of course. James Boswell called a good pun 'among the smaller excellencies of lively conversation.' And when I'm around you, everything is lively."

I raised one eyebrow and so did he. Was there a double entendre in that statement? I wasn't about to ask, but I swear, even his eyes were grinning. I could feel everything including my stomach starting to blush, which is totally unacceptable at my age.

I cleared my throat. "Shall we go get that drink?"

His face changed from teasing to disappointed. That's one of the things I like about Nate: he's not afraid to be alive. I also like that every cell in my body goes on red alert when he's around.

"Kitzi, I'm sorry, but I can't. Cordy has a

sinus infection, and I just ran into town to drop off the necklace and pick up her prescription. I can't stay." I'd have argued, but I want him to be the kind of man who takes care of his sister. Who knows, I might need him to take care of me sometime. "But, I could stay long enough to get your cell number. And you could walk me to my car."

"Absolutely. I'll add it to my new exercise program."

We went out through the kitchen door, and I was surprised to see that there was a security guard sitting at the opening to the tent. "Good evening," I said, reaching out to shake his hand and introduce myself. "I didn't know we'd have protection on the premises."

"Yes, ma'am. I'm Charles Jones. I'll be here until 2 a.m., and then someone'll take over for me. It's just to make sure that everything in the booths is safe."

I hadn't thought much about that either way, but at least I didn't have to be responsible for all the jewelry inside the tent. "It's nice to know you're here," I said. "If you need anything to eat or drink, just ring the bell on the back door and I'll let you in. Or better still, I'll put a key under the mat for you."

"Thank you."

I waved good-bye as we started toward the parking area. When Nate slipped an arm around me I noted again what an amazing effect he had on me. An hour ago I was tired and cranky, and now every part of me, including my hair, felt animated.

"I'll be coming back in town tomorrow evening," Nate said. "Would you like to have dinner?"

"With you?" I stopped. "Are you ever amazed at what comes out of your own mouth?"

By this time we'd reached his car. In the darkness I wasn't sure of the color, but I thought it was between bronze and sand. A Lincoln Navigator. The man traveled in style, much better style than when I'd first ridden with him. That day he'd been in an old beat-up Camp Green Clover van, but it had still been pretty wonderful, if I remember correctly.

"So, dinner tomorrow?" he asked again. "How about if I pick you up around seven? We could listen to some jazz afterward."

He leaned against his car and slid both arms around me, pulling me to him. Then, his arms tightened and I could feel the muscles as he brought me even closer. I don't think I was breathing. Then his mouth came down on mine. I've had some hot flashes in my days but nothing to equal the heat of that moment.

The first kiss was soft. The second was longer and harder. I kissed him back, and for a minute thought I was going to melt right down through his arms and become part of the parking lot.

"Hey, you two cut that out!"

I jumped. It was that darn Bruce, coming up the walk behind us. He was with his wife, and she was shaking her head at him. He was grinning and even his beard couldn't hide it. "Did I scare you? I didn't want you to get carried away."

Nate said, "You mean like this?" He bent me over backward and kissed me dramatically.

Once I could stand again, I said to him, "Let me guess, you wanted to grow up to be the sheik."

"And you are my blonde heroine."

"That's hellcat to you," I said.

Nate was smiling. "So, my blonde hellcat, seven tomorrow night?"

"I'll be ready."

Once Nate had closed the door, Bruce and Delphine walked by. Bruce said, "New boyfriend? You look like you're about three feet off the ground. Just don't fall off your cloud."

"I'm not a bit worried," I said. Nate drove away with a last wave, and I saw Bruce and Delphine go toward their pickup, which was in the neighbor's driveway behind a Dumpster.

I let out a sigh. Maybe I was three feet above the ground. What's more, I intended to stay there.

Just the thought was smug and seemed to tempt the fates. No one stays on a cloud all that long; seems there's always something sooner or later to knock you off. In my case it was sooner.

I was off my cloud first thing in the morning.

Six

The sky was the sort of deep turquoise–cobalt blue mix that Austin is famous for. The grass was sharp emerald green, and the tent was still teal and white stripes. It would have been a nice mix to look at from my bedroom. With me still in bed.

"Why don't we do about forty minutes?" Beth said. "Then we'll be back and still have time to change before the tea officially opens."

It was too early in the morning; we were wearing shorts and T-shirts ready to go for the gusto, or whatever it is that you get as a result of a forty-minute walk.

"We could drive down to Sweetish Hill and get some croissants first," I suggested.

"We had whey shakes and that's plenty. Think of them as milkshakes," she said as we passed the tent. I didn't see anyone outside, and it was closed off, so apparently the guard was asleep inside.

"Why don't we set a route," I said, "and if we get done before the time is up, then great. And maybe it will take us longer than forty minutes."

"You're conniving."

"I'm back-timing. It's now eight fifteen. If we walk forty minutes, that's nine."

"Five of."

"Close enough. The volunteers will be arriving, so we won't have time to shower and get dressed."

"They aren't coming until nine thirty because they got everything ready last night. Nothing officially starts until ten. We have plenty of time."

I growled, but I didn't say anything. Who can argue with that kind of logic?

We cut through the bushes to the parking lot, and I heard voices coming from over the fence where the house was being renovated. "Sounds like a party."

Beth, slightly ahead of me, picked up her pace. "A bad one. The cops are there."

I caught up with her and saw that not only were there police, there was also a special crimes unit SUV and a coroner's van. That's when I started running. Bruce might have broken up my good-night kissing with Nate, but he was still one great guy, and he'd been my closest *neighbor* for over a year — the whole time he was renovating the house. He and his wife had been at the Manse several times, and when I had a problem with the garage door, he was the one who'd fixed it. That was on a Saturday and he'd never let me pay him. When his wife made tamales or *posole,* guess who got some?

I was almost out of breath when I rounded the corner and saw the big Dumpster with a ladder leaning against it.

There were people everywhere, including a few in uniforms, and several more in plain clothes. I went up to the man who seemed to be in charge. He appeared about fifty, dark straight hair, cut in a style you'd call clean-cut or all-American. He had a bit of a belly hanging over his belt, and he was taking some notes on a handheld computer.

"Good morning," I said, still breathing hard. "I'm Kitzi Camden from next door."

"Yes, Ms. Camden, nice to meet you. I'm Senior Sergeant Dwayne Granger." He put away the stylus he'd been using on his Dell Axim and shook hands with me. "Nice to meet you, ma'am."

I hate when people over twenty call me "ma'am." "It appears that something terrible happened here. I knew the contractor and several of the workmen. Are they okay?"

He stared at me, saying nothing, until finally a voice from behind me said, "I'm okay, and so are all my crew." It was Bruce.

I turned around and saw that he looked worn. "Oh, Bruce, I'm glad." I took a huge breath. "You seem tired."

"I am."

The cop said, "Ms. Camden, I understand that you had a party at your house last night."

"What? Oh, yes, but it wasn't actually my party. It was the opening reception for the Bead Tea that's being held. It starts today. It's sponsored by the Ovarian Cancer Organization and the Bead Society."

"Do you have a list of the guests?"

I shook my head.

Beth said, "I'm sure we can get you one. Judy would have it. I'm sorry, I haven't introduced myself. I'm Beth Fairfield. I have a booth in the tent this weekend. The big teal and white striped tent? There will be vendors and I'm one of them."

He seemed interested. "Doing what?"

"Selling jewelry."

"Ah." He nodded. I was relieved to be out of the conversation. "And who is Judy?" Granger asked.

Beth explained that she was the president of the Ovarian Cancer Organization. "I have her number someplace. I'm sure Kitzi has it, too."

"Any chance you can get it for me?"

I shivered in the morning sunlight. Judging from the coroner's van and the ladder against the Dumpster, I could only conclude that someone had been killed and their body left in the Dumpster. And this sergeant thought that the people who had been in my home last night might have something to do with it. Maybe one of those people was dead, lying not twenty feet away, hidden by the steel walls of the Dumpster.

The sight of all the police vehicles had surprised and frightened me. Once I had known that Bruce and his crew were safe, I hadn't thought much more about who had died, or why they were here. The nonchalance of the sergeant had lulled me into a false calm. I wasn't feeling calm now, and the ease of the conversation between Beth and him wasn't helping.

"Not a problem," Beth said to Sergeant Granger. "We can get Judy's phone number to you in less than an hour. Unless you need it sooner. We were just going for a walk."

"That will be fine," he agreed and handed her a card. They had a conversation about which number she was to call.

I was staring at the Dumpster. What kind

of a person killed someone and then just threw the body in a trash receptacle?

"Excuse me," I said. "Can you tell me who is dead? I assume someone is dead." I gestured to the coroner's van.

Sergeant Granger's expression held surprise as he turned to me. "I'm sorry, but we aren't ready to release any names yet." He turned back to Beth. "If you'd give me your phone number, I'd appreciate it. I'd like to set up an interview."

Bruce had stepped a few feet away, and I followed him. "Are you sure you're okay?" I asked. His coloring was normally ruddy from all the time spent outdoors, but this morning his skin was a dreary ash.

"I'm fine." He continued walking and I stayed with him.

"You want to talk about it?" I asked.

"Are you going to give me a choice?"

And then I realized the source of his drained appearance. "You found the body, didn't you?"

"And the blood. And what killed him."

I glanced over my shoulder, but Sergeant Granger was deep in conversation with Beth and paying no attention to us. "Him?" I said. "It was a man?"

"Yeah."

"Damn. But why? I mean, what were you

doing? You can't see into the Dumpster unless you're seven feet tall, and you aren't. And there — wasn't anything in there — well, it was supposed to be empty, wasn't it? How did you happen to find him?"

"You writing an article?"

"Inquiring minds," I said. "I just want to know how you happened to find him. Do you mind telling me?"

He thought about it for a second. "When I came up the drive I saw a trail of" — he swallowed — "of something dark coming out of the Dumpster. At first I thought it was oil, and I was pissed because it was staining the driveway. As you know, the owners aren't going to stand for that. Then I ran my boot through it and there was red. I needed to figure out what it was so I could get the stain off." He rubbed his face with his hand. "I could see through a seam of the Dumpster, but I couldn't see enough, so I climbed up the side. He was on his stomach, and the back of his head was . . . wasn't there."

"My Lord." I held back a gag and took in some air. "Did he fall into the Dumpster? An accident, maybe? I mean, what did you do?" I hoped I was sounding clinical, and I hoped my stomach believed that I wasn't upset by this.

"I climbed in and checked his pulse, but there wasn't one. And no, it wasn't an accident. The bottom of the Dumpster is flat, and he couldn't have fallen from the top and done that kind of damage. Besides, I'm pretty sure I found what did it." A shudder ran through his body. "Anyway, I turned him over."

"Did you recognize him?" I lowered my voice. "Was it someone you knew?"

"I don't think I'm supposed to tell you that."

"But you're pretty sure this was murder? You can't possibly think that I killed him. Come on, Bruce. That's ridiculous." We had continued walking and now we were nearing the corner, out of earshot and sight, and I hoped, out of mind of the sergeant. "Well? Are you going to tell me, or do I have to beat it out of you?" His lips turned white, and for a second I thought he was going to vomit. "I'm sorry. Damn. I didn't mean that." But now I was pretty sure of the murder method, and it gave me chill bumps on my arms.

Bruce leaned over and picked up some nails that were scattered in the dirt. Then he looked back to see if we were being watched, and when he realized that no one was paying any attention, he stood and said,

"I knew the guy who was murdered. He probably deserved killing, but I didn't do it."

"I believe you. Who was it?"

"Andrew Lynch."

I could feel my eyes strain outward. "Houston's . . . protégé . . . assistant, whatever he was? That Andrew Lynch?"

"That's the one."

I leaned back against a telephone pole. This was a shocker. Andrew Lynch was dead. I looked up at Bruce. "You said the back of his . . . uh, you said that you found what you think killed him. What was it?"

"A big brass candlestick."

"A brass —" I had to take in air. "About this big?" I held my hands about two feet apart, and Bruce nodded. "And the base had brass leaves? And two more sections on up the candlestick?"

Again he nodded. "How'd you know?"

"And really heavy?"

"Yes. Now tell me how you know?"

I had to stop the whirling of my brain. "I think," I said, "I think that Andrew was killed with my candlestick from the conservatory."

Despite early morning death, Beth and I had power walked for over thirty minutes. I wanted to tell her what Bruce had said, but I held back at first, not wanting to make the morning as frightening for her as it was for me. Then, because of the intensity of the workout, I couldn't talk anyway.

By the time we got back to the Manse, I felt frightened and violated — more so because it appeared likely that my candlestick had been used to kill Andrew. I wanted to go back to bed. That's what I do when I'm stressed — I sleep. Unfortunately, sleep was not an option. I had promised to make myself available during the day, greeting guests and acting as hostess.

Beth was energized and she practically flew up the back stairs to shower. I detoured to the living room, hoping against hope that the candlesticks were still on the sofa table. They weren't. Neither one, which seemed a little odd. One of them should have been there.

I checked the conservatory, which had been turned into a tearoom, with dozens of small white tables and white wooden chairs. Each table had teal cloth napkins, with a beaded napkin ring of clear glass beads interspersed with sparkling peach beads. The conservatory had never looked so charming.

Unfortunately, the fireplace had never

looked so bare. The mantel had nothing on it. Not two candlesticks, not even one. The tourmaline necklace wasn't there, either, but I thought I remembered that it was going to be shown in a booth in the tent.

It was disconcerting not to find the candlesticks, but not surprising. What I couldn't figure out was why both of them were missing. That made no sense. It also meant that not only had Andrew been in my home last night, but so had the murder weapon, and probably the murderer. While Andrew hadn't been a completely upstanding business person, I couldn't see him trying to steal two decorator items. And why? I personally never liked them all that much. They were okay, and they were part of the legacy of the house, but certainly not easily hidden. They were two feet long, and they were heavy. You couldn't hide them under a coat, which, of course, no one had been wearing last night, given the Austin weather.

A part of me wanted to tell the police that the murder weapon had come from my house, but I wasn't supposed to know about the murder weapon. If I said anything it would put Bruce in a bad light. It might even make him a suspect.

I yawned and went up to my room and showered. I was dressed and starting to put on my makeup when Beth raced in.

"I called Judy with the Ovarian Cancer Organization; she's on the phone now. She wants to fax me the guest list, but your fax doesn't work. The rubber is all messed up."

"Sinatra ate it. Why don't you talk to Granger? I'll bet the station has a fax number."

"Thanks." She was halfway out the door when I stopped her.

"Why don't you let me handle that, since you have so much more to do for the booth?"

"Uh . . ." She paused. "No problem. I'll take care of it." Then she raced out again. The speed of that woman was increasing in direct proportion to the amount of weight she was losing. It needed to stop soon or our almost-fifty-year friendship was going to end; I wouldn't be able to keep up with her.

By the time I made it downstairs, the volunteers were everywhere, and there was a line of people at the front door waiting to get in to have tea. Luckily each ticket had a seating time, so the line wasn't too long. Others were milling outside the tent waiting for it to open.

I was on a mission. That damned candlestick had to be somewhere, and that somewhere had to be in my house. I looked in the conservatory again, just in case I'd missed it earlier — as if that were even possible. I went around the entire room, looking behind plants and under tablecloths. I was practically under a serving table when someone spoke to me.

"Hi. Did you need some help?" It was Lauren from Houston's office. I crawled out and smoothed my hair as I stood up. "Oh. Miss Camden." She backed up. "I didn't know it was you."

"It's all right, Lauren. I'm not going to bite you."

"Oh, I know." But she didn't look like she believed me.

"I am looking for a very large brass candlestick. Actually two of them that were on the fireplace. Have you seen them?"

"Uh, no, ma'am."

"Thank you. And don't call me 'ma'am.' "

"Yes, ma'am," she said, then stopped. "Uh, I'm sorry. I just forgot."

I looked at her for a moment. She was not dressed quite as top-of-the-line as she'd been yesterday in Houston's office, but she still looked nice in black slacks and a white shirt, which was standard fare for the servers at the tea. I couldn't help but wonder if she knew about Andrew.

I decided she didn't. I could only hope that when she found out she was back at Houston's, fending off visitors or whatever her main job was. I didn't want her here. I didn't want that murder any closer than it already was.

She was still watching me warily, which was her problem, not mine. "Lauren, I didn't realize you were going to be here. You must be a member of the Bead Society. Or the OCO."

"Uh, no, ma'a . . . I mean, no, I'm not. Houston sent me down here, kind of as a donation. He's paying me to be here, since Rebecca can't work this hard, and he's busy."

I nodded. "That's very nice of him. Thank you."

"It's a really pretty house."

"Thank you." She was so ramrod straight I was tempted to say "as you were, soldier," but I didn't. I went looking in several of the coat closets and even the pantry, but by that time the front doors were open and guests were coming in.

When we have big events at the Manse, my mother and I become minor celebrities. Not movie star status, no secret service or hulking bodyguards, but we do make a point of walking through and visiting with people. We also end up getting our picture taken with dozens of guests, and we autograph menus or tickets or such. No one has ever asked me to sign a body part, and I'm just as happy with that. I did sign several T-shirts one year, after a bike race, but that's all.

Our family has always figured if we aren't willing to do such things, then we should simply stay out of sight. Nowadays my mother can go to the gatehouse and she isn't bothered. In the Manse itself we have some of those velvet ropes to close off areas we don't want guests in. We don't use them often, since we know people like to look around, but there are times when they are quite useful, like when I had the flu and I was upstairs with several boxes of Kleenex, bottles of aspirin, and two good books. I also had a box of chocolate-covered cherries, which I'm positive have vitamin C in them. Well, they are fruit. In any case, I didn't want people seeing me that way.

Another classic example is the time Sinatra had accidentally been closed up in an upstairs bedroom for a full day. The room was not fit for company when the Juvenile Diabetes Research Association had a fundraiser that evening, so the velvet rope went up. I'm sure people think there's an exotic reason that we close off certain rooms, but the smell of cat poop is exotic enough for me.

On this particular day I had insisted that my mother rest and only show up for the last two or three hours, which meant I was to be out front, at least for a while. And that's exactly what I did during my first hour: I greeted people, visited with friends and supporters of the organizations involved, and even snitched half a scone — a bite-size scone — which I did not intend to tell Beth about.

During the second hour people started coming in with my phone jewelry, asking me to sign the instruction cards that were attached. I was pleased to do that, since it was all helping to raise money and awareness to fight ovarian cancer. It was also during that hour that I found someone who could tell me why Tess, my former assistant, wasn't there.

"Kitzi." Judy O'Bannon, the president of OCO, caught me just as I was coming back from the bathroom. "I heard that you were looking for Tess Lewis," she said.

"I was and I am. Last I talked to her she was going to be here."

Judy looked concerned. "When was that?"

I had to think about it. "Not too long ago.

Maybe about a month. Why? What's happened?"

"She's in the hospital."

We stared at each other, and I had the feeling that Judy knew things about ovarian cancer that I would hopefully never know. Her expression frightened me. "Is she — I mean, is her cancer . . . ?"

Judy patted my arm. "I don't know anything, Kitzi. Last night someone told me that Tess's doctor put her in the hospital. It hasn't been that long, just since Tuesday. I was planning on stopping by this weekend."

"I'll go see her this afternoon," I said. "Damn it. Someone has to do something about this cancer. Find a cure. Get the word out on how deadly it is, and how tricky the symptoms are."

Her smile was sad. "We're trying, Kitzi. This weekend is a start, remember?"

I was not only preaching to the choir, but I was also griping at the choir director for not doing enough. "I'm sorry. I just get frustrated. Do you know which hospital Tess is in?"

She told me, then added, "It could be nothing. Maybe just an intestinal blockage. It's not uncommon after women have a very aggressive surgery where some of the intestine was removed."

I agreed, and thanked her. Our conversation had made me even more aware of the importance of what we were doing, which sent me back to my hostessing duties with a renewed smile. I took pictures with guests, and huge tables of guests. We had a roving photographer who put the shots on a bulletin board for purchase, proceeds going to the OCO.

That was the second hour of my duties, and the third hour was lunch, which is when I left the house to spell Beth, who was selling things. I hoped. It was the first chance I'd had to really think about Andrew's murder. It seemed as impossible now as it had earlier, but through the foliage around the parking area I could see snatches of yellow crime-scene tape. I wondered what our guests thought about that, and if any had realized what a terrible crime had taken place. With my candlestick.

And somehow I had to talk to the sergeant about that. I just couldn't figure out how without making Bruce look bad. I unjumbled some ideas about that, and finally set aside the whole mess. There would be plenty of time later, after lunch and a few more hours in the conservatory and some time at the hospital with Tess.

The tent was busy, which I took to be a

good sign for the Bead Society and the OCO. It was so crowded that even the food booth had been moved outside to make more room. I started down the first row of vendors and forgot all about illness and murder. I was busy ogling all the beads and the items made with them. A bead-induced trance.

The first display that caught me had stunning flowers, all created with tiny seed beads. Purple bead gladiolas and elegant white lilies stood in a tall vase. Delicate hyacinths were nestled in an Easter basket, and colorful gerbera daisies all of beads sat in a maple-syrup bucket.

The crowd moved me forward, and I was facing a booth filled with watches. Hundreds of watches, all with beaded bands. Some were strung with semiprecious stone chips and looked southwestern. Others had bands of delicate pearls, which gave them an elegant and formal look. There were crystal bands and some of seed beads and some with unique mixes of all types of beads. I had no idea how I could select just one watch out of so many beautiful ones. I'd have to have one for every facet of my personality, which would certainly break the bank . . .

In the corner of the tent Jill Bartel was

doing a demonstration on how to crochet a beaded fringe over stone cabochons. The one she was working on was a mix of green, taupe, and peach; I was guessing it was unakite. It was stunning, and the crowd around her was in rapt silence. She saw me and smiled, which is when I remembered that I was also supposed to be working. Beads make me forget almost everything.

I found our table where Beth was busy putting together some simple, yet really beautiful earrings. Each had a flat, white coin pearl with a faceted stone bead. It was blue lapis on the earring in her hand. Several other pairs weren't on cards yet, but they were complete. One had pearl and garnet, another pearl with pink crystal, and a dozen pairs with pearls and teal beads. Back to teal again.

I watched as she slipped two beads on a head pin and connected it to a fishhook earring with the wrapped loop. I call that technique the dreaded wrapped loop, but then I'm a beader with terrible hand-eye coordination. Or maybe I don't have any.

"Very nice," I said. "How are things going here?"

She was glowing. "Great morning."

"No kidding? What'd we sell?"

She held out the display with the earrings.

It had only two pair on it. "I'm making them as fast as I can, but I haven't even had time to hang them up yet. I've sold twenty-seven pair."

"Very impressive." Again a large portion of the profit was going to ovarian cancer research.

"Yes, well so are the sales of your phone jewelry." My cell phone was on display, showing off a crystal dangle like those we were selling. "How many did you bring out here? Didn't you tell me two hundred?"

"I did. How am I doing?"

"Either we priced them too cheaply, or your name is worth more than we thought. So far I've sold sixty-three dangles! Guess we know what you'll be doing this evening."

"I'll take beads to the hospital and make them there. Tess is sick."

Her glow dimmed. "Oh, Kitz, I'm so sorry. Is it serious, I mean . . ."

"I don't know." I let out a sigh. "I guess I'll find out this afternoon. I hate ovarian cancer — and peritoneal cancer and breast cancer and all the cancers that women get. I guess that means all of them. Or maybe not testicular or prostate cancer, but I hate those, too. Did I ever mention that?"

"Once or twice. I know it's hard for you."

"Not for me. It's hard for everyone who

has it and their families." I took a calming breath. "I'm sorry for venting —"

"It was a short vent."

"That was lucky." I sighed. "I actually came to relieve you. Why don't you go eat something?"

"Because I'm not hungry. Not at all."

"That's ridiculous. You have to eat or you'll get sick."

Beth pulled out the wrapper of a low-carb protein bar. "I ate part of this. And I've had two bottles of water. I'm fine. Go shop. You'll feel better."

"I'm okay."

"That's why you keep sighing."

"Short vents, long sighs. It's my new way of life." I glanced around. "Have you visited the ovarian cancer booth?"

"Not yet. I plan to do that tomorrow, or maybe this afternoon. One of the women from the Bead Society is going to sit in for me."

"That's good. Anything else happening?" I asked.

She thought about it for a moment. "Oh, Shannan called this morning. She's all packed, and she told her dad he'd have to take her shopping in San Francisco. She sounded really excited about it." I expected Beth to say something about Mo-Ron, or rather Ron, her almost, soon-to-be, I hoped, ex-husband, or how she was missing the two of them, but she went on blithely as if his trip with their daughter were no more interesting than the weather. "Something else. Keep your cell phone with you this afternoon." She unhooked it from the display. "Sergeant Granger is going to call you."

"Me? Why me?"

She looked around and lowered her voice. "Because there was a murder behind your house last night, and you had one hundred and fifty people here. He'd like to talk to you about them. He wants to set up an appointment."

So she still didn't know who was dead, and how he'd died.

"Okay. But he'll have to get in line — I'm a little busy."

She smiled. "I don't think he stands in line for much of anything. I already spoke with him this morning."

I took the phone and waved a distracted good-bye. The problems in my life were multiplying exponentially. My cousin was trying to take away my house, my cousin's assistant or partner or whatever had been found dead in a Dumpster behind my house with one of my candlesticks. Could it get any worse?

The short and simple answer was yes. At almost exactly three o'clock my cell phone rang. It was Aunt Miranda, and she was hysterical.

Seven

"Katherine," my aunt Miranda said. "Is that you?"

"Yes, Aunt Miranda. It's me." Our cell phone connection was a little difficult on her elderly ears, and it wasn't helping that I was in the conservatory, where lots of other conversations flowed around me. "Wait just one second, and let me go into the living room."

I actually ended up in a closet under the back staircase. It was the only place where I could find sufficient quiet and privacy on short notice. I pulled the chain to turn on the bare overhead bulb and tripped over a Christmas wreath that had fallen off its wall hook. "Aunt Miranda? I'm sorry for the delay. Are you all right? Is something wrong?"

"Yes, something is very wrong. Houston is at the jail. They think he killed that young man who worked with him. Andrew."

"Wait a minute — Houston is in jail?"

"Not in jail, at the jail. Be precise with your language, dear. It's especially important for you, as you remain in the public eye."

I love my aunt Miranda probably as much as Houston does. She is kind, private, and sometimes overzealous when it comes to language. She was an English teacher for several years and the language is her joy.

"I'll be more careful," I said. "I'm sorry that Houston is having to speak with the police, but I'm sure it's routine. The police want to know more about Andrew, and Houston can tell them that."

"Don't sugarcoat things, Kitzi. I hate that kind of bullshit and you know it. I have this awful premonition that Houston's conversation with the police is merely a prelude to his arrest. A homicide charge."

"Oh, Aunt Miranda, I'm sure that's not going —"

"If you don't want to help, then just say so."

"That's not it at all. I don't know how to help. I don't have any political pull, and if they haven't charged Houston, there's nothing I can do. What about Rebecca?"

"Rebecca certainly can't help. She's not well, you know. She has cancer and she's taking chemotherapy treatments."

I hadn't wanted Rebecca to go sit at the police station; I just wanted to know how she was doing with all this. I didn't bother to explain, though. "I'll see what I can do," I promised. "I'll call you this evening, if not sooner."

She hung up almost before I finished talking. That's never a good sign with Aunt Miranda.

I was on my way back to the conservatory when my cell phone rang again. "Ms. Camden?" a male voice asked.

"Yes?" I sounded suspicious. "And who is this?"

"Senior Sergeant Granger. We spoke this morning."

I knew who he was; I just wasn't in the mood to talk. "Yes, we did. What can I do for you?"

"I received the guest list from Ms. O'Bannon, but I have some additional questions I'd like to ask you. Would it be convenient for you to come by the police station and talk with me?"

"Sure," I said. "I can make it about three Monday afternoon. Shall I ask for you at the desk?"

"Did you say Monday? I'll need to speak with you sooner than that."

I turned around and headed back toward my closet, veering around guests and servers. Once inside I said, "I am a little busy today, as you might imagine. If you could hold off until this evening, I'd be very appreciative. Say about eight o'clock?"

"I could come by the Manse if that would help."

"I'll see that you get a cup of tea and if I can find some, a few scones."

"That will probably be my dinner."

"Well, in that case I'll throw in a bowl of strawberries."

He almost laughed but cut it off in midsound. "I'll see you at eight this evening. And, Ms. Camden, please don't speak to anyone about last night's party, the guests, or the murder until we've had an opportunity to talk."

"Guess I'll be nice and quiet for a while. However, it would help me to know who died. And was it murder? I suspect so, since you're homicide."

He sounded a bit more respectful as he said, "How did you find that out?"

"Senior sergeants are only in homicide. Now, can you tell me who was killed?" Like I didn't know, but I wanted to make it official.

He told me it was Andrew Lynch, and I

said, "Can you tell me how he died?"

My plan was to tell him about the candlestick now, but he didn't give me the opportunity. "I'm sorry, we're still not releasing all the details."

So much for my chance of becoming an honest woman. "Oh, and one more thing," I said. "My aunt is quite concerned because she believes you are holding my cousin, Houston Webber, hostage at the police station. If you could let him go I'd be much more popular with Aunt Miranda."

This time I swore I heard a half laugh. "Your cousin is here, but he came voluntarily."

"The government said the Native Americans went on the Trail of Tears voluntarily, too, but not everyone believed them."

"Except Mr. Webber did come here of his own volition. He's helping us."

I caught myself sighing. "Will he be voluntarily leaving any time soon?"

"He's with my partner, Sergeant Hagen, so I can't answer that."

"Well, thanks for everything."

We hung up, and I leaned against the wall. It had been my intention to visit Tess in the hospital, but it didn't look like I'd be able to stay long. Not unless I got a move on now.

I turned off the light and opened the door in time to see my mother leaving the conservatory. Her eyebrows went up as she spotted me coming out of the closet.

"What in the world were you doing in there?" she asked, looking around to make sure that none of the guests observed my social transgression.

I held up my cell phone, the beads dangling and catching the light. "I needed someplace quiet."

"I see." She looked around at the bustle of people in the house and said, "We'd better go upstairs. We have to talk."

I followed her up the front staircase and watched as she moved the velvet rope away from my door and went in ahead of me. Whatever was troubling her was big, and I hoped it wasn't about Houston trying to take possession of the Manse. The other possibility was the murder. I should have told her about it myself, but I couldn't remember what I was legitimately supposed to know and what I wasn't.

"You seem upset," I said as she seated herself in my favorite reading chair. "Are you all right?"

"I'm fine, but your aunt Miranda is beside herself. The police have arrested Houston for the murder of someone who worked for him. Miranda says you refused to help."

I would have groaned or rolled my eyes, but I knew it would only annoy my mother. She and Aunt Miranda are very close. "Mother, that's not quite the way it is."

"Oh, really?" The icy tone was one that could put anyone from a reporter to the queen in her proper place.

"I talked with the sergeant in charge of the case," I said. "And Houston is certainly not under arrest. He is helping the police with their investigation."

"Oh?"

"Absolutely. The young man who was murdered worked with Houston. I'm sure Houston's giving them Andrew's address and the names of his relatives. His friends and clients. You know, all those things the police need to figure out who killed Andrew." My mother thought about that for a few seconds. She would never watch any of the more realistic police shows on television these days, but she has an entire collection of Agatha Christie's books and she used to love watching *Columbo.* I added, "I haven't had a chance to call Aunt Miranda back. Actually, it might be better if you did that, since she's unhappy with me."

Her lovely, ladylike face remained bland, but I knew she was thinking. Finally she said, "So you did talk to the police and Houston is not under arrest. He is helping them. Is that correct?"

"Yes, exactly."

"That is so typical of Houston. He's a fine man." She looked at me. "You could be helping, too, you know. I understand the young man was at our party last night."

"A detective is coming here this evening."

"Before she passed away your grandmother told me that when Austin was much smaller, several murders took place in this area." She rose as gracefully as a swan despite her years. "I'm sorry that one more happened. Now Kitzi, you have to do everything you can to get this murder solved. And do it quickly, please, because we don't want it to hurt the Bead Tea. This cause is far too important. We also don't want to upset your aunt any further."

I followed her to the door in my own less-than-elegant style. "You know I'll do my best."

"And if that's not sufficient, do more."

I was on my way to the hospital, wondering if Houston would actually be arrested at some point, and if that would be a good thing or bad. Personally, for my family, it looked like a good thing. Then his attorney,

Mr. Edward Harrington, could learn a new specialty and spend his time trying to get Houston out of the clink. I had a momentary, but very satisfying, visual of Houston, his silver hair gleaming, wearing bold black-and-white stripes, his hands pitifully clutching jail bars. The fact that inmates now wear orange jumpsuits didn't get in the way of my fantasy.

If it weren't for Rebecca I might have bribed the sergeant to put Houston in jail. It would be mean-spirited for another reason, too: I didn't really think Houston had anything to do with Andrew's murder. I could believe Houston was a sleaze, and I could carry his lack of scruples all the way to con man or crook, but I just couldn't give it the final *oomph* to murderer. More's the pity.

My cell phone rang, and it was my mother. "Is everything all right?" I asked.

"Yes, but your aunt and I had an idea. Why don't you go by Houston's office and see what his secretary can tell you?"

"Lauren? She's serving tea at the Manse."

"No, she was serving tea, but someone called and told her about Andrew. She was in the tent at the time and everyone must have heard the scream. I'm told she left immediately."

Which didn't mean that she went back to the office, but it was only five minutes out of my way. "Consider it done," I said.

It was nearing five o'clock and the parking lot of Houston's building was empty except for a white convertible BMW. It wasn't the newest model, but it still wasn't a cheap car.

I pulled in, grabbed my purse, and made one of those executive decisions to turn my phone off before I went up the steps. It was a precautionary measure in case my mother or my aunt got another wild hair. I didn't mind my cousin in jail, but I didn't want it to be me.

Once up the stairs I opened the door and stepped inside. Lauren was sitting at her desk. At the sounds of the door opening, her head came up, and when she saw me her mouth opened as if she were going to scream.

"It's just me," I said to reassure her. "Are you doing okay?"

"I'm fine. Fine. Houston's not here."

"So I heard. I thought maybe you could give me a little information."

Her eyes were so wide she looked like an old Keene painting. "Now's not a good time. I'm pretty busy. My life is busy. I'm on my way to the police station — they're expecting me right now." She had backed her chair up almost to the screen behind her.

"Is that true?" I asked.

"Of course."

"Okay, then answer this: why are you afraid of me?"

"Who says I'm afraid?"

"Your face. Is it because I said I'd like to pinch his head off and throw him in a Dumpster?" She stiffened, eyes still wide. I said, "I was talking about Houston because he's trying to take away the Manse. I didn't have a thing against Andrew except that he was annoying. People don't get killed for being annoying." I spotted a chair against the wall and sat in it. It gave her a clear path to the door in case she thought she needed one. "Houston is at the jail talking to a Sergeant Hagen, and his mother is very worried. Houston's mother, not Sergeant Hagen's. She understands, in theory, that he went to the police voluntarily, but emotionally she's concerned that he'll be arrested for Andrew's murder."

Lauren's shoulders came down half an inch. She wasn't completely relaxed, but she was thinking about it. "Miss Camden, that's not realistic. Houston wouldn't hurt anyone. He doesn't even raise his voice when he's upset."

"I'm glad to hear that." I put my purse on the floor and got more comfortable. "Did you know Andrew very well?"

She let out a long sad sigh and her proper posture deteriorated as she slumped in her chair. "I've worked with him ever since I came here. Four months. I mean, we weren't close or anything, but he was nice. Monday night I had to make some phone calls for him so he sent out for Thai food. It's my favorite. The next day he even gave me a gift card to Green Pastures." An upscale, old Austin restaurant on the south side of town.

"You never argued with him?"

"No," she said. "Why would I? I mean, I worked for him. You don't argue with your manager if you want to get ahead. A good reference is important."

"Were you planning on leaving?"

"Someday." She shrugged. "When the job market is better, but not right away. This wasn't my dream job, but Andrew and Houston were both starting to let me handle some of the research on investments. Due diligence. I was learning a lot and I consider that important."

"Of course." I didn't see Lauren swinging a candlestick against the back of Andrew's head, but then we can all be naïve about other people when their appearance doesn't match the crime. I imagine that's why defense attorneys dress murderers up in suits to take them to court: it confuses the jury.

I studied Lauren for a minute. She was slender, which meant she probably worked out regularly. She was taller than I was, maybe five seven.

"Do you by any chance play tennis? Or baseball?" I asked.

She frowned. "A little tennis, but that's all."

I nodded. At least she was relaxing. Her longing for the door wasn't quite so intense.

"Lauren," I said. "Was Andrew married? Did he have a girlfriend?"

"Neither. He is — was — pretty focused on business and that's how he spent his time. You know, researching investments, attending functions to meet clients, anything that would make him money."

"Would you mind just telling me about him? Anything you can think of?"

She nodded and gave me what she knew about Andrew Lynch. He was thirty-one years old. They'd had an impromptu birthday dinner for him in April. Houston, Rebecca, Andrew, and her. Seemed a little sad to me since neither of the young people had dates.

Andrew didn't drink much, only red wine or beer, and he lived in an apartment near Braker and U.S. 183. Upscale and very nice. He'd never had any friends come by the office, although he did get some calls. Lauren thought most of them were from clients or potential clients.

At that point she pulled out an employment file and scanned it quickly before saying, "He went to UCLA, but moved back here about three years ago and had worked for Houston for over two years. He graduated with honors. For his birthday he bought himself a used Infiniti."

I was almost nodding off from Andrew's exciting life. "Did he ever ask you out?"

"No."

"Did he ever talk about dating? Do you know if he did?"

"No, he didn't."

"Did he ever talk about doing something just for fun? Movies? Car racing? Going to the lake? Sky diving? Frog jumping?"

Lauren lifted her shoulders in a shrug. "He kept his attention on business."

"Talk about a guy who needed a life —"

"Wait." Lauren thought about it and reached for her computer. "He did do something — he never said exactly what, although . . . he put it on his calendar. In Outlook. I can check."

She moved the mouse around and stared intently at her computer screen. It was a flat panel and probably a nineteen-inch. I still have one of those big hulking things, but at least it isn't one of the green ones.

"Here," she said, turning the monitor so I could get a better look. Since she no longer seemed frightened of me, I stood up and moved closer. "See, Sunday evenings, 5 p.m."

The notation read "TX H'em Tour." And then there was a phone number.

I frowned, looking at it from various angles. "Golf? Was Andrew playing in a golf tournament?"

"No, he thought golf was boring. He did play a little, but just to spend time with clients."

A hem tour. The only thing I could think of was sewing. Sightseeing in various alterations shops? Overseas clothing factories? "Why don't we take a look at Andrew's office?" I said. I used the *we* so she wouldn't think I was going to pillage and plunder.

"We can't. The police must have been here, because everything is sealed up."

"Well, hell." I thought about it for a while.

"What about his car?"

"I don't know where it is, but it isn't here."

I was about out of places. "Can you think of anywhere we might look?"

"Well . . ." She hesitated. "I guess you could look in Houston's office, but I can't. Not if I want to keep my job."

The whole idea didn't seem to be getting me anywhere, not that I knew where I wanted to go. I pulled out my card. "Lauren, I know this isn't easy for you, but I'll do anything I can to help, and I hope you'll do the same for me. Here are all my phone numbers, and you can call me at anytime if you think of something, or if you need help."

She took the card, shaking her head. "Oh, I'm fine. Really. I guess I'll just go home. I mean, it's Friday, and I don't work again until Monday."

Something about her tone wasn't right. "Do you live with someone?"

"No. I have a little house in Hyde Park." An old, upscale area in central Austin, very near the university. She paused. "It's nice."

"But you'll be alone all weekend?"

"Well . . . I kind of thought I might come back and work at the Bead Tea some more. If nobody minds."

Now I understood. Lauren did not want to be by herself this weekend, and I could hardly blame her. Too many unpleasant thoughts and maybe even some bogeymen to keep her company.

"We could use your help on both days," I said. "Would it be more convenient if you stayed at the Manse? We've got lots of guest bedrooms, and you can eat all the leftover tea goodies you can find. Beth is staying, too. You remember my friend Beth Fairfield? She was with me when I came to the office yesterday."

"Yes, I saw her today. She had a wonderful booth. I especially loved her earrings."

"If you ask, she'll show you how to make them. She's a great teacher. As far as I know I'm her only student who was a bead-class dropout. I can't do the dreaded wrapped loop." I picked up my purse and pulled a key off my key ring. "This will let you in the back door. I'll call Beth and tell her to expect you. Take the blue room — it's my favorite.

"Oh, one more thing," I went on. "A police detective is coming by at eight tonight, so if you aren't inclined to talk to him, you might want to stay in your room. It won't be a hardship — there's a TV, DVD player, movies, books, and even a small refrigerator. You can stock it with whatever you want."

Lauren took the key and her sophistication disappeared. "Wow! Cool."

That settled, I headed out to accomplish my next mission.

EIGHT

Tess's hospital room held two beds with a hanging curtain between them and a window at the far end. Her bed was next to the door; a fluorescent light flickered from a fixture on the wall at the head of her bed. It was mostly white, dreary, and dark. It didn't smell all that grand, either. It was a combination of disinfectant and dead flowers.

Tess was lying down, her eyes closed. Her hair, which had always been a rich, luxuriant brown, was now mostly gray and short. A chemo cut. Her cheekbones were more prominent than I remembered, and her skin was waxy looking.

She opened her eyes, saw me, and her smile was as beautiful as ever. "Kitzi. How did you find out I was here?" She began raising the head of the bed with an electric control.

I went to her side and gave her a hug. "I've been stalking you for weeks," I said, handing her a dozen Lammes chocolate-covered strawberries that I'd picked up on the way. They were fresh and in a box that looked like an egg carton. "Something for us to nibble on while we talk."

"You're so sweet."

"I am not, and you of all people should know better."

She smiled again, but some of the brilliance had worn off. "I can't believe you found me."

"I can't believe you'd go in the hospital without telling anyone. Anyone being me. I was at the Bead Tea and I asked about you." I opened the top of the strawberries. "Eat one. So, why didn't you call me?"

She pointed to a chair near the foot of the room. "Pull that over so you can sit down." She ignored the strawberries but settled in more comfortably while I brought the chair close. "I know how you hate hospitals, but I'm so glad you're here."

For just a moment I thought Tess was going to cry. Smart, brave, wonderful Tess.

She was wearing a hospital gown, one of those faded things, with some nondescript pattern that was partly worn off. The edges were frayed and one shoulder was slipping. I reached up and straightened it.

She had an IV going into her arm, and a

full dinner tray was on a hospital table that had been pushed back against the wall. This wasn't the first time I'd seen Tess in the hospital, but every time was harder than the last.

It was years ago that Tess Lewis had showed up at my campaign headquarters; in fact, it was the first time I'd run for the Texas Senate. The office was a storefront near Thirty-eighth Street that had three scavenged desks in it, three telephones, and enough boxes of flyers and such to cause a world paper shortage.

Although Tess had been a touch soft-spoken on that first meeting, her bright clothes spoke for her. She had on a lime green suit with a navy shell under the jacket and a navy flower on her shoulder. Her hair had been dark brown, thick, and wild, seeming to stick out in all directions. She'd held her big black purse in front of her with both hands. My first impression — that here was a woman of many inconsistencies — was right on target.

"Hello," she'd said in her lovely voice. "I'm Tess Lewis. I'd like to talk to someone about volunteering for Katherine Camden's campaign."

"I'm Kitzi Camden," I'd said, gesturing her to a chair across the desk from me.

"Will I do?"

She'd nodded as she sat. "Actually, Miss Camden —"

"Kitzi."

"Kitzi. I wanted to ask you a few questions before I jump on the bandwagon. I hope that isn't rude."

"I consider it smart, but then my mother tells me I'm sometimes rude, so what do I know?"

For the first time she'd smiled and it lit up that office. "I worked on your father's campaign for governor when I was in school. I thought he was a wonderful man — I'm so sorry he passed away."

"Me, too. Besides all the selfish reasons for wishing he was still around, he'd also have made a bigger difference if he'd had more time in office. Unfortunately, that's one of those things that they don't let me control." I remember trying to keep my voice light, but Tess had looked so sincere and so damn sad I had trouble. I made one more attempt. "Sometimes I think if I were in charge the world would be in better shape, but I can't seem to find the place to run for that office. I figure this will do for a start."

She nodded, and I got the feeling she was weighing everything I said. "You aren't doing all that well in the polls."

"I blame that on my staff." I gestured to the empty room.

"Are they all out?"

"Mostly they don't exist. I have some part-time people who help stuff envelopes and such, but I jumped into this race at the last minute, and as my mother has pointed out, I wasn't well organized. I'm working on it."

"Ah." Tess sat back in the chair and began asking me questions. She wanted to know my views on education and on funding education. She wanted to know how I felt about toll roads, property taxes, the gun-control laws, and the death penalty. The thing is, she was so good at asking questions and encouraging answers that I just blathered on until she knew almost as much about my opinions as I did. She was smart, that much was for sure, because when I hedged she'd make just the right comment to force me to explain myself.

I don't remember how long we talked, but I do know that when we were done it was dark outside and I was hungry. "How about if I buy you dinner?" I'd suggested. "We can finish our conversation then."

"Don't you want to know if I'm going to work for you?"

I'd stood up. "You are."

"How do you know?"

"Because if you weren't going to you wouldn't have wasted so much time." I picked up my purse and a jacket. "You know anything about the media or public relations?"

"I used to work for an ad agency."

"Past tense?"

"It was my husband's, only he's divorcing me." She stood up. "He's handling your opponent's campaign."

Now that was very telling, just as her earlier comments and questions had been. "So, in part," I said, "this is a grudge match."

"In part, yes, but not completely. If I'm going to spend time doing something I want to make a difference. I'm tired of writing macho commercials for boats and cars and RVs. Anybody can hawk a pickup, but not everyone can change lives."

I reached out and shook her hand. "Tess, you're hired."

That had been so many years ago. It seemed as though we'd both been about ten, although that can't be true. She'd been an amazing person to work with. From the moment she joined the campaign, she energized it. She softened the look of my logo, created a campaign slogan, and recruited a volunteer staff. Then she booked me on more talk shows than I knew existed.

She was always bringing someone new into the office. "Kitzi, this is Karen. She's an image consultant." "Kitzi, this is Rose. She's going to place our radio commercials." "Kitzi, this is Ann. She is going to book your travel."

When it came to important issues, though, it was Tess who did the research and gave me her opinions. We didn't always agree, but when we were finished with our spirited discussions, we understood both sides of most topics and I could debate them with anyone. And I did. I got elected, too, and I always say it was in big part because of Tess.

Right after the election, I offered her a full-time position as my assistant in the Senate. She had a few reservations, but I didn't have any. She did a heck of a job, and we made a difference. Oh, once in a while something would get past her, and we kept a running total of those. When I left office she had a total of eighteen and I had something like eighty-nine. If it hadn't been for my name we'd have been better off running her for the Senate.

For me, the worst part about leaving office had been the stretch in our friendship.

We still felt the same way about each other, but we no longer spent as much time together. I'd started my training company and wanted to take her with me, but Tess loved politics as long as she could remain primarily behind the scenes. She'd gone to work in the governor's office. She'd gotten married and three years later, divorced. I'd taken over the Manse. She'd been diagnosed with ovarian cancer.

"What are you doing in the hospital?" I asked, helping adjust her pillow. "What are they saying?"

"It's nothing really."

I gestured at the IV bag and realized that what was inside was red. "Which is why they're giving you a blood transfusion? For nothing. Your vampirical tendencies?"

"I don't think that's a word."

"I don't think you're answering me."

"It's actually a long and very involved story."

"You don't tell that kind," I said. "Just hit the highlights."

And so she did. She'd gotten a cough that wouldn't go away, and she had become more and more tired. The doctor had tried antibiotics. They'd done some sort of scan and found some unusual spots on her liver, although a biopsy had come up negative for cancer. I took a deep breath when she said that. One doctor told me that ovarian cancer doesn't move to the liver, but then we'd both been told things that hadn't proved true.

"My body can't fight the infection — if that's what it is — because I'm anemic," she said. "That's the primary reason they put me in here. Also, I can get twice as many tests and see twice as many doctors in half the time. I'm not sure that's a good thing, but it is easier. I just don't like this place."

"What's your CA-125?" I asked.

Tess sat up straighter and said, "Now that's a little personal, don't you think?"

"I didn't ask about your underwear. I'd tell you my blood pressure."

"Because you don't have any blood pressure."

I waited. The CA-125 is a blood marker used for ovarian or peritoneal cancer. A CA-125 level above thirty-five is considered suspicious — it may even mean you have cancer. After a diagnosis this is the one test that tells doctors if the cancer is spreading, if it's in remission, if the chemo is working to kill it — all those questions that are so vital to treatment.

"Well?" I asked again. "Are you going to

tell me?"

"It's at 850, but that doesn't mean anything. It's just high."

Way damn high. My heart hurt, even as I pretended I wasn't concerned. I knew what it meant: the last type of chemo hadn't worked and the cancer was taking every advantage to spread. "It means," I said, "that I am going to have to speak sharply to your doctor. Or perhaps we'll have to try some voodoo. I can also light a candle at several churches, and I may have to take control of the universe."

"Forget me. Tell me about the Bead Tea. I really wanted to be there."

"You can be at next year's," I said. Then I went on to tell her about the cocktail party and about Rebecca in the blonde wig. She smiled and patted my hand. I don't think it mattered much what I said, she just wanted some company.

I talked about the vendors and the booths in the big tent, but I didn't mention Andrew or his murder. I also didn't talk about Houston or how he was trying to take away the Manse. Even though Tess had bigger problems of her own, I knew she'd worry about what Houston was up to, and how my mother and I would fair. I tried to keep my conversation light and interesting.

When I wound down she said, "How are your grandkids? Is Cliffie still the most brilliant child on the planet?"

"In the universe," I corrected. "And, of course, he is."

I could tell Tess was trying to keep the conversation light, and I wanted to as well. If I didn't, I was afraid I was going to cry. It's almost unbearable for me to have to face someone I love and know that they have a disease that's going to take away their life. When Tess was first diagnosed, I saw a grief counselor; she was wise beyond her years and told me that we're all dying, every day, from the moment we're born. She reminded me that I could be the next one to go, maybe in a car wreck or in an airplane crash.

Even sitting in the counselor's office, looking at the calming blue painting on the wall, the words didn't help. Oh, some part of me knew that she was right, and I still know it's true, but there's a difference. With someone who's terminally ill, death seems more prominent. Every day it's in your face and in your heart. Every day you're looking for that piece of magic that will stop the disease. There are also those days that you just don't believe it's true. Mostly though, you know it is, and your heart feels as if it's going to break with the fear.

I thought about Andrew Lynch, so young and still dead. Unexpectedly. Sometimes life made no sense at all.

"Does he read yet?" Tess asked.

"Cliffie? Well, he's only five, but he has mastered reading in two languages. We're working on several others."

She smiled and we went on to talk about my kids.

I have two. Will is twenty-nine and a marketing whiz for some techno-geek company. He's also single and a workaholic. My daughter, Katie, is thirty-one, married, and going through a snippy phase. Since she is the mother of my three adorable grandchildren — twins Cliffie and Shelby, five, and Gabrielle, three — I try to humor her. Or appease her.

Tess doesn't have children, just two ex-husbands and a marvelous Airedale terrier named Rafferty. "How is Raff doing?" I asked.

"Wonderful. He's just a great guy."

A nurse came in, interrupting the conversation as they do. She was wearing scrubs in orange and gold with some kind of tropical print on the top. "I need to get some vitals." She checked the IV bag.

I stood up and noticed that the bed on the other side of the curtain was empty.

"Hey, Tess, did you know there's no one over there?" I asked.

"The woman just left a couple of hours ago. It's nice, isn't it?"

"Very. Can Tess move over there?" I asked the nurse. "It's a lot brighter and cheerier."

The nurse nodded. "No problem. We can do that right after I finish this, but I'll have to get someone else in here to help. We're not allowed to move patients alone."

Tess looked up at me. "You're still changing the world —"

"One bed at a time," I finished. She smiled.

While they went on with the hospital routine, I stepped into the patient bathroom in the corner of the room. There was a toilet, a sink with a mirror over it, a box of rubber gloves on the wall, and a string hanging from a switch near the toilet. It was marked *Emergency*.

The bathroom was overly bright and smelled funny. Actually, I think every inch of every hospital smells funny, so I stay out of them as much as possible. I took my time going to the bathroom, then washed my hands and ran my fingers through my blondish hair. I needed a brush. My purse was outside, so I opened the door to find that I was blocked in by a bed. They were moving Tess over.

I reclosed the door and looked around. Actually, this bathroom was not nearly as clean as I thought it ought to be. The top of the chair rail was dingy, and there was some kind of greenish stain on the wall above the toilet. It didn't bear thinking about, but I could clean it. Tears welled in my eyes. If only it was so easy to clean the cancer out of Tess's system . . .

Sometimes the only thing you can do is keep yourself busy — do something constructive. I couldn't do anything about the cancer, but I could at least give Tess a clean bathroom. I slipped on a couple of the plastic gloves, grabbed some paper towels, and squirted them with antibacterial soap. Then I went to work.

First I cleaned the mirror, then the sink, then around the toilet. Finally I tackled that chair rail. I was only halfway done when there was pounding on the door.

"Are you all right?" someone demanded.

"Open the door!" another said.

"Who's in there?" a third voice yelled.

Good lord! I jumped and threw the paper towels in the trash.

"I'm in here," I said.

"Are you all right?"

"Of course!" I said. "I'm fine."

"Open the door. Now."

I ripped off the gloves and trashed them as well. Who knew it was illegal to clean the bathroom?

I opened the door to find three nurses staring at me. "What?" I asked.

One of them pointed to the string and the emergency switch. "You must have hit that," she said.

"Oh."

"You need to turn it off," another added.

I flipped the switch and tried to look calm. "I'm so sorry."

As they walked away, one of them stopped to add over her shoulder, "Oh, and the bathrooms are only for patient use."

I straightened my slacks, and stepped out into the hospital room to find Tess in her new spot only a few feet from the window. She was smiling. "Leave it to you," she said, "to make even this place exciting."

An hour later the sun was going down, and I had coaxed Tess into eating a little of the food off her tray. Most of the time we'd sat in silence, but I knew she was glad not to be alone. I thought her color looked better, but I wasn't sure if that was because I was getting used to it or because the transfusion was working.

When she finally drifted off to sleep, I went outside on a patio to make a quick cell-phone call. I didn't want to break any more rules, and this place seemed to have a lot of them.

I'd forgotten that I had turned off my cell earlier, so when I turned it back on, I was surprised to find that I had missed five calls. That worried me. I never have more than one or two messages. I flipped through the recent calls. There were three from the Manse, one unknown, and one from Lauren.

I hit the button to call the Manse. I could only hope that the abundance of people trying to get a hold of me didn't mean that something had happened to my mother.

"Let her be all right," I whispered, listening to the distant ringing.

It was Beth who answered. "Hello? Camden Manse."

"Beth, it's me. Is everything okay? My mother —"

"She's fine, but there are a few other things you need to take care of."

"Me? What? What's up?"

"Well, let's see. First, Sergeant Granger is on his way over. He got loose a little early and he'll be here at seven forty-five."

"No problem," I said, looking at my

watch. It was seven thirty. "I can be there in ten minutes. Just give him some food and tell him to wait."

"Great. But you forgot one more little thing, too," she said.

I wracked my brain and then I remembered. "If you're talking about Lauren, I meant to call and tell you she was coming. You let her stay, didn't you?"

"Of course. No, Lauren is all taken care of, and she told me she has some information for you," Beth said. "But that's not what you forgot. I'm talking about your date."

"My date —" And then I remembered. I had a date with Nate Wright.

A half hour ago.

Nine

The parking lot was empty, and the Bead Tea had ended its first day. The only sign of its existence was the big teal and white tent. The guard waved as I started toward the house.

"Hey, Charles," I said.

"Good evening."

"Do you need anything to eat or drink?" I asked.

"No, I'm fine. Thanks."

And that's when it occurred to me that Charles might have information about the murder that I could use to appease my mother and Aunt Miranda. I wasn't feeling exactly guilty about not going by the police station, and I wasn't feeling exactly good about it either. God knows I didn't owe Houston any favors, but there were other people involved. I always wonder if other families have the same convoluted standards that mine does. For the sake of everyone I know, I certainly hope not, but I'll bet they do.

"Charles," I said, moving closer so I didn't have to shout. "Did Sergeant Granger talk to you today?"

"About the murder? My manager called me at home and woke me up to meet with the sergeant."

"Sitting here, you have a pretty good view of the parking lot."

"Well, not the whole thing, but I can see through that split in the bushes." He gestured and I turned to look.

I could see the light pole rising up above the hedge, and I could see the Dumpster, or a corner of it, beyond the fence. "I guess everyone's doing their part. My cousin has been at the police station for hours giving information to the officers. Houston Webber. Do you know him?"

"I know who he is." Charles grinned. "He has a horse that he runs at Retama Park, Rebecca's Cinder Sage. That horse never loses."

I presumed by the grin that Charles often bets on the horse, but I didn't ask for clarification. "I'll remember that," I said. "Charles, did they give you a range of times when Andrew Lynch could have been murdered?"

"They asked about some times, and when I saw people leaving."

Aha. Now I was getting somewhere. "What times did they ask about?"

Even before he spoke, his sorrowful look told me I wasn't going to get the information I wanted. "I'm sorry, Miss Camden, they asked me not to discuss my interview with anyone."

"Oh, of course," I said. I wanted to tell him that I wasn't *anyone,* but I didn't. "Well, thanks anyway." I finished with a wave. I didn't offer him any additional snacks since he wasn't cooperating with me.

Through the kitchen window I could see the breakfast table, with several people gathered around it. There was my mother, Beth, Lauren, my brother Stephen, and Nate Wright. Seems I was missing a party.

If Charles hadn't been guarding the tent I think I'd have backed up and done some primping, but it was too late for that. As they say, plunge ahead anyway, so I did.

"That looks good," I said as I entered. In the center of the table was a big pot of tortilla soup. "Nate, I'm so sorry I forgot our plans."

He stood up as I came in. I expected his devil-may-care smile, but instead I saw concern. "Beth said you were at the hospital with a friend. How is she doing? How are you?"

"She's having a lot of tests, so that's the first step."

"And you?"

"I'm fine," I said. "A little worn, but that could be age more than the day."

"Never," he said, pulling out a chair for me. "Your mother was thinking of making soup for herself and we all pitched in." I noticed that around the soup pot were smaller bowls that held all the fixin's, such as sliced avocados, grated cheese, tortilla chips, fresh chopped tomatoes, and sour cream.

"It's wonderful," Beth said. "You'll be glad you aren't going out to dinner."

My brother was *tsking* at me. "You know, if you carried a Blackberry or an Axim, you wouldn't forget appointments. You could set an alarm to remind you —"

"If I had one of those," I said, putting my purse on the counter and taking a chair beside Nate, "I'd spend my life trying to figure out how to make it work." My arm brushed against Nate's, and the electricity was so strong I expected to see an arc of light between us.

Stephen already had his Axim out. "Look, I'll show you. It's so simple, even you can figure it out."

"Why, thank you, Stephen." I rolled my eyes and caught Nate grinning in my direction. It made me think of my first date and how Stephen had done the same kind of thing then. At the time I'd been mortified, and Stephen had been totally unaware of what he'd done. Kind of an innocent Brad Pitt. Always adorable, never quite on this planet. "You can show me the blueberry another time."

"It's a Blackberry, only I have an Axim."

"Stephen, let her eat," Beth said, handing me a bowl. "She looks tired."

I ladled soup into it. While I added a small dollop of sour cream and a few chips, my mother patted Nate's arm, then said to me, "Kitzi, I want to know why you haven't introduced me to your Mr. Wright before this."

I'm sure I stuttered before I remembered that Wright was Nate's last name and my mother wasn't assuming things about our relationship.

"Uh, he's, he hasn't been around much."

"So I understand, but we've enjoyed him so much. And how in the world could you have forgotten a date with him?" She smiled up at Nate. "Our family is partial to charming men, and missing a date with one isn't something usual."

"I was a little early," Nate explained. "I refuse to think I'm that forgettable."

My mother laughed with delight, and said, "I assure you, even at my age I would never forget you. A handsome man who can also cook is rare."

"It's nice that you appreciate my cooking talent. I just call it assembling and heating."

Stephen was still playing with his handheld computer, Lauren was eating, seemingly stunned by the flirtation between my mother and Nate, while Beth was openly enjoying every second of it.

"I don't cook at all anymore," my mother said. "I tell people the kitchen just came with the house."

Nate smiled. "You know what Katherine Cebrian said. 'I don't even butter my bread. I consider that cooking.' But I think she was an extreme case."

Mother patted Nate's arm again. "And you're erudite as well. Kitzi, you really have to treat Mr. Wright better in the future."

"I promise I will," I said.

She nodded. "Good. Now, just to prove that I'm not as pampered as Katherine Cebrian, I am going to contribute something to this meal. I think ice cream is called for. If Kitzi doesn't have some up here, I do have some in my freezer."

Nate gave her a crooked smile. "I knew you were the kind of woman who could lead me astray."

"You can stand a little ice cream," she said, eyeing him.

Beth laughed and even Lauren appeared to be enjoying the flirtation at this point. I wanted to smile, but I had a sudden vision of Tess, twenty years younger than my mother, alone in a dark hospital room.

The soup suddenly wasn't very tasty.

The doorbell rang and I jumped up. "I'll get it."

"No, I will," Beth said. "It's Sergeant Granger."

Stephen put his handheld away, stood up, and headed toward the back door. "I'd better go."

"Stephen," I said, "wait just a minute. I'll walk you out." I turned to Nate and said, "I'll be right back. Don't let my mother carry you off anywhere."

Once outside Stephen's steps grew longer, like he was trying to get away from me.

"Slow down," I said.

"Kitz, I need to go. I'm meeting Debby."

"What?! Why in the world —" Which was not a very polite question to be forming, since Debby is his ex-wife and the mother of his one child, my niece, the adorable Lily. "Is Lily okay?"

"Oh, yeah. Sure. She's fine. She misses not seeing me so much. You know." He had his hands in his pockets like a kid.

"I can understand that Lily misses you, but that doesn't explain why you're meeting Debby."

He sounded belligerent. "I guess I should just tell you — I'm trying to get us back together. Debby and me."

"Oh." I nodded, trying to look interested rather than appalled. "I'm a little surprised. I mean, your divorce has only been final, what, a year? It took forever; I'd think you'd want to enjoy your freedom." Besides, Debby was never going to be happy with Stephen, at least not until he won a big lottery or fell into a gold mine.

When they'd gotten married, Debby was thrilled to be Mrs. Stephen Camden. At the time Stephen was a wealthy man. However, once she and Stephen had emptied his trust fund and she'd realized no one was going to refill it, she became a very unhappy woman. An uncle on my mother's side took Stephen in on some real estate investments. Those had kept them going for a while, but then Uncle Jack retired. Then they borrowed money from everyone in the family, and at some point I refused to loan them any more. While that annoyed them both, I think they assumed they could change my mind. I didn't, and worse, at least in their eyes, I wouldn't listen to their whining. I thought it was perfectly obvious that both of them needed to get real jobs and cut back on their spending. Debby thought it made more sense for me, or my mother, to keep them.

Debby had perfectly good reasons for thinking we should "help them out"; at least they were good reasons for her.

First, she saw our funds as "family" money. She's from the what's-mine-is-mine-and-what's-yours-is-also-mine school of thought. She also said that Lily wouldn't have to go to day care if we supported them. I countered that if just one of them would get a full-time job the other could stay home with Lily. Debby said that the job market was tight, she'd been blackballed by some former employer, and Stephen was holding out for a management position. Neither of them seemed to grasp that an employer didn't just give you a job — you actually had to work.

More than once Debby and I had exchanged some rather pointed words.

Stephen shrugged his shoulders at my comment about his freedom and continued to look toward the driveway. "I've had my freedom, now I want us to get remarried." He turned back to me just long enough to say, "And, Kitzi, I may have to borrow some money from you. I can't explain, but it's important. I'll pay you back."

Right. "Why do you need money?"

"You wouldn't understand."

"Stephen," I said, trying my best not to sound exasperated. "This whole thing makes no sense to me."

"We have a complicated relationship."

Maybe they did, but I didn't see how since I was pretty sure that Debby was simple-minded. "Stephen, can we have a talk about this before you go off and do something rash? Say, next week? You come over and I'll fix your favorite shepherd's pie, and —"

"Kitzi, it's not something I want to talk about. It's . . . well . . . it just is." He didn't seem happy with me, but I wasn't the one who wanted him to remarry a not-very-nice gold digger with claws longer than my cat's. "I'd better run."

"No," I said. "Give me just five minutes. I have to tell you what's happening —"

"I can't. Not now. Maybe later." And with that he took off toward his car at a lope. I hadn't even gotten to tell him about Houston's bid to take over the Manse.

I could feel myself getting angry. Stephen was adorable, but that cuter-than-thou appearance didn't hold up for long in the grown-up world. If he couldn't find a job, Stephen could at least focus long enough to be of some help to me. He knew the entire family, and he cared about the Manse. Not as much as I did, but his incentive would be Mother — he did love her.

I walked back into the house wishing I had a wand that I could wave to make everything the way I wanted it. I might even use it to smack a few people around. On the driveway near the front door was a rather nondescript white car. That would be Sergeant Granger's, which meant it was time to talk to him about Andrew's death.

My anger was giving way to sorrow. No matter what I thought of Andrew, he was young with a major portion of his life still in front of him. And there was Tess, younger than I was, in her hospital room. There was so much to lose in life. It didn't seem right or fair.

In the dark hallway I stopped and leaned against the wall. Sometimes things are just hard. I put my hands over my face. The stupid house could go — I would gladly give it away if someone would find a cure for ovarian cancer now, soon enough to save

Tess. She had looked so terrible. So weak, and just not herself. I felt like someone had thrown a javelin through my heart and I wanted to cry to wash out the pain, but no tears would come.

Maybe I didn't have anything to cry about. I was healthy; I would survive. It was Tess and others like her who should be crying, but they were the brave ones. I pressed on my eyes with the palms of my hands until I saw spots. Sometimes life just pissed me off.

I felt hands on my shoulders and I opened my eyes in surprise. Nate was watching me.

"Hi," I said.

"Hi, yourself. Are you okay?"

"Oh sure." I let out a long breath. "Nothing but a few little bumps on the road of life. Isn't that what the poets say to expect?"

"That and they like to talk about rain. Into each life a little must fall."

I straightened up. "That's probably in the forecast since I seem to have black clouds following me around."

He smiled and kissed me lightly on the nose. After a pause he said, "Now I have to give you bad news. Sergeant Granger wants to talk with you."

"More fun," I said.

"When your interview is finished, how

about if I buy you a drink? Or some dessert?"

"Either," I said as he wrapped an arm around my shoulders and steered me toward the kitchen.

As we walked through the doorway together, Lauren looked up from the sink and blushed. "Oh." She looked embarrassed, but then she's young. She said, "I'm sorry. I was going to clean up . . ."

"It's okay. Never apologize for doing someone else's work," I said.

"I'll help," Nate offered. To me he added, "You'd better go see the sergeant. Do you want to take anything with you?"

"Cyanide?" I asked.

"I was thinking more of tea or coffee, or maybe a glass of wine."

"That's okay," I said. "Oh, I did offer the sergeant some food earlier."

"Beth took him some."

"Then I'm on my way."

The sergeant was in the small downstairs office, a tape recorder in his hand. It's a room of navy and oak, dominated by the huge antique desk that had been my grandfather's. Dwayne Granger wasn't exactly sitting behind it; he was at the side, using it to hold one of my Mexican trays with his bowl of soup and a plate of crackers. The bowl was almost empty. He also had a pen and a notebook.

Beth was sitting on a loveseat across from Granger and they were both smiling. When Beth saw me her expression changed to concern. "Are you all right?"

"I'm fine," I said. "Bad day and it caught up with me."

Beth nodded and patted my arm. "I'm sorry." Then she turned to the sergeant. "Go easy on her, okay?"

He raised his eyebrows. Beth left the room, and I had to wonder what I'd missed. That wasn't a remark I'd expect from Beth to a police officer.

"Ms. Camden, would you be seated?" he began.

Once before I'd had to give a formal interview to the police, only then I was holding things back to cover up for Beth's daughter Shannan. This time I was ready to tell the detective anything and everything he wanted to know. I was even going to tell him things he wasn't expecting.

First he asked if I minded the tape recorder, which I didn't. Then he wanted my full name and address. Next he read me my rights, which surprised the hell out of me.

"Am I a suspect?" I asked.

He smiled and did a small wave in the air.

"Primarily I'm asking for information to help us find the person or persons who killed Andrew Lynch; however, you still have the same rights under the law. You don't have to speak to me without an attorney present." I suspected that was something he'd said many times before.

"No thanks. My attorney, Howard Voelkman, is probably asleep in front of the TV set about this time, and we wouldn't want to disturb him. He wouldn't be near as comfortable sleeping in a chair here."

Granger smiled. "First," he said, "I have to ask you not to mention any details of the crime scene to anyone."

"Like the fact that he was found in the Dumpster?"

He nodded.

"Fine."

"Good." He checked the tape recorder, then said, "Did you know Andrew Lynch?"

"I've known him for a couple of years," I said. "Let's see, about two — ever since he went to work with my cousin Houston Webber."

"And what was your relationship with Mr. Lynch?"

"Mostly I didn't have one, and I preferred it that way."

"Oh? Why was that?"

"Because Andrew and my cousin had an investment company, and Andrew was always trying to get me to let them invest some of my money. I have always believed that relatives and money don't mix, and that's even true of the business partners of relatives."

"But personally you liked Mr. Lynch?"

Now that was a rotten question. I could lie and say "sure," but that just seemed silly. I straightened up in my chair. "Actually, I didn't care all that much for him. He was pushy, and he was always trying to sell me something." I thought about it. "It wasn't that I disliked him, but he annoyed me."

The sergeant nodded in acceptance. "Okay. When was the last time you saw him?"

I told him about our very brief conversation the night before at the party.

"Did you see him with anyone else?" he asked.

I thought about it, started to say no, and changed my mind. "Yes, I did. He was with an elderly couple." I corrected myself. "Perhaps elderly is the wrong term. They were in their late sixties or early seventies. Is that elderly?"

"I have no idea," he said. "Have you ever

seen them before? Do you know who they were?"

"No. I thought the woman looked familiar, but not . . ." I was struggling to remember. "Maybe I've seen her at the bank or the grocery store or something like that, but I can't place where. I'm pretty sure she's not someone I've ever talked to. At least, I don't think so."

"Would you recognize her name?"

"I'm not sure I'd recognize her face."

He let that go and pulled out a list of the guests. It was a copy, and together we went through every name. Did I know them? Did they know Andrew? What time did they arrive and what time did they leave?

I knew about twenty of the people, and many of those were artisans who were setting up their booths. "Can't Charles help place them?" I asked. "The guard who was watching the tent?"

"I've already spoken to him; most of the vendors were gone by the time Andrew Lynch was killed."

"What time was that?" I asked.

He smiled. "We aren't releasing that information just yet."

"But he was killed here; I mean, in this neighborhood. At the neighbor's. Is that right?"

"That's close."

We continued down the list, one by one. I told him that my mother had been escorted to the gatehouse by my brother around eight thirty or nine at my insistence. She'd been pale with exhaustion, and I knew she'd leave if Stephen suggested it. He came back to the party, but I couldn't say when he left for the night.

Beth and I had gone upstairs around eleven, and we had locked up the house, so everyone had been gone by then. I knew what time Nate Wright had driven off, and I could tell him about Bruce and Delphine Burnett's departure.

Houston and Rebecca had arrived about seven thirty, and I'd seen them at various times during the evening, but I couldn't say when they'd left. I did realize that I'd seen Houston at the end of the party. It was close to ten, but Rebecca hadn't been with him, and there weren't that many people at the Manse except the volunteers who were clearing the last of the refreshments.

Then he asked, "Do you know if any of these people had a reason to be angry with Andrew Lynch?"

That morning Bruce had said Andrew needed killing, but then Bruce had also said he hadn't done it. My cousin Houston certainly wouldn't be pleased with Andrew if he knew about Andrew's plan to move out and start his own business. It would be especially bad if Andrew was taking some of Houston's clients, but I didn't know any of that for sure.

Lauren might or might not be telling the truth about her relationship with Andrew. They could have dated, and he could have dumped her.

Even my brother had done some investing with Andrew, and I hadn't heard how that turned out. If that was part of the reason, besides rampant spending, that Stephen was broke, he might be very upset with Andrew.

"You know," I said after thinking it through, "I didn't know Andrew very well, and I'm sure it wouldn't help for me to guess at his relationships."

"Different generations. Makes sense."

I thought I detected a touch of condescension, but I was annoyed with him and that always colors how I hear things. The problem was that he hadn't given me an opportunity to tell him about the candlestick.

"You know, there is something —"

He cut me off. "Tell me about the lights in the parking area."

"There's not much to tell," I said. "We have a security company that checks them.

Because of its size my mother was always concerned that the Manse would be a target for thieves, so that's just one of the security measures she had installed. Of course, we have an alarm system, too. I'm sure you've already talked to the company."

"This afternoon," he said.

"Good. Which reminds me, I need to report a crime. It completely got past me, because it was so busy today. And then with the murder . . ." He didn't look terribly interested; in fact, he continued flipping through papers in front of him. "So here's the thing," I went on. "A pair of brass candlesticks was stolen."

His head came up. "Stolen from here? Are you sure they were taken yesterday?"

"Not just yesterday, but last night." Now that I had his attention I explained that Beth and I had moved them yesterday evening less than an hour before the party started, and they had not been here this morning.

"You're positive?"

I didn't roll my eyes, or say "duh" like my granddaughter, Shelby, but it did cross my mind. "Yes, of course, I'm sure."

"Would you describe them?"

And so I did. Size, color, ornamentation. All I couldn't tell him was the weight, but that didn't matter much. He could weigh the one he had in his evidence closet or whatever they call it. At least now he knew where the murder weapon had come from.

"You said two are missing?"

"Two."

"And were they valuable?"

"Well, they were my grandmother's, so I assume so." I hadn't thought about that.

When we finished with all his questions, I walked him out of the small office. "Is there anyone else you need to talk to?"

"Who else is here?" He flipped through his notebook.

"My mother, but I bet she's gone back to the gatehouse. Beth Fairfield, and Lauren, Andrew's assistant."

"I spoke to Lauren, I mean Miss Kestler, earlier today. She was at his office last night."

"Also," I said, "the guard, Charles, and Nate Wright."

"He's on the list, isn't he? He was at the party."

"For about half an hour," I said. "He left early."

"I'd like a minute of his time. Could you send him here?" He gestured toward the office.

"Not a problem." Somewhere in the

background a phone was ringing, and I hurried off to answer it.

Ten

"Did Dwayne leave?" Beth asked.

This time *I* raised an eyebrow. Beth looked wonderful, her skin rosy and her eyes twinkling like Santa's. My, my. "No . . . Dwayne is still here. He's in Grandfather's office and he wants to talk to Nate."

"I'll get Nate. You get the telephone. It's Rebecca."

She went in one direction, I went in the other, toward the old wall phone in the kitchen. "Hello?"

"Kitzi, I can't believe what's going on!" Rebecca's voice was high, her words rushed. "Andrew was murdered. Did you know that?"

"Yes, I'm afraid I did."

"It's just too horrible, and Houston is still at the police station. He's been there for hours. I'm terrified that he's going to be arrested. And then his mother keeps calling me every twenty minutes; she's practically in hysterics."

Rebecca used to be a first-grade teacher who could corral twenty-five six-year-olds without ever raising her voice. I'd seen her in action at two school events; she was the poised one who could catch a marauding child with one hand and fend off a demanding parent with the other.

Before she and Houston married, my mother and my aunt Miranda took Rebecca to lunch. I had liked Rebecca right away, so I showed up halfway through the meal in case someone needed to pick up the pieces and like all the king's horses and all the king's men, try to put them together again. I found the three of them having a wonderful time telling stories about Houston. All charming stories, of course. When it was time for dessert they ordered two different ones and shared like college roommates.

Rebecca had handled children, the family elders, and even cancer with a grace that I could only admire. It rattled me that she was so upset over Houston's absence.

"Rebecca," I said, "I talked with one of the detectives just a minute ago. He's here at the house, and he's doing what looks like a normal and very thorough investigation. Houston is not going to be arrested."

"But he hasn't come home and he doesn't

answer his cell phone. When I talked to him earlier he said he couldn't leave." She took a long shuddering breath. "Kitzi, this whole day is like a nightmare."

"I know it is, but it's going to turn out fine. Trust me on that, okay? Look, why don't I come over there and keep you company? I can be there in ten minutes —"

"No, that's not necessary. Thanks anyway, but I'm fine." She did sound somewhat calmer. "My concern is Houston. Don't you know someone who could get Houston away from the police station? Miranda said she asked you to help and you refused. Did you?"

"Oh, brother, of course not." I let out a frustrated breath. "Problem is that I don't know anyone to call except the detective who's here now. I'll just go talk with him. Right away. And, here's something you need to know: by law Houston can walk out of his interview anytime he wants to. They can't keep him unless they charge him. Or he can at least have an attorney join him. Important thing is, they can't keep Houston unless they charge him."

"But I can't get a hold of him to tell him that." Her voice was rising again.

"I can, and I will."

"Oh, God, Kitzi, I wouldn't ask, but that

stupid chemo just wiped me out. I don't have the strength to get up and do battle."

"Of course you don't," I said. "And you don't have to. After I talk to the detective I'll call Aunt Miranda —"

"No, I'll do that. As long as she knows you're helping she'll calm down."

"Good. Tell her I'm talking to the police this very moment. Then you take a sleeping pill and go to bed. Houston will be there to wake you up."

"I don't think that's a good idea; I hate taking drugs."

Here was a woman who'd had poison in the form of chemotherapy pumped into her body and she was afraid to take anything to make her feel better.

"Rebecca, that's just nuts. If it were me I'd be on Valium IVs."

"No, you wouldn't."

"Sure I would. And I'd certainly take a sleeping pill. If you don't have any, I'll send something of Mother's. It will be herbal and you might grow a beard, but you'll sleep."

Her laugh was shaky. "Oh, Kitzi, thank you so much."

"You're welcome. Now I have one question: did you go home before Houston last night?"

I could hear a crinkle on the phone. "Yes,

I was tired. Houston asked Judy O'Bannon, the OCO president, to bring me home. She even waited here with me until I was ready for bed."

"And why didn't Houston take you home?"

"Does it matter?" There was a touch of defensiveness. "Don't tell me you have doubts about him, too?"

"Rebecca, I do not believe that he had anything to do with Andrew's death. However, I'd feel a whole lot better if I knew why he didn't leave at the same time as you."

There was a pause before she said, "It had something to do with Andrew and some investment. I don't know the whole story. Houston keeps trying to protect me from everything. I don't like it, but he thinks he's helping me."

"Because he adores you." I didn't have any more time to spend on the phone; I wanted to be sure to catch Sergeant Granger before he left. "You go get some rest, and I'll get Houston home. Don't worry about a thing."

"Thank you." She sounded relieved and exhausted.

"And take a stupid sleeping pill. That's an order."

"Yes, senator. Good night."

" 'Night." I hung up the phone and marched to the office. The door was closed and I could hear masculine voices coming from inside. I opened the door and stuck my head in. "Sergeant Granger, when you're done I really need to talk with you."

He looked surprised but said, "No problem." I closed the door.

"Ms. Camden?" Lauren appeared, wineglass in hand. "Beth and I were having some wine. She said you might want some, too."

"Lauren, at this point I'd drink Everclear," I said, walking with her to the conservatory. "And please quit calling me Ms. Camden. My name is Kitzi."

"Yes, ma'am."

"That's even worse." I stopped and took the wineglass from her. "If you call me that, you can't drink my wine."

I was half kidding, but Lauren took me seriously. Her lovely skin turned scarlet. "I'm sorry. I didn't mean to offend you."

"You didn't, but if you're old enough to drink, then you're too old to call me *ma'am.*" I sniffed her glass. "What is this? Did Beth pick it out?"

"A chardonnay."

"Let me get you some good wine." I handed her back her glass, walked into the concervatory, where Beth was sitting at one of the tables, and went to the small built-in refrigerator hidden behind a pullout bookcase. It was stocked with soft drinks, bottled water, and several different kinds of wine, including Muscovito, which happens to be my favorite.

Beth said, "Lauren, whatever you do, don't drink the stuff that Kitzi's getting. It's not really wine; it's just some kind of soft drink that, I swear, she makes with Kool-Aid and fizzy water."

"I do not." I poured myself a glass and brought the bottle to the table where Beth was sitting. She had a fluffy white towel spread out in front of her, as well as an open bead box and two pairs of pliers. She'd already made a dozen phone dangles and a couple of pairs of earrings. "This wine is made from muscadine grapes," I said. "Which happen to be delicious and a little sweet. May I join you or is this place taken?"

Beth made a sweeping gesture to indicate the room with all its empty tables. "I think we can squeeze you in."

The volunteers had cleaned the floors, reset the tables, and even spritzed the plants. The room was lovely and waiting for the guests who would be arriving tomorrow morning.

I had to stop and think what the next day was. Saturday. We'd have our biggest crowds and the tea began at 9 a.m.

"Lauren," I said, "come join us."

Beth held up a dangling earring with a turquoise chip, a thin liquid silver tube bead, and a larger piece of turquoise. "I sold four pairs like this today. I thought I'd make a few more. What do you think?"

"Very pretty. Could you make me something similar with blue crystals? Or aquamarine?"

"Sure. The price would be higher, but it's for a good cause."

I smiled and Beth went back to her beading, while Lauren sipped her wine. I kept turning to check the door. I had to get a promise from Granger that Houston would be home within the hour. I was willing to resort to bribery, coercion, and even violence if necessary, but I was not about to let the police do anything else that would put more stress on Rebecca.

"Lauren," I said, abandoning my vigil, "Beth told me earlier that you wanted to talk to me. Did you have some information about Andrew?"

She put down her glass. "I almost forgot. Let me get my purse." She dashed out of the room.

Beth took the opportunity to say, "Rebecca didn't sound good on the phone. Is she okay?"

"No, she's frazzled, and it doesn't help that Aunt Miranda keeps calling her. We've got to get this handled, and I think I'm going to need your help."

"Of course —"

Lauren was back; she tossed a cell phone and a hot pink sticky note on the table before she sat down. "Remember that appointment we found on Andrew's Outlook?"

"Right. The hem company. Something like that."

"What's this?" Beth asked.

Lauren explained about his twice weekly appointments with TX H'em, then added, "That wasn't the first time I'd seen that notation. In fact, it's there almost every week, Saturdays and Wednesdays. I went back through the whole year, and eventually I found a phone number that went with the appointment." She handed over the sticky note. "This is the number." She looked proud of herself.

"Have you called it?" Beth asked, looking up from her work.

Lauren's demeanor and expression went from expecting praise to insecure. "I thought about it, but if I called, I don't know what I'd say."

"Oh, you'd think of something," I said.

Beth said, "Then let Kitzi do it. She was in politics, you know."

"Like that makes me some kind of liar." I picked up the phone and dialed the number. The answer was a simple hello; the voice was a woman's. "Oh, hello," I said, not quite sure where I was heading with this. "I'm calling for Andrew Lynch."

"Is he going to be at the tournament? Or is he canceling again?"

"Actually, there's a problem," I said. I really wished I knew what we were talking about. "He won't be able to be there."

"I'm short two players as it is." She sounded thoroughly disgusted. "You wouldn't want to fill in for him?"

I looked at Beth and Lauren, then said to the voice on the phone, "Sure. I'd love to take his place." Beth's mouth dropped open, and I went on. "You'll have to give me directions. And the rules. Any special rules?"

"No special rules, just simple no-limit Texas hold 'em. Entry fee is eighty dollars, cash at the door."

"Okay," I said. At least I knew what I'd be doing, but I wasn't sure how I felt about it.

"You have anyone else you could bring?"

"Well . . ." I looked at Beth and Lauren.

Surely one of them could play. "I do."

"Let me get your name first. Go ahead."

I hadn't counted on that. "It's Katherine Zoe — Zoelnik. Katherine Zoelnik. And my friend is Luby Muscadine."

"Luby? Is that a man or a woman? We don't usually have a lot of women. Spell it."

"Lupe. L-U-P-E. Sorry, I must have mumbled. Let me get a pen and write down the address."

In less than three minutes I was off the phone, and grinning.

"Well?" Beth demanded. "What kind of a tournament? If it's golf you are in big trouble because your golf is terrible. Your tennis is worse."

"Luckily this isn't tennis or golf. This is poker. *H'em* was apparently Andrew's shorthand for *hold 'em.*"

"Do you play poker?" Lauren asked.

Beth smiled. "Oh, she plays."

"Except it's no-limit hold 'em, and I need to brush up on that one. I don't necessarily have to win the tournament, but it would be nice not to embarrass myself."

"If you're going as Katherine Zoelnik, why does it matter?" Beth asked.

"Personal pride," I said. "Luckily, I know who can give me a little practice before tomorrow night." I dialed my daughter

Katie's number, and when she answered I asked how she was doing.

"Oh, we're fine," she said. "How is the tea going? I was planning on coming over tomorrow. You aren't letting Grandmother exhaust herself are you?"

"No, Katie, I'm not. She took a nap this afternoon, and she's already home tonight."

"Good. I worry about her. She's not young, you know." Katie believes that she is the keeper of the family well-being because I don't pay enough attention to it. I don't know who she thinks raised her. I've told her repeatedly that she didn't get her manners from a pack of wolves.

"Can you get me a couple of extra tickets?" she asked. "I only have two, and as it turns out Mark has to work so I'm going to have all the kids."

She was playing right into my hands. "That won't be a problem," I said. "You and Gabrielle can have tea. I'm sure you'll meet lots of your friends." The upwardly mobile mommies had packed the place this morning, and Katie probably knew half of them. "I'll keep Shelby and Cliffie. In fact, why don't you just drop them off at the gatehouse, and you can shop before you have tea?"

"Are you sure? It would be about nine

thirty. They can be a handful."

"They just need something to keep their minds occupied — it won't be a problem."

Despite the fact that they were not quite six, Cliffie is one of the sharpest little poker players around, and Shelby is not only good, she's ruthless. She'd take her grandmother for her last dollar. Come to think of it, she has.

"That will be wonderful, then," Katie said. "Thanks, Mom. I'll see you tomorrow."

"Thank you, dear. I love you," I added, but she'd already hung up.

Lauren was frowning. "Your daughter is going to practice poker with you?"

"No, no. She's useless at poker, although at Scrabble she can whip almost anyone. My grandkids are the poker players."

Beth said, "I don't see how you can learn techniques from them that will help against real players. They're only five."

"Almost six," I said.

Lauren said, "And they play Texas hold 'em?"

"Yes, but their mother doesn't like them gambling, so when Katie gets here, don't mention it, okay?"

"But wait," Beth said. "If you're the Katherine Zoelnik who'll be playing tomorrow, who is Lupe Muscadine?"

"That would be you, unless we can make Shelby look twenty-one."

"No, we can't. And I don't know if I'm willing to go with you. I'm not very good at Texas hold 'em."

"Fine. Send me off to some illegal gambling den by myself." I drank more wine. "I wouldn't let you go alone."

"Really?" Beth said. "You know, I don't remember that you were this good with the guilt when your kids were small."

"I wasn't, which is why Katie has this perfection complex. I'll have to work on it."

Beth finished another pair of earrings and set aside the round nose pliers. "Before I make any decisions, I need you to explain all of this to me. Andrew played poker and now you're taking his place at some tournament. I don't understand. Why?"

"Because it's all we have. He didn't date. He didn't have friends that we know of. He just had work and poker. I'm hoping to find out if someone there could have killed him."

"Really?"

Except that poker didn't seem a likely reason for murder. This isn't the old west, and official tournaments have a director who closely watches all the action. I'm not exactly a poker expert, but I've watched it on TV and I've never seen anything that would lead to a killing.

The only other thing we knew about Andrew was that he made investments. Those don't have to be so precise. When I was going to UCLA for two years, before I came back to Texas, I worked part-time in a brokerage house. Twice we'd had irate clients come in the door shouting about how some broker had given them bad advice and lost them money. One of the men had found himself at practically zero in his account after pouring funds into the commodities market, which is volatile to begin with. He brought a gun and actually shot his broker, although it was just in the arm. The client went to jail for six months, and the broker got more sympathy than I thought he deserved. He'd been giving bad advice, and he'd made money whether his client lost or won. That's not the way I think it should work, but then shooting people doesn't work, either.

Houston and Andrew weren't handling stocks and bonds, which kept them from being as closely regulated as the securities industry. I had no idea what investments Andrew was so proud of, or if he was really good at making money for people like he claimed. I did know that Houston had put together some limited partnerships to purchase commercial buildings, acreage, and even two private jets. Some investments had been successful, and others hadn't been, according to my brother.

"You're sighing again," Beth said to me.

"There's something else we have to do," I said. "We have to find out about Andrew's business. What he bought, what he sold, and if he made a profit." I changed my mind. "Actually, it doesn't matter if he made a profit — it's whether his clients did."

"How do you propose to do that?" Beth asked.

"I'm thinking about it."

Lauren sat up a little straighter. "There might be a way. I don't want to get in trouble . . ."

"With Kitzi?" Beth said. "Never happen."

Lauren wasn't sure whether Beth was kidding, but she went on with only a little hesitation in her voice. "Our computers are linked. Andrew's and mine. I can operate his remotely. I don't know if I can get into the files you want, but I could try. I have my laptop upstairs."

I could feel myself smiling. "Lauren, you are a genius. No rush to get it done — whenever you have a minute."

I heard the office door open, and I stood up. "Be right back." Nate wasn't around, and I caught Sergeant Granger just as he was picking up his notebook. "I need five minutes of your time," I said. "Maybe less."

He sat back down. "Certainly. This sounds important."

"It is." I took a place on the loveseat and began. "I know you said that Houston Webber was at the police department voluntarily, but however he got there, he needs to leave. Now. Right now. I don't care what he's telling you, or what else you need to know, but he's got to be with his wife."

"I'm really not the one —"

"Doesn't matter, because you can make it happen." I slowed down and remembered to ask nicely. I'd use a bludgeon later if this didn't work. "His wife has cancer and just finished chemotherapy. She's alone, ill, and stressed to the limit. If you don't want another death on your plate, you need to get him home."

Beth walked in the door in time to hear the last of what I'd said. Granger looked at both of us, and thought about it.

"Look," I said. "I know why you're keeping him there. You think he has a solid motive to kill Andrew, but nothing is as important to him as his wife. He wouldn't risk leaving her."

Granger said, "You don't know anything

about his motive —"

"Yes, actually, I do. Andrew was starting his own company and taking some of Houston's clients." I wasn't positive, but I hit the mark.

Granger's face turned red. "How do you know that?"

"Andrew told me last night."

"And you didn't bother to pass it along when I asked who might be angry with Lynch?"

"I didn't think it was worth mentioning." I gestured toward the phone on the desk. "One of us needs to make a phone call. Either you need to call the station, or I've got to call lawyers. As Beth will tell you, I don't care for lawyers."

Beth said, "Please, Dwayne. This is important."

His heart was warring with his testicles. I never trust that a man in that position will do the right thing.

A cell phone rang in the distance and I jumped up. "We'll be right back," I said, taking Beth out the door with me. Once we were down the hall I said, "Maybe he'll come to the right decision if we don't sit there and pressure him."

"And if he doesn't?"

"We'll get Cliffie and Shelby to mug him."

We followed the ring of the cell phone to the dining-room table, where Beth's purse was on a chair. She spent a minute digging for the phone and finally pulled it out. "Hello? Who?" She listened. "I can't hear . . . hello? Hello?"

"Who was it?" I asked.

She punched a button to hang up the phone and turned to me. "I think it was Ron, but who cares? I need another glass of wine while I put my beads away."

In the distance I heard the voice of Sergeant Granger, but it was just a rumble, not distinct words. I said, "Be back in a minute." Then I went toward the office.

"Just cut him loose," Granger was saying into the telephone. "Unless you want to be slammed with a dozen high-powered Camden lawyers."

I'd won — with a bluff.

I tiptoed backward and bumped into someone. By the sparks, I was pretty sure I knew who it was. "Hello," I said, turning to find Nate. "What are you doing?" I asked.

He was watching me with a half smile. "Just standing at the corner —"

"Watching all the girls go by?" I finished. "How's it going?"

"Well, it was a bust until about thirty

seconds ago. Things are looking up now, though."

Eleven

One of the nice things about a house as big as the Manse is that it has many places where you can go to find some privacy, which is what I had in mind with Nate. I went through my list of options and chose the front balcony, which is attached to a seating area at the top of the front staircase. It's not as big as the balcony on the White House, but it's still a favorite spot of mine, especially for a tête-à-tête. We had with us two wineglasses, a bottle of Muscovito, a cheese ball, a spreading knife, and some crackers.

I opened the drapes slightly and led Nate outside. It was a beautiful night. The sun had gone down, and all the lights of Austin were glittering in a myriad of different colors. I sometimes forget how pretty it is.

"Very nice," he said, pouring wine. He smiled, looking at me. "Yes, I'd say just lovely."

"Thank you, and the view's nice, too, if you want to give it a glance. If you don't, that's okay by me, too." Actually he couldn't see me except in the slight glow coming from inside, because I had left the outside lights off. It makes for a nice atmosphere, and just as important, you don't have to fight so many bugs.

Nate smiled and gestured to the old glider. The pillows are cushy, and I'd vacuumed them just a couple of days earlier. "Perfect," I said.

I took a seat and he sat beside me. "Now," he said, looking square at me. "You are about as distracted as anyone I've ever seen. Not only that, you have a line between your eyebrows that has been there before, but it's getting more prominent." He used the tip of his finger to smooth it away. "Want to talk about what's going on?"

And here I thought I'd been behaving admirably, at least normally. I'd have loved to ask what he saw, other than the wrinkle, that had given me away — the *tell* as they say in poker.

I didn't bother to ask, because I didn't want to get off track. I needed someone to listen to me. My brother had failed miserably in that role. Beth, Tess, and Rebecca had their own troubles; my mother was the one I was hiding things from, and I didn't have a therapist.

Still, I held back. Nate and I had been on only one real date, and that was three months ago. I'm pretty sure it was Helen Gurley Brown who said you're supposed to hold off on the blue eye shadow and that much honesty until at least the fourth date.

"Think I could have a little wine first?" I asked, holding out my glass.

He poured some for both of us, and we touched glasses. "To the view," he said.

"The view."

Beth makes so much fun of my taste in wine, I wondered what Nate would say. "Well," I asked. "What do you think?"

"It's nice. Sweet, smooth. Definitely a dessert wine. A little like a Riesling, but softer." He paused. "Did I pass some kind of test?"

"I didn't plan it that way, but I suppose I was curious to hear your opinion."

He took another sip and didn't make a face, which made me think he was telling the truth. "Okay," he said. "Now, tell me what is happening in your life."

"You're sure you want to hear this?"

"Very sure."

I took a breath, opened my mouth, and began. I didn't just talk — I spewed. I started with Houston's call for a board meeting that would, he hoped, take the Manse away from me.

"Nice guy," Nate said. "And you just made sure the police let him go?"

Now that my eyes were adjusting to the lack of light, I could see that a lock of Nate's dark hair had fallen across his forehead. His eyes were watching me closely, and they were sympathetic. Damn. I hadn't expected that. When people feel sorry for me I've been known to cry.

I said, "I didn't do that for Houston. I did it for Rebecca. His wife." And then I told him about Rebecca and that she had ovarian cancer. That cancer was like the thread that ran through all our lives, bringing us together. Houston's wife had it; my friend, Tess, had it; Bruce's sister had died from it, as had Nate's mother. It was why we were all involved in the Bead Tea and why we wanted to make a difference.

"That was a nice thing for you to do," he said. His tone was matter of fact, maybe because he didn't want me to get emotional. Little did he know there was more to come. "So what are your chances of fighting off Houston's takeover?"

"I don't know. It depends on who changed their vote, and if they might change it back. Maybe there's a loophole in the voting process. I'm looking for a really sharp lawyer. The kind who won't stop until we win."

He nodded. "But you haven't found one yet."

"No, so if a name comes to mind, don't hesitate to say it out loud."

"Promise. What's going to happen to your mother if Houston gets the Manse? Will she be able to stay in the gatehouse?"

I almost laughed. "No. I'm going to look for some kind of super duplex for the two of us. I don't mean one that's huge, but one that will be in this area so she'll feel comfortable, and with a connecting door between us."

"Now that could be bad. I'll ask around about a lawyer."

"Thank you." Asking didn't mean finding, but it was nice that someone else was on the hunt. It was especially good that the someone was Nate. In case he did another round-the-world work tour, he'd at least have to call me if he found a lawyer.

"Besides the lawyer," he said, "is there anything else you can do?"

"Well . . ." It was the first time I'd actually stopped to think, something that should have come first. My approach had been ready, fire, aim.

I looked at it like a senate vote. "I should be polling the family. Find out who is voting which way and who might be swayed in our direction. I need some big guns, too." Lobbyists were always useful to move a vote in the right direction. They were smart, persuasive, and presentable. Some had large ranches, hunting leases, and great golf club memberships, not that I could see any of those things working with my family. "I need some staff and some lobbyists," I said.

"Any family available? Or are they all on Houston's side of this fight?"

"That's what I don't know, since we've never had anything like this before. I'm sure I have a list of everyone with voting shares somewhere in my office upstairs." My brother would be the perfect one to make the calls since all the relatives love him, and since he usually isn't busy with anything important. Wouldn't you know he'd pick this particular time to woo back his ex-wife?

Obviously Houston wasn't going to be any help. Aunt Miranda and my mother were out. I mentally went down the list of family members who would be willing to get involved.

Nate said, "Could you get Lauren to work for you for a couple of days?"

"I could, except she's actually employed

by Houston, and that's considered crossing enemy lines."

"I forgot about that."

"I do have a couple of people who might help. My kids. Katie and Will." I was looking at the lights like they might form an answer. There was really no way to know what my offspring would say until I talked to them. Katie is always busy, what with three kids, a husband, Junior League, the twins' soccer, softball, swimming, Spanish lessons, piano, and three-year-old Gabrielle's lesson of the week. Baby basket weaving or marathons or some such.

Still, Katie loved the Manse. She might be a perfectionist, but she was very much like my mother. A fighter on the inside, a lady on the outside. Not only would she shop and have tea tomorrow, but she would also be a charming emissary for the Camden clan, despite the fact that her last name was now Spencer.

Katie had also made it known to me that when the time came, she wanted to live in the Manse. Her husband Mark was a lawyer, and there had been talk of him running for office. The Manse would be perfect for them, but we still had to have possession of it.

"My daughter Katie will be able to make

the phone calls, if she has the time."

"Katie?" Nate said, and then he was silent for a moment. "Short for?"

"Katherine. We're all Katherines. Actually it only goes back four generations. My mother is Katherine Lillian, and she goes by Lillian. I was initially called Kit, now, of course, Kitzi, and my daughter is Katie."

"And her daughter?"

"Shelby Katherine."

"Now that's a dynasty."

Our thighs touched, and the resulting sizzle was so astounding I started babbling. "But the men have had most of the power. So far," I said. "I mean, I was a senator, but that's nothing to my father and grandfather."

"I think it's very impressive."

I took a few good breaths before I said, "Thank you. Okay, I'll talk to Katie first thing in the morning. And maybe Will. My son. You haven't met either of them, have you?"

"Not yet."

"We'll put that on the list of to-dos."

Nate smiled. "First I get to meet your mother and now your children. I'm definitely moving up in the rankings." He slid an arm around me, and it felt so good I leaned back into him. "Your shoulders and neck are tight," he said. He moved around until he was able to massage them.

"That's wonderful," I said. "I suppose I didn't realize quite how much stress I was carrying around."

His fingers gently manipulated my shoulder muscles until I was tempted to purr. "George Burns said, 'If you ask what is the single most important key to longevity, I would have to say it is avoiding worry, stress, and tension. And if you didn't ask me, I'd still have to say it.' "

"Yes, and do you know what Lily Tomlin said about stress? 'Reality is the leading cause of stress among those in touch with it.' "

Nate laughed. "You win. And I suspect that right now you've got plenty of reasons to be stressed."

That's when I mentioned Beth and her ex-husband, Mo-Ron.

"Ah," he said. "The one who was having the affair." I had met Nate the day after I caught Ron in a tryst with a woman other than Beth.

It was when Beth and I, along with her daughter Shannan, had been attending a craft retreat near Wimberley. It was held at the same camp where Beth and I used to go as kids, and now it's owned by Nate's sister.

He was there for a visit. It was actually Shannan and I who caught her dad with another woman, and the following day there had been a murder. It wasn't the kind of camp experience we were used to, but the good that came out of it was Nate.

"Beth and Ron are separated?" he asked.

"Hopefully forever."

Beth's voice came from inside the house. "Kitzi. Kitz. Where are you?"

I stood up and opened the door. "We're out here. Did you need me?"

She poked her head outside and saw Nate. "Oh. Hi. I didn't mean to interrupt. I just wanted to tell you that I'm leaving for a while."

"Oh?" I kept my voice noncommittal. "That's nice."

She dipped her head a little. "Just going to grab some coffee. You know."

"In the kitchen?"

She let out a disgusted sigh, which was directed at me. "No. I'm going out. I'm taking the kitchen-door key, so don't set the alarm, okay?" she asked.

"Sure. Have fun," I said. "Oh, and say good night to Dwayne for me."

"No comment." She waved and went back inside.

"You know," Nate said, settling himself

back on the cushions, "that might be the beginning of the end of Beth's marriage."

I'm sure my upper lip curled. "You think she's interested in Dwayne Granger? He's too macho. I might think Ron is a Mo-Ron, but Dwayne doesn't seem any better for Beth, just different."

Nate gave me a half smile. "I didn't say she'd end up marrying him, but I think it's a good sign that she's at least willing to have coffee with someone other than her husband."

I wasn't sure I was convinced, and if I were, I wasn't sure I'd have been comforted. Beth was in for some hard times no matter what happened. Divorces hurt, because you're not just leaving a spouse, you're leaving behind a piece of yourself as well.

If for some reason Beth and Ron stayed together now, eventually there would be another split. It wasn't that Ron would have another affair, but he would still be the dampening factor in Beth's life and art. At some point she would have to rebel. Lots of people would push her to it, and I might even be one of them.

I would also be distraught if she ended up seriously dating Dwayne Granger.

Nate must have seen my look. He touched my arm, and I could feel my hair tingle.

In the distance the capitol building glowed. It's an exact replica of the nation's capitol in Washington DC only ours is a little larger. It's what you'd expect in Texas. Farther out, the University of Texas tower was lit up to a bright orange against the dark sky. It meant that one of the many UT sports teams had won.

Farther downtown, to the right, there were so many new buildings along Congress Avenue I couldn't name them all. Funny how many had sprung up, including the newest, the Frost Bank Building with a shining art deco glass pyramid on top. I could see several huge cranes outlined on the skyline, too, a sure sign that more buildings were on the way. During the height of the building boom, we'd kidded that the state bird of Texas was the crane.

"How's your friend doing?" Nate asked. "The one you went to see at the hospital?"

"I guess you heard that Tess has ovarian cancer," I said. "She was at a stage IIIc when she was diagnosed. Her gynecologist, a man, wouldn't take her seriously, and then it was too late." Stage IV is when they send you home to make out your will.

"I'm sorry." He knew what Tess was going through, because he'd watched his mother die of ovarian cancer. He knew about the false hopes and the hurts, and how it almost always ended. "I'll listen anytime you want to talk about it."

I nodded, but I didn't have anything to say just yet. I didn't want to explore my fears or my feelings — I only knew that every time I thought of Tess my heart hurt so bad I was afraid it would splinter into pieces.

"And," he went on, "if you want to change the subject, we could talk about the murder at your back door. That can't have been easy."

I took in a long breath, focusing my thoughts on the murder, which was just as tragic as Tess's illness, but not so close and personal. "It wasn't easy, and it's gotten harder with my mother and my aunt Miranda involved."

I'd have explained more but someone else was calling me. "Ms. Camd— I mean, uh, ma'am, uh, hello? Are you here?" It was Lauren.

I stood up and said to Nate, "Popularity is not all it's cracked up to be." Then I opened the door. "Out here."

"Oh, great! I did it. I got into Andrew's computer." She was holding her laptop, practically running up the stairs. "I couldn't get into everything of his, but he kept copies of all his bank statements electronically. I have those." She came out the door and stopped dead when she saw Nate. "Oh. You've got company."

"Don't worry about me," Nate said. "I've sheltered Ms. Camden from the police before. I love illegal activities."

Lauren looked stunned.

"He's kidding," I said. "It was a misunderstanding, that's all. I was hiding from the police behind a rock and Nate just happened to find me." I closed the door, just in case she was tempted to run back in the house. "Have a seat and show us what you've discovered." We moved the cheese and glasses so Lauren could put her computer on the small table.

What she had was interesting, especially since she had decoded most of it already. "This is Andrew's bank account," she said, sliding her finger around her touch pad. A long list of numbers came up. She used the cursor to point. "It's pretty straightforward. I have to assume that this is a car payment, this is for groceries, and this is rent."

"That much? You could buy a house for that."

"This is Austin," she reminded me. "Most of these expenses are easy to figure out. Now, here, it appears he put a portion of his money into a 401(k) at a brokerage firm. Some went into his savings account. Nothing really very astounding." She moved the cursor some more. "By following transactions I could see the money go from his checking to his savings. Then it started getting interesting, because the money didn't stay in savings all that long. About every three months it moved. I think I know where it is. You see," she said, clicking around so that an entirely new screen appeared, "this is his business account. Lots of money going in and lots of money coming out."

Nate and I both leaned forward for a better look.

Twelve

"His business was doing pretty well," I said, looking at the numbers. Half a million dollars had gone in, then another half million. It looked about $250,000 of Andrew's personal money was deposited as well, before there was a withdrawal of $400,000.

That's the way the numbers went, the dollars piling up and then a large amount coming out. I couldn't tell where it was going, and neither could Lauren.

Lauren said, "I don't have access to his Quicken files just yet, but I'll bet I can find them. Then we'll know where the money is now."

"Hello?" Beth's voice came up the stairs. "Kitzi, I'm back."

"Come on up," I called.

She appeared in the doorway. "Hi. I won't stay; I just wanted you to know I was here."

"That was fast," I said.

"Dwayne got a page and had to go."

"Come on out. Lauren found something very interesting. Take a look."

She squeezed in beside me, pushing me a little closer to Nate, and scrolled through the numbers in the business bank account.

"Am I cynical," Nate asked, "or does this suggest a Ponzi scheme to anyone else?"

"I was just thinking that," I said, going over the dollar amounts again.

Lauren nodded. "Me, too."

Beth leaned back. "I am not a numbers person, and I don't know what a Ponzi is. Can anyone give me the short version?"

"The name comes from Charles Ponzi," Lauren said, jumping into an explanation. "In the 1920s he found that by changing foreign stamps for American ones the exchange rate made him a profit. Something like 400 percent initially. He began telling people that he could double their money in ninety days."

Beth looked puzzled. "Very creative, but there was obviously some flaw."

"Several," Lauren said. "He had to get things through customs, and there were delays, but that didn't stop him. There were people literally lined up around the block to give him money, and the average was three hundred dollars. That was a lot of money back then. He had to hire staff to keep up with the demand, and of course he was spending money like mad, too. He bought a mansion, jewels for his wife — things that people do with newfound wealth.

"At first, he paid the early investors off, with the funds that came in from the second and third tier. This made everything look legitimate. Then a Boston newspaper ran a story about him, questioning whether his company and the money were legitimate. Quite a few people demanded their money back."

Nate added, "He actually paid off a lot of them, but when the government did an audit they discovered he'd returned so much money that he was bankrupt."

"Part of it was," Lauren said, "that he'd never purchased all the stamps or international reply coupons to make the plan work."

"Which," Nate concluded, "is why his last name, Ponzi, is synonymous with pyramid schemes. End of story."

Beth looked at me. "Do we get college credit for this?"

"I already knew it," I said. "Pretty interesting, though, isn't it? Ponzi always maintained his innocence, and I've wondered if he could have pulled it off if he'd been just a little bit quicker on the uptake."

Lauren shook her head. "It wasn't possible. He was collecting too much money. We did the calculations in one of my business classes and if you start with just eight people, by the time you reach the ninth level, or maybe the eighth, you'd have to have everyone in the United States investing."

Beth put up her hand to halt the discussion. "Very interesting. So Nate, you're thinking that Andrew was doing a Ponzi scheme instead of legitimately investing the money?"

"Something just suggests it to me," he said. "Lauren, you know more about his business than the rest of us. Was he? Could you tell?"

"I don't know," she said. "I was hired to help Houston when Rebecca was sick, and so primarily I handled Houston's correspondence and his clients. Once we got caught up I did research on commercial real estate and potential subdivisions for him. Andrew was my go-to guy when I had questions. It wasn't until a couple of weeks ago that he talked about other investments — I guess the ones that were just his. He was researching something in Corpus Christi or Galveston. And something at the lake here."

We all stared at the computer screen with

its lines and rows of numbers. They all represented Andrew's money. Or perhaps his clients, but in either case, we were peering into his private world. It gave me a very odd feeling — as if we were being voyeurs and we couldn't even apologize to him for being so rude.

"You know," Beth said, "almost every account in the world has money going in and out, so that shouldn't be odd. We have to find out where the funds were going, don't you think?"

"That's our next step," I said. With some regret I added, "If only we'd gone into that meeting Andrew was having on Thursday."

"He invited us to come in afterward," Beth corrected. "Not during it. I thought I heard arguing in there."

"There was," Lauren said. "The Yancys were furious with Andrew. I was afraid Mr. Yancy was going to have a heart attack. I was sitting at my desk and I could hear him yelling."

"Really?" I said. "What were they so mad about?"

"Money. I didn't hear the whole story, but I think their statement had an error on it. Andrew kept saying that it was a simple computer error — some kind of glitch in the program, but they either didn't believe him, or they were using it as an excuse, because they demanded their money back. Andrew told them it was too early and they'd have to wait, which really set them off."

Nate leaned forward to ask, "Did it ever get resolved?"

"I don't think so," Lauren said. "They did finally leave, and they seemed calm by then. I asked Andrew if they were okay, and he said something like, 'Oh, sure.' He said it was all a misunderstanding. How were they during the cocktail party?"

"They were here?" I asked.

"Andrew gave them tickets last week, and Mrs. Yancy said she was looking forward to seeing the Manse. I don't know if they actually came, after the argument, but it would seem silly to waste the tickets. And they didn't have to talk to Andrew." She looked at me. "Did you meet them?"

"No. I wish I had." I tried thinking back to the party and the dozens of people I'd spoken to, not to mention all the faces I saw in passing. In retrospect I felt like I'd spent half the night in the closet and the other half in my room being lectured by my mother. "What did Mrs. Yancy look like?"

"White hair. Pretty old. Taller than me.

Kind of thin, but rangy looking," Lauren said.

I thought back through the evening and remembered Andrew talking with an older couple. They could have been the Yancys.

"Are you done with this?" Lauren asked, pointing to the computer. "I'd better plug it in or the battery is going to go dead. I'll keep looking, though."

Beth yawned. "I'd better go in, too. I'm tired, and tomorrow is going to be another long day."

Except neither of them moved, and the computer screen flashed of its own accord, creating temporary darkness, then came back on at the screen saver — a beach and palm trees.

"What happened?" I asked.

Lauren was frowning. "I don't know. Probably just lost the wireless connection." She put her index finger on the touch pad, moved it around a bit, and once more the screen changed. "That's strange. I'm still connected —" Then her mouth opened and she made a little sound.

"What?" I said.

"I just had this weird thought of Andrew coming back from the dead to stop us from looking at his information."

I put an arm around Lauren. "Luckily we

know that's not possible. I'm betting you have a more logical explanation."

"Well, it has happened a couple of times before. At the office. Andrew had asked me to edit letters for him, and I was, but then I got kicked off. Just like this time."

Nate said, "Wait a minute, I think I missed something here. This is your computer and it's linked with Andrew's?"

"Uh-huh. I could sit at my desk and work on his things. It's really convenient."

"Yes, but why would you suddenly stop being connected?" I asked.

"Well, if someone locks me out from his computer. Andrew would do that sometimes — I guess if he was working on something private. But the other way is when he shuts down."

"Turns his computer off?" Beth said.

"Yes."

"Okay," I said, "we know that Andrew didn't lock us out, so we can dismiss that possibility."

Lauren said, "Then someone just turned Andrew's computer off."

"But why would it be on?" I asked.

"He always forgets — forgot, I mean — to turn it off," Lauren said.

We silently thought about that, watching the computer that remained eerily glowing.

I felt like a peeping Tom who'd been caught; it was almost as if the screen was watching us.

"It could be Houston," I said. "On the way home from the police department he stopped and turned it off."

"Or," Lauren countered, "it could be the police. If they decided to take the computer with them."

I stood up, which felt wonderful. I'd been inactive for too long. "There's only one way to find out."

"Are you kidding?" Beth demanded. "You're going to break into Houston's office?"

"You wouldn't!" Lauren said.

Nate was smiling.

"Break into his office?" I said. "It's up a flight of stairs and I don't pick locks." I shook my head in disbelief. "Of course, I'm not going to break in. *If* we were going to Houston's office, then presumably Lauren has a key."

"I do, but —"

"But we aren't going to the office. I'm going to call him on the telephone and see if he's home."

Nate started laughing.

Since I'd been so adamant that Rebecca take a sleeping pill, I called Houston on his cell phone and discovered that he was safely at home, getting ready to take a shower.

"How is Rebecca?" I asked. Nate, Lauren, and Beth were standing behind me in the upstairs office, not quite listening over my shoulder, but close.

"She's just fine. I think she took something to help her sleep, so she should be out in a few minutes."

"That's good," I said. "Well, I was just checking. Have a good night."

"You, too." And he hung up. Of course, he didn't know how he'd gotten away from the police, and I wasn't going to tell him.

"You realize what this means?" Nate said as I hung up the phone.

"That Houston Webber is an even more rotten SOB than I'd thought?"

"Maybe, but it also means that you can't get any more information on Andrew's investment business. Even if Lauren downloaded everything we saw, it isn't much help."

"I didn't," Lauren said. "Shit." We all looked at her in surprise. "I mean, damn. Uh, sorry."

"Doesn't matter," I said. "There are other ways to get information. In fact . . . I already have some ideas . . ."

Lauren looked at Beth. "Is she always like this?"

"Always," she said, and punctuated it with a yawn. "I'm sorry, but I've got to get some sleep."

"Me, too," Lauren said. "But I would like to hear what you're going to do."

"Tomorrow I'm going to call Bruce, the contractor next door. I have a feeling he knows about Andrew's investments." I smiled at Nate. "And I'll track down the Yancys, and someone will go to the office."

"But what if Houston is there?" Lauren asked.

Nate reached over to slide an arm around me. "Then we should go when he's not there. Like right now. I hope there's a light on." He turned to me. "Are you driving, or am I?"

"Oh, I can. But, Lauren, we're going to need your keys, too."

"My keys? But if you go in there, isn't that illegal? They've sealed off Andrew's office."

"We won't touch anything," I assured her. "And if you're not comfortable about this, just tell me where your purse is and I'll borrow the keys and bring them right back."

Lauren started into detailed descriptions of what I needed to do when I got to the office and how, if the police had just turned the machine off, I was going to have to get into certain programs and do certain things to be able to get information. I could see why Houston had hired her. She was as detail oriented as anyone I've ever met.

After about five minutes she went to get paper and pen to write instructions down, and after another five minutes I gave up.

"Won't work," I said. "Either you come with us, or I'll have to steal Andrew's computer and bring it here."

Lauren was appalled by that, especially since there would be no sign of forced entry, which would, of course, point to her complicity. And we had to make sure that her computer was properly prepared to accept things, because she certainly didn't want to send anything by e-mail, which would leave a trail.

Nate looked at me. "I'm just waiting for her to say that the moon has to be in the second house —"

"And Jupiter aligned with Mars?" I finished.

Beth pulled her bead bracelets off and began shaking them like a tambourine. "Then peace will gui-ide the planets —"

Together we sang, "And lo-ove will steer the stars . . ."

Before we could really get rolling, Lauren

stood up and said in what I thought was a rather prim manner, "I will get my computer set up here, and then I'll go with you. However, I want you to know that my father will not be happy if I end up in jail." When none of us responded, she added, "I think one of you should go start the getaway car."

Thirteen

We took Nate's Lincoln Navigator because it had an innate respectability that Beth's PT Cruiser couldn't match; it was also cleaner than my Land Rover Discovery. When Nate started up the car, the radio came on, playing eighties rock and roll. "Walk Like an Egyptian."

"Might be good advice," Beth commented.

The rest of the trip was spent reassuring Lauren that we were not doing anything foolish, and that we were not going to go to jail. It was her office and she had a key. Houston had never specified that she was not to come back to work after five o'clock.

"Who are you trying to convince?" Beth asked. "Lauren or yourself?"

"Slow down and drive past the building," I said to Nate. "We can check on lights, first."

Which we did, and there was a faint haze

from the back, but no cars in the parking lot. Nate pulled in and parked as close to the stairs as possible.

"Why are we parking here?" I asked.

"If we're not doing anything wrong, then we shouldn't be hiding," Beth reasoned.

"Makes sense, I guess," Nate said.

I wasn't sure if I agreed, but I didn't want to do any additional backseat driving. One does not get another date that way.

After some discussion I suggested that Lauren and I go up while Nate and Beth waited in the car. Nate wasn't particularly thrilled with letting us go alone, but I reminded him it was just an empty building. And if the police should drive up, he and Beth could make some excuse as to why they were sitting in the dark in a parking lot. They could also hit the horn a couple of times so Lauren and I could find a place to hide.

It was Beth who vetoed that plan. "You two go up. I'll stand at the back corner of the building and play lookout. Nate can park on the street behind the building, and if the police come, I'll whistle." Beth can whistle louder than a steam engine. "If you hear the whistle you two hide, and Nate can —"

"Tell me again how there is nothing wrong

with this," Lauren said.

We went with Beth's idea. Lauren and I gathered our things and headed to the unobtrusive door on the side of the building, with Beth right behind us. Once we had it open, Beth waved and left. Lauren and I slipped on our gloves. Mine were black leather; hers were bright yellow dishwashing gloves, because that's all I had that would fit her hands. We also had a flashlight, which we weren't going to use unless we had to.

The inside of the building wasn't what I would call pitch-black, but it was dark. The streetlights outside gave us some very bright spots and lots of shadows.

We paused long enough in Lauren's office to let our eyes adjust, and then I followed her around the corner to Andrew's door. It was closed, and there were half a dozen crisscrossings of crime-scene tape. I tested the knob.

"Locked," I whispered. "Do you have the key?"

"In my desk."

It's funny: when you're in a dark office after hours, all your primal preservation instincts kick in, whether you need them or not. We were whispering and tiptoeing like it mattered, but I doubted anyone would have heard us if we'd screamed.

Back in the front office I watched Lauren fumble to open her desk drawer because of her bulky gloves.

"Just take them off," I said. "The police would expect to find your fingerprints, remember?"

"Oh, right."

Finally we were opening Andrew's locked door. His blinds were closed, so it was like looking into a cave; I couldn't see anything. We spent a minute or two studying the tape. Removing it was going to be a dead giveaway, in case anyone looked.

"We could crawl under," I said.

"I have another idea." She flicked on the flashlight just long enough for us to see Andrew's desk. There was no computer. "Well that stinks," she said, clicking off the light.

"I'll say." Neither of us moved, still standing near the door staring into the black hole like there was something to see. "Who do you think took it?" I asked.

"I don't know," she said. "Houston?"

"Could be. Or the police." I had an idea. "Let me borrow your flashlight."

I put my hand over most of the lens and clicked it on, running the light along the doorframe. The paint had been lifted off in a couple of places, as if the tape had been moved. Or maybe removed and replaced, which I'd have to think about later.

"Where are Andrew's files?" I asked. "Contracts, papers, and things like that?"

In shadow I saw her shrug. "The police took the files on our clients. I told them that Houston was going to be unhappy, because we use those all the time. Andrew didn't have any separate files that I knew about. Well, maybe there were a few in his office on investments that he was still researching. Or his apartment."

A sharp whistle pierced the air as a graze of light touched the blinds in Andrew's office.

I grabbed the door and pulled it closed. Lauren dashed off, and by the time I rounded the corner she was already reaching for the knob of the side door. "Get down," I snapped.

"What do you mean?"

Another loud whistle. "No one out front can see the door, but they will see you. Crawl out. Flat, on your belly."

"These are my new jeans —"

"You can't wear them in jail."

She opened the door, which luckily swung inward, and then she crawled out. "This hurts."

I was right behind her, inching over the

doorjamb and onto the cement walkway on my stomach, partly pulling myself with my elbows. It did hurt. I could see the car in the parking lot, its lights shining toward the building, but we were far enough away from it that I didn't think the occupants of the car could see us.

I couldn't get the door closed. I didn't dare stand up and grab the knob, and I couldn't shut it with my foot. Not only that, I was lying on several large acorns.

"You go ahead," I whispered.

She had already covered so much ground I didn't think she heard me.

Which still left the open door. I was going to have to turn around, close the door with my hand, and then crawl like a centipede to get out of there. I didn't cuss, but I did consider it. My body was beyond the age when crawling was acceptable, and it certainly wasn't comfortable. Just as I was halfway through the maneuver, the car in the parking lot swung around. I watched, not moving, as the lights went from pointing toward me, to away from me. The car stayed in the driveway facing out for a few seconds then pulled into the dark street.

Slowly, stiffly, I stood up and brushed myself off.

"Are you all right?" Beth called from the

darkness nearby.

"Of course."

I had skinned my elbows, scared myself, and thrown away a perfectly good evening that I could have spent with Nate. And why? To save Houston's hide — and maybe to placate my relatives. It was a waste of my time and talents. Not my intelligence, because I obviously hadn't used a lot of that.

Why did I care who killed Andrew? That was a job for trained professionals like Sergeant Granger and his partner Hagen. What I cared about was my mother and my house. The Manse. And here I was just outside the office of the man who was trying to take it away from me.

I had done it again.

Ready, fire, aim.

"Are you coming?" Beth called.

"Not yet." I left the door open and went up to where she was standing with Lauren. Nate was in the Navigator with the window down.

"Ready to go?" he asked.

I shook my head. "Not quite. I have one more thing I need to do."

"What's that?" Lauren asked.

"You know, for someone who doesn't want to get into trouble, you sure want to know a lot. Maybe it's better if you don't ask questions," I said. "This time, Lauren, I want you to stay here and be lookout. Can you whistle?"

"Not like Ms. Fairfield did. Maybe a little tune —"

"Nate? How about you?"

"Sorry, no. But, I can do an owl call and howl like a coyote. That one's pretty convincing."

I flashed him a look. "You sure it doesn't sound more like a wolf?"

"Might," he admitted with a smile. "But it's loud enough for you to hear, and that's all you really care about, right?"

"Absolutely. Lauren, you'd better give Beth your gloves."

Nate climbed out of the SUV. "I'll stand at the corner of the building, and Lauren, you can drive the getaway car." He gave her the keys, which she took quickly enough.

"Let's go," I said.

Beth followed me to the door, and I closed it quietly once we were inside. "I hope we're not going to do anything too illegal," Beth said.

I thought about that while I waited for my eyes to get used to the darkness again. "I don't think this is a mortal sin, if that's what you're asking. Just a venial one."

"Should I say a prayer to St. Jude, the

patron saint of lost causes?"

"As long as you do it quietly and you don't take too long," I said. "Lauren is getting antsy, and I don't want her to call the police on us." I started around the mahogany screen. "Come on. We're going to look through Houston's files to see if we can find out anything about the Manse." I tripped over something and almost fell. It wasn't big, but it was hard. "What in the world?" I got down on my hands and knees and felt around. "There's something down here," I said. "Help me find it."

"If it's a body you are in so much trouble . . ."

"It was small. Wait, I've got it!" I could feel the cool metal cylinder. "The flashlight." I aimed it at the floor and turned it on. "I guess we dropped it when you whistled. This is a good omen."

I could see Beth put her hands on her hips. "Next we'll find a lock pick and a gun," she said. "Wouldn't those be good omens?"

"Come on."

We went straight to Houston's office and closed the door and the blinds before I turned the flashlight on. It was like a showcase room with no clutter and no personality. Even the little silver computer was gone

— probably at home with him.

I moved the light beam around the room. Amazing how clean his bookshelves looked. "Maybe in those drawers," I said, pointing at the two drawers beneath the shelves.

She took one side and I took the other, with the flashlight on the ground between us, pointing directly at the drawers. Someone had done a very meticulous job labeling each folder. I pulled out one — it was green and marked *New Century.* It contained background information on a real estate investment trust that was developing land in Chappell Hill, a community about a hundred miles southeast of Austin. There were plans, deeds, and projections, as well as deed restrictions and lots of other things that didn't interest me.

I skimmed through half a dozen more before I concluded that green folders were about investments. I fingered through them one by one and found a blue folder.

It was marked *Linder.* It contained several sheets of information on John and Marion Linder who lived in Pflugerville. A time sheet listed every meeting Houston had with them, and a final paper showed where he had placed their funds. Very precise.

What I found noteworthy was the precision of the filing. I never imagined Houston to be so diligent in his business procedures. Just two years ago Houston's company was not doing well, which is why he'd borrowed money from me. I guess I figure if you're that careful, you're bound to make money. Especially when you're as good-looking and personable as Houston. My impression was that people liked doing business with him.

Maybe it was Lauren who had made everything so orderly.

"What have you got?" I asked Beth.

"I'm not sure what all is here. Are your files color coded or is that random?"

"Green for investments and one blue for a client. Apparently the police missed that one. Why?"

"Well, then I have yellow for ovarian cancer in general; orange for Rebecca's tests, diagnosis, etc; and red for insurance filings," she said.

"Anything on the Manse? Or on attorneys?"

"Wait, I think I do." She pulled out a tan folder, and I crawled over beside her. "Houston's personal business."

Together we flipped through the folders. Beth found bank statements for the past three months in one but nothing earlier. "Do you want to see them?"

"No. That would be just plain nosy of me,

and they won't tell me anything about the Manse, anyway," I said.

She put away the files. "Nice to know you still have your scruples."

"Not to mention my standards and morals."

"Although they may be sagging in spots."

"That comes with age," I said. "Here we have paid bills, and this folder has travel brochures. Someone's thinking about going on a cruise."

Beth was putting everything neatly back in the drawers when she said, "We missed one color. Brown. Business expenses. Promotion, travel receipts, professional dues, employment taxes, employee files, office expenses — do you want me to go on?"

"No, thanks." I stood up and stretched. If this was the way my luck was going to continue to run I might as well go home.

Beth was rubbing her back. "Want to try his desk?"

I circled around the expensive mahogany piece and rolled his chair to the back of the plastic mat it was on. There were drawers on both sides but not a center drawer. I guess that's what you get with modern furniture.

"We might as well," I said. "I feel my scruples drooping."

The small drawers on the right-hand side held little things like breath mints, paper clips, pens, a pair of sunglasses, and such. It was the left-hand side that had a file drawer. I slid it open and began to smile. The very first folder was labeled *Camden Manse.* The second had one scribbled word on the label: *Harrington.*

"You try this one." I handed her the one for the attorney, and I took the Manse.

The folder wasn't as thick as I might have expected, but then Houston didn't live in the Manse and didn't have anything to do with the day-to-day workings of it. Instead he had kept the corporate reviews that were sent out every year. Expenses, repairs, taxes paid, and alterations to the grounds or the house. Big sloppy check marks went through most of the expenses. He had put exclamation marks — large ones — beside some of the expenses that came out of the corporate funds. One notation was *Bullshit!* It was beside the cost of new drapes for the sitting area upstairs. Apparently my cousin didn't like the fact that I was keeping up the Manse.

I was getting very tired of files. "This is so boring," I said.

"I have the letter of engagement for Harrington and a copy of the letter he sent out to all the stockholders. Oh, and look at this." She was holding one paper closer to the flashlight. "This must be Houston's handwriting."

"Big and messy?"

"That's it. This is a time sheet for Harrington," she said. "His rates aren't outrageous, but it appears he spent an inordinate amount of time trying to call you. The notation says he repeatedly spoke with your mother. Guess she didn't give you the messages."

"Good job, Mother." I flipped over the last of the papers. "Finally! This list of stockholders and voting shares. And guess what? They all have Houston's notes. This is it!"

A male voice came from the front office and called out my name. "Kitzi?"

For just a moment my heart stopped.

The voice came again. "Kitzi? Beth?"

It was Nate. I heaved a breath that was so deep I almost fell over. "Back here."

Beth opened the door and held up the flashlight so that we looked like Halloween spooks. "We're almost done. Is everything okay out there?" she asked.

Nate came in and shook his head. "Lauren is not a patient young woman. She's driven off twice and come back. Are you about ready to leave?"

I said, "I have to make one quick copy, and then we're out of here."

Except I couldn't find the copy machine immediately, and by the time I did, and it had warmed up, all of us were getting antsy. Finally I was done and had everything put away. Beth had gone back to the car, and Nate was at the front door, holding it open for me. I pulled the desk drawer open and carefully refiled the folder; the original was right back where it had been, and I tucked the copy in my waistband.

On the way out I made sure the copy machine was turned off.

I can't say how relieved I was when I was finally outside, breathing fresh air.

Lauren had the SUV running with the lights off. Nate and I jumped in the backseat and closed the doors. "We can go," I said.

"Do you realize you were gone for over twenty minutes?" Lauren asked, switching on the lights and taking off. "I was afraid something terrible had happened."

"I'm sorry," I said. "There are a lot of files."

"You went through the files?" She was appalled. "Which files? Can anyone tell?"

Beth reached over and patted Lauren on

the shoulder. "Relax, Lauren. We didn't take anything. Kitzi remained scrupulous throughout our quick look around the office."

Lauren was driving a bit faster than I would have preferred, but I suppose it had been hard sitting in the car wondering what we were doing. I wasn't going to show her the two copies I had tucked away.

"And it's over now," Nate said. "Consider it an adventure. How often do you get to break and enter with a senator?"

"Former senator," I said. "And I didn't break a thing, except maybe my elbow. I have a new rule for life: never crawl on concrete."

"Yes," Beth said. "And go to the bathroom before you leave the office. Which is where I'll be running to as soon as we get back."

We weren't far from the house, and when we pulled into the driveway I reached around to pick up the flashlight. Everyone was out of the car so fast it looked like a Chinese fire drill, especially since Nate went to the driver's seat. Beth said good night, then dashed off toward the Manse. Lauren was right behind Beth on the walkway.

The flashlight wasn't on the backseat, so I felt under the front seats and between them. Nothing. It wasn't beside me, and I couldn't remember the last time I'd seen it. In Houston's office? At the copy machine?

"I guess we're alone," Nate said, interrupting my thoughts. "Thank you for another fun evening." He slid his arms around me.

"It was only fun because you were along."

He smiled and kissed me like he really meant it. I kissed him back a couple of times just to show that I meant it, too.

"I'll call you tomorrow," he said.

"I'll look forward to it," I said.

I hurried to the house. Nate stayed until I turned and waved from the back door, then he drove off. I loved kissing Nate, but this time I'd been distracted. It was that damned flashlight.

I went straight up stairs, turning off lights as I went. Lauren's door was closed. I didn't really want to talk to her anyway. She didn't have the flashlight, and she'd be upset that it might have been left behind. My only hope was Beth. Her bedroom door was closed and a light shone under it; I knocked softly. "Beth? Can I come in?"

No answer. I knocked again. "Beth?" I was louder this time.

We're good enough friends that when she didn't answer this time I opened the door and walked in. As I'd guessed, Beth was in the bathroom. The water was running in the shower. I looked around the room quickly, but I didn't see the flashlight. Damn. If she had it, she wouldn't take it in the bathroom with her. It would be sitting on the dresser or someplace out in the open.

I looked around again, like maybe I'd missed it. It's a fair-sized room, but there wasn't much in it. Beth's suitcase was zipped closed, the shoes she'd worn were beside the closet door, and the bed was neatly made.

As I stared at the bed I saw something poking out from under the bedskirt. Of course! She'd brought the flashlight in and put it on the bed, but it had rolled off and kept right on going.

I knelt down and put my hand under the bed to pull it out. I found something metal, all right. And it could provide light, but it was much heavier than the flashlight.

It was one of the big brass candlesticks from the conservatory.

FOURTEEN

I would like to say that I sat up all night worrying about why my dear friend Beth had the missing brass candlestick under her bed. Or that I stayed up reading the copies from Houston's office. Or even that I went over the rules for Texas hold 'em, but the truth is that I have my own method for dealing with stress. I sleep. That night I slept long and hard.

Not only that, I didn't wake up until almost nine in the morning, so apparently my mother, Beth, or maybe Lauren, opened the doors to let the volunteers in. The day was getting away from me, and there was a lot I needed to do.

"You want a shower?" I asked Sinatra, who was sleeping on the foot of my bed. He looked up but went immediately back to sleep, which wasn't a surprise. He didn't even help me make the bed.

I showered as quickly as possible, put on

some makeup, which I can do in seven minutes flat, and brushed my hair. I was carefully avoiding thinking. My daughter and grandkids would arrive by nine thirty, probably a little earlier if Katie was true to form. This morning I would concentrate on poker and the Manse. Life and death could come later.

There was a tap on my door, and Beth's voice said, "Kitzi? I'm going down to open up the booth. Are you awake?"

"Yes, I'm just getting ready."

"I'll meet you at the gatehouse." Her steps grew fainter as she moved toward the stairs.

Life supports you when you vote to avoid things. The Beth problem neatly sidestepped, I looked through my closet and skipped over what I call my senator suits and went to the next level down: professional casual. I selected an emerald green knit top with three-quarter-length sleeves. That sleeve is always a good length — covers enough of my arms in case I get carried away and start waving to people. The top went nicely with charcoal slacks and black shoes.

I added some emerald-crystal drop earrings that I had made myself, and a matching bracelet. I might not have been ready for the red carpet, but I could sure knock them dead at the senior citizens center.

Last thing I did was take the two-page copy I'd made at Houston's office, the one with all the voting shares and who owned them, and folded it neatly into my pocket. A lot of things had to happen today.

Below me I heard voices; I took a look out the window and discovered that the tent flap was open and the place was ready for business. Guests were already arriving.

I closed my door and put up the blue rope, then hurried down the back stairs. In the kitchen I did my best to stay out of everyone's way while I grabbed a handful of strawberries and a scone. Beth might question my choice of the scone, but I could make up the calories by walking briskly to the gatehouse. I was on my way there when I spotted my mother.

"Good morning," I said. "Another gorgeous day."

"Yes, and look how busy everything is already! I was just going to thank everyone."

My mother can be truly wonderful. I knew that she would thank each of the volunteers, then go booth to booth, telling the vendors how grateful she was that they were donating a portion of their profits to the Ovarian Cancer Organization. I've watched her do it at every event at the Manse, and everything she says on these occasions comes straight from her heart.

While my father made his contribution in office, my mother made hers every day in the small ways that have a personal impact. In her younger years, I had seen her work in soup kitchens and treat everyone she served like a guest in her home. She was one of the first to have extra meals from banquets taken to homeless shelters. She made sure that the workers got fed, too, not just the homeless who were in off the streets.

When she couldn't be there in person, she did what she could from a distance. As first lady of Texas she would have thousands of thank-you notes printed every year at her own expense. Then her assistant would go through the paper each morning and give my mother a list of people who had been involved in a charitable event, done a heroic deed, or achieved some special distinction. Mother would send them a handwritten thank-you.

She spoke to so many kids at so many schools, they should have given her a teaching certificate.

It's not that she's a saint. She's still a perfectionist, and sometimes downright critical, but she learned at the side of her mother-in-law, my grandmother, that giving back is the one thing that everyone can do.

"I owe you a thank-you, too," she said before going on her way. "Your aunt Miranda said that Houston was allowed to go home last night. For whatever you did, we are all very grateful."

"Just a conversation," I said. Then I smiled, thinking of the Camden lawyers. "And a touch of arm-twisting."

"You get that from your grandfather." She shook her head. "I suppose there are times when that's necessary. Oh, and Katie is already waiting for you at the gatehouse. That little Gabrielle is so adorable."

"Isn't she?" She looks, and has begun to act, more like her mother and my mother every day. She doesn't get a thing from me, but I love her dearly.

I went to my mother's house through the sliding glass doors and found Katie just closing her cell phone.

"Gran Kitzi!" Three-year-old Gabrielle reached up and threw her arms around my hips. "You're late! We missed you." I had to laugh. First thing and already there was that slightly problematic tone. She was fine — I was the problem.

"I missed you, too," I said, giving her a hug. "Want a strawberry?" I held it out to pop it in her mouth when Katie intervened.

"No, we don't want anything messy on your clothes," she said to Gabrielle. "Besides we're having tea in half an hour." She ran her hand across her daughter's cheek then raised her eyes to me. "Hi, Mom. How are you doing?"

"I'm fine, honey." I gave her a hug, and she hugged me back with one arm. "Where are the twins?" I asked.

"They're with Beth in the tent. She said she'd bring them over."

"Oh, great. You're going to love all the booths. Take a look at the French beaded flowers; they're amazing. And the tea is divine." I held out my half-eaten scone. "These are my favorites."

"Careful, you're getting crumbs on the rug. Gabrielle, run and get Gran Kitzi a napkin from the kitchen." After Gabrielle raced off, she said, "Mother, I wish you'd set a little better example for the kids. We have rules. You have to follow the rules."

"No, no, you've got that wrong. I am the grandmother. At my house we follow my rules. Unless you want to be the family crone."

She shuddered. "That's disgusting." Gabrielle returned with a napkin. "Thank you, honey," she said to Gabrielle. "Maybe Gran Kitzi should sit at the table. Do you think that's a good idea?"

Gabrielle nodded. "Yes. Then she won't make a mess."

It was clear that Gabrielle needed to spend more time with me and less with her mother. Or, maybe her mother needed to spend more time with me. I had obviously done something wrong if Katie was more concerned with crumbs than hugs — especially since I hadn't seen any of them in two weeks.

However, this was a discussion better left for another time. I had plenty to deal with, and I also needed Katie's cooperation if we were going to fight the vote on the Manse.

I went to the breakfast table and gestured for Gabrielle to sit beside me.

"I have to go potty," Gabrielle said. "And I don't need any help. I can do it myself."

"Good for you," I said. "You're a very big girl."

"Yes," Katie said, as Gabrielle headed for the bathroom. "And don't forget to wash your hands. If you can't reach, call me."

Nice timing since it gave us the privacy I needed to enlist Katie to help me. "Do you have time to sit down and have coffee?"

Katie shook her head. "Not if we're going to see any of the booths."

"Then come by after your tea. I'll be here."

"Mother, I really can't. I have to pick up some groceries and wrap a present for a birthday party that Shelby has at four."

"That's five hours to wrap a present."

"Yes, but we have to buy the present, too."

"Buy a gift bag to put it in, Katie. And please sit down. I can't talk at this angle. This is important. I'm going to need at least a half hour of your time."

"Mother —"

"Your future and the future of the free world depend on it."

She rolled her eyes. "What could possibly be that important?"

"How about a corporate takeover of the Manse? Does that get your attention?"

She went pale and sat at the table. "You're kidding. This is a joke, right?"

"You'll have to ask Houston, since he's the one who's instigated it. His attorney wasn't laughing." I looked around. "And, Katie, I haven't told your grandmother. In fact, no one knows but Beth, so don't say anything."

She had her hand over her mouth either from shock or to stop herself from vomiting. "I don't believe it."

"It's true."

She took her hand down. “How can he do that? After all the money you’ve put into the house and the grounds, and the time and effort. Does he have any idea how much work it is? You know he isn’t going to be cleaning the gutters, and it will all go downhill again.” She was so agitated she was practically twitching in her chair. “How is Rebecca going to deal with the Manse? She’s sick, for God’s sake. Doesn’t that man have any brains at all?”

I crumpled my napkin with the crumbs of the scone in it. “One assumes he does, but it doesn’t seem he’s using them.”

Katie jumped up. “I’m going to talk to Rebecca. She —”

I grabbed Katie’s arm. “Sit down. Please. Calling Rebecca would be the worst thing you could do. She doesn’t need this.” Katie was still undecided. “Especially now,” I said, “with Houston’s business partner murdered. And Rebecca’s scared that —”

“What? Who was murdered? No one told me that!”

“Well, yes.” I struggled with words. I hadn’t meant to let that slip out. “It was his young partner, Andrew Lynch. Rebecca and Aunt Miranda are concerned, as you can well imagine. It really doesn’t have anything to do with us.”

"When did it happen?"

"Two nights ago. Katie, that isn't what's important; it's just another reason we have to keep this from Rebecca and handle it ourselves —"

"Where was he killed? Was it downtown? Was he out partying? Drunk or something? Who did it?"

I had well and truly stepped in it this time. "I don't have all the details." Which was true. "I do know that the police talked with Houston at length yesterday, which is why Aunt Miranda and Rebecca, and your grandmother, asked me to step in. I didn't do much. I just talked with the detective and they let Houston come home. He wasn't being charged —"

"That was all you did? You just talked with him and he let Houston go?"

"It wasn't quite that simple, but close."

"This whole thing —"

"Mommy!" Gabrielle said, racing in. "I put the lid down, just like you tell Cliffie to, so then I could standed up. See? I washed my hands."

Here was my reprieve. "Good girl," I said, pulling her onto my lap. "You made your own stepping stool. You're very clever."

"Yes. I know."

Katie was still stewing, but she wasn't

about to have a conversation regarding murder with Gabrielle there. "I think we need to talk later," she said. "After the tea?"

"Perfect," I said, since that had been my goal all along.

Katie lifted Gabrielle off my lap. "Please don't say anything about this to the twins, and I won't mention the other thing we talked about to Grandmother. I'm sure we can work something out."

Our family keeps so many secrets it's a wonder that we all even know we are related. Unfortunately, until Katie grows up and realizes that the world happens and you just deal with it, I much prefer to keep it that way. If she learned that Andrew had been here the night he was killed, or that he was found behind our property, she was perfectly capable of taking the children home because there was some kind of bad influence around. I love my daughter very much, but she isn't always rational. She prefers to be right.

Beth arrived with the twins, and there were more hugs and kisses. "Gran Kitzi!" "We've missed you!" Shelby was climbing on my lap; Cliffie was hugging my arm.

"What are we going to do today?" Shelby asked.

"I'm so glad we don't have to have tea,"

Cliffie said, kissing my neck. "Thank you, thank you, thank you. I don't like tea. Gabrielle says you have to stick your little finger out. That's stupid."

Shelby flipped her blonde hair back. "She was just making that up. She only does it to make you go all weird."

"I don't go weird," he said.

Katie leaned over and kissed them both on the head. "Be good for Gran Kitzi. We'll be back in an hour or so."

"Okay, Mommy," Shelby said.

Katie left with Gabrielle, and Beth began pulling things out of the armoire in the living room. "We need your help," I said. "Beth and I have to go to a poker tournament tonight, and we have to practice playing Texas hold 'em. Will you help us with the rules?"

"Kewl!" Shelby said. "I taught the kids at kindergarten to play, but the teacher got mad because I won all their cookies."

Great. "Did she call your mother?"

"No." She flipped her hair again and sat in a chair next to me. "She said if I gave everything back and promised not to play poker at school again, she wouldn't call Mom."

"Sounds like a good deal to me," I said.

"Me, too," Shelby agreed.

Cliffie took the chair on my other side and said to me, "I told her not to play at school, but she didn't listen. I told her it would get her in trouble, too."

Beth was busy counting out poker chips, and I began shuffling cards. "Yes," I said. "Luckily it didn't. So, here's what we want you to do. Play tough."

"How?" Cliffie asked.

Beth said, "Bluff, go all in, do whatever you can to beat us. And if we do something wrong, tell us, okay?"

Shelby nodded. "Kewl."

"Yeah, kewl," Cliffie added.

I shuffled one deck as I watched Beth hand out our stacks of chips. Shelby and Cliffie accepted her like a favored aunt. They weren't on their best behavior, or their worst. They were just themselves, and Beth was one of the family. Isn't it said that children have an instinct for people? Wouldn't they sense if she had done something . . . something . . .

Beth said, "Red is five, blue is ten, white is twenty-five, and black is fifty."

Cliffie restacked his chips. "And a black with a white and another black is an Oreo!"

It didn't matter whether the kids liked Beth or sensed anything. Beth was my friend. She had been my friend for almost fifty years and *I* knew her. If she hadn't killed Mo-Ron in all those years of marriage, she wouldn't bother with someone she'd just met.

As for the candlestick under her bed, there was a good explanation. One that would make me laugh — once I heard it — and she would tell me when we had a free minute. But I wasn't going to ask, just in case the answer was embarrassing to her. Whatever that could be.

"I'll deal," Shelby said.

"Excellent," Beth said.

I put the all thoughts of candlesticks back in some barely accessible portion of my brain. I was here to refresh myself on poker and pick up a few tips. I needed to concentrate.

I sat up straighter in my chair and said, "This is going to be fun."

Shelby's a little slow at dealing, since the cards are big for her hands, but she knows what she's doing.

The object of Texas hold 'em is to make the best five-card poker hand using your own two cards and the five community cards on the board. There are four chances to bet on each hand, and the game has a language all its own that I hadn't quite mastered.

"Put out the blinds," Cliffie said. I was ready to close the miniblinds when he added, "Miss Beth, you're the small blind. Five dollars."

"Oh, right." She put out a red chip.

I had known about the blinds, I just didn't have my poker brain in gear yet. The blinds are like the ante in regular poker, except only two people put up money, the small blind and the big blind. Cliffie put out two five-dollar chips, and Shelby was dealing the cards, two for each of us, facedown.

Now we did our first round of betting, based on what we thought the hands would end up being. I had a king and a ten. Both hearts. Well, I could get a flush, which is five hearts, or I could get a straight, or pairs —

"Gran Kitzi," Cliffie said, "are you going to bet?"

I put out three chips, although I couldn't remember what each one was worth. "There."

Shelby said, "If you're going to raise, you're supposed to say 'raise.' If you're only going to call, then you say 'call.' If not, people get confused."

"That would be me," Beth said.

"I raised," I said. "I have out more chips than you do."

"I call," Cliffie said, matching his stack to mine.

"Fold," Beth said, tossing her cards facedown on the table.

"I call," Shelby said. "I'm a very good poker player. I'm usually the winner, except when I lose." Once her chips were out she said, "Now comes the flop." She put three cards faceup in the center of the table, or at least as close to the center as she could reach. "A pair of queens and a ten."

Beth frowned at me. "Are these two practicing for the World Poker Tour?"

"Don't talk to me," I said. "I'm concentrating." I knocked on the table. "Check."

Cliffie bet a hundred, and Shelby said, "I'm folding. Cliffie, I hate it when you get all the good cards."

I matched his chip, and Shelby put another card faceup. "Fourth Street."

I checked, he bet, I called. The last card was another ten. As the kids would say, kewl. Except when the hand ended, I had three tens, while Cliffie had three queens. Not kewl. Or cool.

"Where did you learn so much?" Beth wanted to know.

"Hold 'em is on AOL Games," Cliffie said. "We used to play a lot."

Shelby put the cards back into a neat

stack. "And it's on TV, too. The Travel Channel."

We played a good forty-five minutes, and I could feel myself getting back into practice. After all, I am the one who taught the twins to play. Twice we had to get Shelby to sit down because she was dancing around the table singing, "I'm a winner, a winner."

At the end I had what I was sure was the top hand. "All in," I announced, pushing my entire stack toward the center.

Shelby watched me for a minute, her eyes narrowed. "I can't decide." She picked up her two cards and studied them again.

"Leave them down; that's for amateurs," Cliffie said. "The cards didn't change."

"Maybe I just forgot," Shelby said. "Maybe I'm trying to bluff her. Don't bug me, Cliffie." She stared at me, then at the cards. Finally she said, "All in."

She won my entire stack of chips, which ended the game, at least for me. I stood up. "We'd better put these away," I said, scooping up cards. "We don't want to upset your mother."

"It's okay," Shelby said. "She doesn't care anymore."

"Yeah," Cliffie added. "She knows you're a bad influence."

Beth rolled her eyes and started to laugh.

"I think the twins should come with us tonight. They can be Katherine Zoelnick and Lupe whatever the name is."

By the time Katie was back, all the evidence of our gambling was put away and we were watching cartoons. I'm not sure if they were parent-approved cartoons, but I can't worry about everything.

"Did you have fun?" Katie asked the twins.

"Oh, yeah," Shelby said. "And I won."

"Won what?" her mother asked.

Shelby rolled her eyes. "You know. I just won."

"Don't do that to me," she said. "It's rude. Now, I have to talk with Gran Kitzi for a while. Can you three play on the patio?"

"Can we go see Sinatra?" Cliffie asked. "I haven't seen him at all."

"Yeah," Shelby added.

"Sure," I said. "He's in the —" I just realized where he was. "I left him closed up in my bedroom. I hope he hasn't torn the place apart. Damn."

"Gran Kitzi said a word!" Gabrielle piped up.

Beth scooped up Gabrielle. "I'll go with the kids, and we'll take care of Sinatra. Want us to bring him back here for the day?"

"Yes," I said. "But if he's done something terrible —"

"I'll clean it up. I'll consider it my penance for giving him to you in the first place."

Katie and I got up and went to the table where we sat across from each other. "All right," Katie said. "Give me the details. How bad is it?"

Fifteen

Katie's face, so lovely, with its smooth skin and delicate bone structure, had little lines that I'd never noticed before. Were those from the seriousness of our topic, or was her outlook on life making her old?

Kate had been such an adorable child, so fair that she was almost ethereal, wispy like she could float away. When she was a baby I remember watching her sleep, as I suppose all new mothers do with their firstborn, and thinking that this had to be the most angelic child ever born. And then she grew. She remained fragile and beautiful in appearance, but her first word had been *no,* as in *not now, not ever, and I really mean it.* We had an old English sheepdog at the time that was short on brains but big on beauty. Before Katie's second birthday she had taught that dog to sit and to stay, not for fun, but because she didn't want a hundred-pound fur ball knocking her down.

In school it became obvious that Katie was both bright and ambitious. If there was a spelling bee, she wanted to win. If there was a math contest, she went into it with the full intention of coming out first. If she wasn't the winner, then she would arrive home not disappointed as other kids would be, but furious that she hadn't worked harder, studied more, or whatever.

Some people said I was driving her to be the best, but the truth is it didn't matter a whit to me. I don't judge people by where they land on the world's scale, and I never have. When I was in elementary school, I overheard my mother telling my aunt that if I made it to sixth grade without flunking out or being kicked out, she would consider me a success. I took her at her word and stayed out of too much trouble and passed all my classes, some of them by the skin of my teeth.

I did a much better job in high school because by then I could see some value in school. Besides, I wanted to go off to college, and that wouldn't happen unless I pulled up my grades. Katie, on the other hand, was valedictorian in middle school and high school. She did very well in college, but she'd finally found other interests: her sorority and boys.

She never lost her early strength. Even when Katie had been pushed around by the class bully in fifth grade, she had handled it in her own style. Apparently she'd been a target because of her last name, because she was wearing braces, and because she was small and thin for her age. Every morning before school, the bully, Jared Marshton, would stop her outside of the building and take away her lunch money. Then Katie took to hiding it in her underwear, which is when he pushed her down and threw her notebook in the mud. At that point a teacher saw the altercation and came running over, just in time to see Katie pick up her notebook and slam it into Jared's face.

I never would have heard about it if it hadn't been for the teacher. Katie might have been angelic on the outside, but like my mother, and I suppose most of the Camden women, she's got that tough core. Problem was, the cover over the toughness was getting hard, too.

I was going to have to take some time and convince her that life was much easier if you didn't try to force everything to your will. I would do that after the battle for the house was over.

She looked up now from the pages I'd copied in Houston's office. "You're sure this is Houston's writing?"

I wanted to brush her light brown hair back from her forehead, but those kinds of endearing gestures weren't welcome at this stage of her life. "I'm positive, honey. It's always been big and bold like that."

"Where did you get this?" she asked, fingering the pages in front of her.

Now that wasn't a place I wanted this conversation to go. "Kate, that's a rabbit hole, as they say in my workshops for the computer industry, and we need to stay on topic. The topic is: how do we stop Houston? Do you have any ideas?"

"Lawyers?"

"That was my first thought, and I have talked with Howard —"

"Mother, he's a dinosaur. And not a very predatory one, either. He's a . . ." She snapped her fingers to help remember the word. "Herbivore. He eats plants and leaves."

"You're right, but he's a very nice herbivore," I said. "And he is my lawyer, so I had Houston's lawyer fax some things to him. I am asking around to see if we can find the kind of lawyer who is predatory. Carnivorous."

"Eats other lawyers for lunch. And dinner."

"Unfortunately, so far I haven't found one, and we don't have all that much time."

"That's another thing I don't understand," she said. "Houston obviously sent out letters, or called everyone in the corporation, and so, how come we're just now finding out about it two weeks before the meeting? Aren't we required to get some kind of notice, too?"

"Yes, but it's something like two weeks' notice if I remember correctly. Yours will probably arrive next week sometime. Something did come to the Manse and someone signed for it, but I never received it. I still wouldn't know about the takeover fight if Houston's lawyer hadn't called me all pissy. I guess I was supposed to respond with a cordial note saying that I would be packing and out of here in two weeks or before the next coven gathering."

"Mother," Kate snapped. "Do you have to talk that way?"

"What way?"

"First you said *pissy,* and then you said *coven.* Shelby and Cliffie ask me about those words when they come home. What am I supposed to say?"

I wanted to roll my eyes like Shelby. "Tell them to ask me about words that I use. The twins are very bright, and they'll be even brighter if you don't shelter them so much."

"That is not true. We live in a very frightening world. It's my job to keep them safe and secure. It's not like when you were raising us. You can't just turn kids loose and say, 'Go outside and play.' "

Obviously there was more behind this perfectionism than I'd thought. Katie actually sounded as if she feared she might fail somehow and endanger her children. I wondered if that was even possible: Katie afraid. The concept was like peering through the looking glass backward. I certainly didn't want it to be true.

"You're right," I said. "I'm sorry. I'll be more careful around the children."

"You're not going to ask me to give you a rule book?"

"No," I said. "I asked for one last year, and you never sent it. So let's go back to the Manse. You didn't receive a letter, right?"

"Right."

"I think I'm going to call Mr. Harrington on that. It might have been some little trick on their part. If you didn't show up at the meeting, that would swing the vote even more in Houston's favor." It was right on the tip of my tongue to say that he was a sneaky bastard, but I didn't. "Since it's the weekend, we can't call the lawyer. So let's look at the list. As far as I can tell, these are all the people who have a right to vote on who occupies the house."

Kate was looking up and down the list. "It looks like Houston has talked to all of them. Of course, he neatly skirted our family. The question is, what do we do?"

"First, call some of the people on our side. See if they still have the letter from Houston. I'd be very curious to see what was in it, what reasons he used for wanting us out. Next, we start with the relatives we think we can swing over to our side."

She didn't look as cheery as she had when she'd arrived this morning, and those tiny lines were more prominent. "And you want me to make the calls?"

"You don't have to call everyone on the list, just enough people to see if Houston's count is accurate, and then a few to see if we can shift the vote in our favor." If Shelby had shown up with the same disgusted look that Katie had on her face, she'd be in trouble. "You do want our side of the family to keep the Manse, don't you? If this doesn't matter to you, then fine. Your grandmother and I can move into a duplex and be done with it."

"That's blackmail. This whole thing feels

like you're blackmailing me."

"Why? Because I'm asking you to do something? That's ridiculous, especially since in the long run it's for all of us." I leaned forward. "You know, Katie, I have a life and a business as well as the Manse. The bottom line is that I can't do it all."

For a moment she looked stricken, as if I'd said something that hurt her. Before I could ask about it, she lifted her head and took a deep breath. "I'll be happy to make the calls." She snatched the papers from the table and put them in her purse as she stood up. "I'll pick up a present on the way home and put it in a gift bag. We'll order pizza for dinner."

"I have gift bags," I said. "Take one of mine. And there's a whole pot of tortilla soup in the refrigerator that you're more than welcome to take."

"Thank you, but I can handle this."

I stood to look her in the eye. "Honey, I didn't mean to make you angry. I simply need some help —"

"Fine. And where is golden boy Will? You have two offspring, remember? He doesn't even have a family, so he's got more time to help."

Will is younger than Katie, unmarried, and working for a start-up company. He puts in sixty hours a week, and those hours have created something like a crevasse, almost as wide as the Grand Canyon, between himself and the rest of us. I keep hoping that it's another of those phases that we all go through, and I hope that it will end soon.

I don't know exactly what drives him, but I'm pretty sure that this is another example of how Will fights against living up to the family standards. It's bad enough to have a family that lives and breathes politics when you're a kid who'd rather be playing with Matchbox cars. It's even worse when your older sister excels, practically over the top, academically. It's not that Will wasn't as bright; he was. He was even more charming than Katie when he chose to be, but Will too often didn't choose. He still doesn't.

Will is the one who loves to point out how screwed up the people in our family are. I've tried in vain to tell him that this is not a topic you bring up at Thanksgiving dinner, no matter how right you are. We have one family member, a U.S. senator, who thinks he was blessed at birth to be better than everyone else. Even sadder, his sons believe they are of the ruling class, too, and their mother is simply the maid who sees to it that they, and their house, always look good. They take dysfunction to a whole new level. Will and I agree on that, but that's still not a good reason to tell the senator and his sons they are "so dumb they could throw themselves at the floor and miss."

Will has a bit of my grandfather in him. That same spirit of the wildcatter, robber baron. My grandfather spent sixteen years as governor of Texas, and he was a thoroughly wonderful person. I adored him. He knew how to channel his rebellious energy; at least, he knew how by the time I came along.

Will is still struggling. One of his first big loves had been a young woman who was a topless dancer, and I think he was thrilled that it rocked the family. I never thought he had much in common with her, but the way some of the relatives talked you'd think he was dating an Al Qaeda terrorist who ran a brothel.

When that relationship ended, as I knew it quickly would, Will decided to become a geek. His word, not mine. He went to work for a start-up company, and now he puts in a marathon workweek every week. He doesn't take vacations, and weekends give him only enough free time to do his laundry before he is back on the computer or back at the office.

You have to be able to hold your own in a family of strong-willed, independent people. Will can, but he's chosen to run away from all of us. Oh, I see him once a month or so, for lunch or breakfast, but I want more, and I know it will happen. I'm just not sure how long that's going to take.

"And," Katie went on, "what's wrong with your brother? Stephen doesn't do anything as far as I can tell. Why can't he make the phone calls?"

A sigh slipped out. Someone once told me they loved driving by the Camden Manse because they just knew the people who lived inside must be really happy.

Well, on some days I am, and on others I'm not. I don't think the house has much to do with it. When I leave the Manse, I'll be just as happy as I was before. I only hoped that day didn't come in the next week or so.

"It's okay," I said, hearing the regret in my own voice.

Katie stared at me for a long time and finally said, "I'm sorry, Mom. I didn't mean to blame you for the way Will and Uncle Stephen are."

I stood up. "I know."

She took in a deep breath. "I know that

you're busy, too, so I'll help. I'll make the calls."

"Are you sure? I did try to get Stephen to help, but he's off on some holy quest to get your aunt Debby to remarry him."

Katie shook her head. "Isn't that just typical? Sometimes I think half the men in our family are stupid and the other half are assholes."

I let my eyes widen. "Katie said a *word!*"

"Don't tell my kids." She looked rueful. "Do you ever think it would be easier if we were just like everybody else?"

"Honey, we are just like everybody else. Trust me on that."

"I always think everyone else is smarter and happier."

"Most people think that — about everybody else. It may be the single biggest problem in the world."

She didn't look convinced. "I'll go round up my kids and get started on my calls. Bye."

"Bye, honey."

I was driving slowly, looking for house number 9038. It would be on my right, and it was the home of the Yancys, Earl and Louise, clients of Andrew Lynch.

The neighborhood was very nice, in a

northwest section of Austin called Balcones Village. The houses were mildly reminiscent of the seventies; they were large, nestled on good-sized lots with full-grown trees making the area lush and green. Between the houses I could glimpse the golf course, and if I went far enough down the road, I knew I'd end up at the Balcones Country Club.

I had a reporter friend who lived nearby, and I'd visited him more than once, except I always got lost in the twisting and turnings of the streets. I had finally located the street; now, if I could only find 9038. I hadn't told anyone I was coming here. Actually I was headed for the hospital when I realized it was Saturday and Tess would probably be overwhelmed with people. I would see her later or the next day. She'd love to hear about the poker tournament. I just had to hope Beth and I would come back alive.

I passed a long ranch-style home with a circular drive and banana trees coming up near the front porch. Next to that was a two-story, tan-brick house that was a little institutional looking, but exceptionally neat. I squinted at the numbers beside the porch — 9038, finally. I had found the home of the Yancys.

Not only had I not told anyone I was coming, but I also hadn't called the Yancys first.

It just seemed wiser to show up and request a few minutes of their time. I didn't want them prepared. I wanted them to tell me the truth about Andrew and his investments. They might give me exactly the information I needed, which would be great, since then I wouldn't have to go to the poker tournament.

There were no cars on the street, so I parked in the driveway and took my purse with me as I went to the door. It was painted a creamy color that matched the trim. Conservative, but in good taste. I rang the doorbell and waited, wondering if they would be there.

"Yes?" The door opened and Mrs. Yancy was standing there. I recognized her from the party and the office. I knew now what had made the identification so difficult at the party: then she'd had her hair pulled up with a magnificent Chinese clip holding it in place. In the office she'd had her hair down and in an old-fashioned pageboy, the way it was now.

Everything about her was classic, lovely, and just a bit out of date.

"Hello," I said, looking up at her. "You're Louise Yancy, aren't you?"

"Yes, I am. And you're Kitzi Camden! We were at your party the other night, and I never had the opportunity to meet you. Won't you come in?"

I followed her through the house, which was a little dark, nicely decorated, and like Mrs. Yancy, a little out of date. The carpet was beige, the couches a light turquoise silk, and there were several glass cases with Hummel figurines. The pinch-pleated drapes were a soft gold and lined.

"We usually keep it dark in here so the energy bills won't be so high," she said, opening the drapes. "Electricity is so expensive these days, and Austin is not going to get any cheaper."

"Oh, believe me, I know about that," I said.

She smiled. "Yes, I'm sure you do. But your home is lovely. Please, sit down, Miss Camden."

"Kitzi."

"And I'm Louise." We sat on opposite couches.

"Your home is lovely, too," I said. "And right on the golf course."

"Isn't that nice? Earl, my husband, and I used to play a great deal, but he had a heart attack a few years ago, so we've cut back. I try to get in a few days a week, and then sometimes I'll be on the back porch and friends will go by in their carts and invite me to join them. It's only the third hole, so I just grab my clubs and go."

"How fun."

"There are some advantages to being this far out of Austin," she said. "Oh, and I enjoyed your party so much the other night. I have wanted to go inside the Manse for years. The conservatory is spectacular. How in the world do you keep the overhead glass clean?"

"I have a company come in four times a year and wash it. Anyone who thinks I'd get up on a ladder that high is wrong." We both laughed. "I'm glad that you enjoyed yourself. It was nice of Andrew to bring you."

"Yes, it was," she said. "Now, what can I do for you? I know you didn't come all the way out here to talk about your party."

"You're right, I didn't. I hope this isn't too presumptuous of me, but I need some help and I'm hoping you can give it to me." She nodded for me to go on and I said, "You probably know that Andrew worked with my cousin, Houston."

"Yes. And I've met your cousin. He's a very nice man."

"Thank you." Amazing how many women like Houston. "And I'm sure you've heard about Andrew. That he . . ."

"The police were here yesterday." She

looked down at the floor, shaking her head. "It isn't right. For a young man to die in that manner, hit over the back of the head with an old candlestick . . ." She trailed off. "And then to end up in a Dumpster like that. It's awful, just awful."

"Did you know Andrew well?"

She brought her head up to look at me, her eyes sorrowful. "We met him when he was just eighteen years old. That was a very long time ago, wasn't it?" She sighed softly. "Our grandson, Donovan, was in the fraternity that Andrew pledged at the University of Texas. In fact, Donovan was his big brother at the fraternity house. They were such good friends. Donovan brought Andrew here for Sunday dinner many times, and then they'd go into the living room with Earl and watch football." She smiled. "They were so full of fun and energy. We loved having them."

Something had happened, I could tell by the wistfulness in her voice, but the patina of gentility in her house kept me from coming straight out and asking what it was. Instead I said, "I thought that Andrew graduated from a college in California. UCLA?"

"I guess that's where he went after the accident. I knew he left."

I waited for her to go on, and after a few moments she did.

"The boys, Donovan and Andrew, were with another friend one night coming home from Sixth Street." Sixth Street is part of downtown where many of the clubs are — a hangout for the college kids. "There was a car accident," she went on, her voice soft but firm. "Donovan was killed. It was such a tragedy for all of us." She sighed, then straightened as though being strong might make it more bearable. "The other boy ended up in a wheelchair. Andrew was in the hospital for a while, and then he went away."

I was too far away to touch her, and I wasn't sure she'd want my sympathy. "I'm sorry," I said.

There was a silence in the dim room. She only let it linger for a minute or so, and then she looked at me with a smile. "When Andrew called to tell us he was back, I was surprised at how excited and happy we were to see him. I guess it's just the energy." She laughed softly. "Being around all that exuberance is better than watching television, that's for sure."

"Andrew helped invest for you, didn't he?"

"Yes. Of all the people in the world, we knew that Andrew would take care of us as if we were family. I suppose in a way, I felt as though we were. He was almost all we had left of Donovan."

She went to the big, old cabinet-style TV. I could see the warmth in her face as she picked up a picture and ran her finger across it as if there might be dust. Or maybe it was just to make contact with the young man who gazed back at her from the photo.

"Is that your grandson?" I asked.

"Yes." She handed me the picture. "Wasn't he a handsome devil?"

And he was. What I held appeared to be his high school graduation picture. He was wearing a suit and leaning forward toward the camera, his smile just a touch cocky but engaging. His hair was long — it came below his ears — and his eyes had a premature crinkle of humor. I think I'd have liked Donovan.

I couldn't help but smile as I handed back the photo. "What a charmer. It's like he's having such a good time — even getting his picture taken."

"That was Donovan. He could find fun anywhere. Even here at his grandparents' house."

She put the picture on the TV and took a new seat in an upholstered armchair of watery turquoise stripes. Her happy smile had faded. “Life is sometimes very hard, isn’t it?”

I was thinking of Andrew and Tess when I nodded. “Yes. Sometimes it is.”

“Some things just seem wrong, don’t you agree?”

“I agree,” I said. “A friend once said if you want fair, go to the carnival.”

“That’s terrible but so true. As we get older, it seems as though we see more — or maybe we just recognize the wrongness of things. Like criminals. Why are they alive when good people die? And why don’t we die in order?” The words seemed hard coming from this gentle woman. “It should be the oldest first. It’s not right that our children and grandchildren leave before us. I know they’re going to a better place, but it’s so lonely without them. I read in the newspaper about a 105-year-old man who is living in France. Now what could he possibly be adding to the world?”

It was a great question and not one that I was qualified to answer. “I don’t know,” I said. “I keep thinking there’s a plan, but I’ve never understood it.”

Mrs. Yancy shook her head sorrowfully. Then said, “I’m sorry. I didn’t mean to make this a sad conversation.” She brought her hands to her lap. “Earl always says to stay in the present. I guess he's right. Oh, and here you came all the way out here and I didn't even offer you refreshments." She stood up quickly. "Would you like something to drink? I have iced tea and sodas."

"No, thank you. Please, stay where you were. I'm fine." She sat again, and I went on. "I really came to see if you could give me some information. I didn't mean to take up so much of your time."

"What kind of information?"

"I was hoping you could tell me how Andrew invested money for his clients. What he was buying. Stocks? Bonds? Real estate? I can't seem to find out."

She thought about it before she said, "Well, he insisted on diversification, of course, but primarily with us he was buying a boat. A yacht, actually. It was very large, and it had been seized because of drugs. Andrew used our funds to bid on it at federal auction and got it for a small percentage of its value. The *High Jinx.* It's in the process of being remodeled, just like a house."

"And when it sells there will be a profit?"

Her chest seemed to deflate. "That was the intention, but investments don't always turn out the way they are supposed to. I'm sure you heard that we argued with Andrew at your party. I should apologize, and I am sorry. That was very rude of us. I was just so upset." She stopped and shook her head, the sadness again evident on her face. "Now Andrew is dead and my last words to him were angry ones. I think I've lived too long."

Her husband was just entering the room, and I swear he growled like a grizzly bear.

Sixteen

He could only have heard her last words: *I think I've lived too long.*

"Louise, don't do this to yourself." He stopped between us, so that I saw just his profile. "Sometimes life is hard," he told her, placing his hands on her shoulders. "But we've always made it through, and we will now. There are lots of good times ahead for us."

Both gentleness and love showed on her face as she reached up and touched his hand. "And you're almost always right, Earl. It's very annoying sometimes, too."

"Yeah, yeah, you've said that before." He was smiling as he turned to me. "You're Kitzi Camden."

I stood up and held out my hand. "And you must be Earl Yancy. Nice to meet you."

His hand was large but the skin was crinkly, like all the juice was out of his body. His voice was welcoming, though. "Likewise. I always like having pretty women at the house."

"Oh, Earl," Louise said. "Why don't you sit down and join us?"

"I'm sorry," I said. "But I really need to go. I didn't realize how late it's getting, and I'm on my way to visit a friend in the hospital."

"Sure we can't talk you into some wine?" Earl asked. "The sun is over the yardarm. Or the yardman. Or someplace."

"No, thanks," I said with a laugh. "I'd better go, but I'll take a rain check." I started toward the door, and they followed. As Earl opened the door for me, I said to Louise, "I really appreciate your help. And anytime you'd like to come by and see the Manse, just give me a call. I'd love to give you a guided tour." I pulled a card out of my purse; for once I didn't have to spend time digging for it. "You can always reach me at one of those numbers."

"That's wonderful. We'll do it," Louise said as I left.

I climbed into the Land Rover and tossed my purse on the passenger seat. Now I had two completely conflicting reports of Andrew's expertise. Louise had said that things didn't turn out well; Andrew had bragged that he was making more money for his clients than Houston was.

I started the car and drove off, thinking about that. Seemed to me there was only one way to prove who was right. Since the police had Andrew's computer, and we couldn't get back in it, and since they had his files, we would just have to track down the *High Jinx.* That big a yacht wouldn't be impossible to find. There had to be a registry of boat numbers, and that would mean the state. I was pretty sure I could influence someone to track down what I needed to know.

I was also curious about the accident that killed the Yancys' grandson, Donovan. Who else was in the car? Who was driving, and who were the other people involved?

If we could get that, we could cross-check the names with Andrew's clients, assuming, of course, that we could find out who his clients were, and we could match it with the guest list. Lots of *ifs* and *coulds* in there, and that didn't take into account the poker players I might meet that evening.

There was something else tucked away in the back of my brain, and it chose that moment to surface. Bruce had said that Andrew needed killing, and I had to wonder why and how those two knew each other.

I stopped at a drugstore and put my cell

phone earplug in. It annoys me when other people have private conversations on the phone while they're out in public, but I didn't intend to do the talking. At least not much talking. I was just going to ask questions.

By the time I was walking through the automatic doors, I could hear ringing on the other end, and then Bruce answered. "Yo."

"Yo, yo-self," I said. "I have two quick questions for you. Do you have time to answer?"

"Is this a marketing survey?"

"No, this is Kitzi." I headed toward the candy aisle and started looking for Tess's favorite kind. "Do you have time?"

"I guess. What's up?"

"How did you know Andrew Lynch?"

"When my sister was sick we met at the Relay for Life. She and I were walking, and he was with a client who had some other kind of cancer. He wasn't walking; he'd just donated some money."

"Did you invest with him?"

"Some."

I was looking up and down the shelves. "Is that when he started talking about investing money, at the Relay for Life?" I asked.

"You knew Andrew — what do you think?"

"That was the day." I found them: Red Vines licorice. Tess used to chomp her way through a bag a week when the pressure was on. "What did he put your money into?"

"Do you have a license to ask these kinds of questions?"

"Nope. Do I need one?" Now I was heading toward hair products. "Are you going to tell me?" I swear that what I was looking for just jumped off the shelf and into my hand. I couldn't help grinning when I thought of what Beth's reaction was going to be. "Well?" I asked Bruce. "Where did he invest your money?"

"A yacht. It was at a great price because the government was auctioning it. We knew going in that a lot of work had to be done on it."

"It wasn't by any chance named the *High Jinx*?" I asked. I was already at the counter, taking out my debit card.

"Yeah. Why? Did you invest in it, too?"

"No, but from the way you talk, right about now it might be for sale cheap." I ran my card through the payment machine. "How much of your money was in it?"

"That's pretty damn personal, don't you think?"

"Okay, then I'll break it down into categories: (A) just a little, (B) a whole lot, or (C) probably more than you should have put in."

"All of the above."

I picked up the sack with the things I'd bought, smiled at the young cashier, and started for the door. "That's all I needed to know, Bruce. It's always a joy talking to you."

It was still sunny by the time I got to the hospital, but it was late afternoon and I had a lot to do. I would have to keep the visit short.

Upstairs I tiptoed into Tess's room and discovered that she had a roommate. A woman who looked to be somewhere in her late seventies was sleeping, and snoring, in the bed next to the door. There was an IV going into her left wrist, and her right hand seemed to be twitching. She must have been sick for sometime because her hair was completely flat on one side, with light brown, matted curls on the other. There was also a good inch and a half of gray roots at the scalp.

I supposed that in the list of indignities that came with illness, that was a minor one, but still, it was obvious that she cared about her appearance and hadn't been able to do anything about it of late.

The curtain between the two beds was pulled closed, and I kept on going, practically tiptoeing around it. On the other side was a wheelchair. Had Tess been too weak to walk on her own?

Tess was lying in the bed, staring out the window. A magazine was spread open on her chest, as if the view outside was better than anything inside. Or maybe she was sleeping. I kept going around the bed until I could see her face. She was awake, and she smiled when she saw me.

"Hi."

"Hi, yourself," I said. "Look at you."

She wrinkled her nose. "I wouldn't like to, thank you very much." She ran her hand over her short hair. "I'm graying, aging, and belching. None of that is good."

I laughed. "Well, on you it's all good." Her skin had color today, and the waxy sheen was gone. Her eyes were brighter, too. "Obviously the transfusion helped. You seem so much better."

"If this is an improvement, I don't even want to know what I looked like when I came in here."

"Dull and boring," I said, handing her the sack of candy. "These ought to perk you up." I sat in a chair and took a good look at her. She really did appear better. Thank God for things like doctors, hospitals, and blood transfusions.

"Red Vines?" She poked a fingernail through the plastic and brought the sack close to her face. "Even the smell is wonderful. Thank you."

"You're welcome."

Soft, squishy footsteps entered the room, and someone who had a professionally cheerful voice spoke to the woman on the other side of the curtain.

"Mrs. Winston, did you turn on your call button?"

"Yes, I did. I told you before, I was supposed to get the bed by the window."

"I'm sorry, but as I said to both you and your sister, we don't have a bed by a window. As soon as we get one, we'll move you."

"They promised me. Before I agreed to come to this hospital, they promised me."

"Can I get you anything to drink? Are you thirsty?"

"No. It's dark in here. I can't stand this dark. Why didn't I get the window bed?"

"Let me turn a light on for you. Would you like the TV on, too?"

"No. I can't sleep with the light and the TV on. I just want my window."

Luckily the woman couldn't see us, because Tess and I were openly listening, and I was making faces. I leaned forward and whispered to Tess, "When did she get here?"

"Last night," she said softly. "She's been asking for the window ever since."

"Oops. I guess that's my fault. I'm the one who got you moved."

"I told the nurse I'd switch, but they said that it was too much trouble now that both of us were here. Something about phones and records."

We couldn't help but eavesdrop on the rest of the conversation:

"I'll be back in just a little bit to take your vitals, if there's nothing else —"

"The window bed. I told you. They promised me the window bed. Why can't I have the window?"

"We'll move you just as soon as one becomes available."

"But I want one, now. I was promised."

We heard the nurse leave the room.

"Has she been like this all day?" I asked, and Tess nodded. "Oh, brother," I said quietly. "So, other than that, how are you feeling?"

"Better. You know. Still not too perky, but a lot better than I was."

"Have they done any tests?"

Tess curled a lip. "I spent half the day with someone either asking me questions or poking at me. Now I know how those presidential appointees feel after Congress gets done with them."

"Have they figured out anything to do for you?"

"Still no treatment plan," she said. "First I'll finish the tests, then they — and I don't know who *they* is — will get the results and consult with some other doctors, so they can come up with a plan."

"I want to know when you get some results. And what they are going to do for you."

"Yes, senator."

"Good. Have you called Melissa?" Melissa is her twenty-five-year-old daughter. A beautiful young woman, bright, and a lot like my son Will. Too busy to take time for parents. "When is she flying in? It won't be any trouble for me to pick her up at the airport."

"I'm not quite sure. How is the tea going?"

"Wait just a minute. What do you mean, you're not sure? Have you called her, or what?"

Tess took her time, raising her bed and

pulling her tray closer so she could sit up and sip some juice through a straw. "I must need the vitamins — this juice tastes wonderful."

"You still haven't answered my question. Have you called her? Does she know you're in the hospital?"

"Kitzi, I'm old enough to run my own life. I called her, we talked, and she probably won't be coming out here."

"Well, now, that's devotion for you. Except," I said, "did you say you were really sick?"

"I'll be fine in a week or so."

"Just because you'll get better doesn't preclude you from being really sick now. I'll bet you told her not to come. In fact, I'd put fifty dollars on it."

She leaned back against her pillow. "Save your money. I told her not to come."

"Did you need something?" We heard a different voice, but still professional, addressing Tess's roommate.

"I want some juice. Real juice, not those cocktail things. And I need something for anxiety. I'm very distressed."

"Yes, ma'am. Just let me check your chart, and I'll be right back."

"I wouldn't be so upset if I hadn't been lied to. I was promised a window, you know."

"Yes, I've heard. You rest, and I'll be right back."

I whispered again. "What's wrong with her?"

"Something on her lungs and something else, but I haven't heard what."

In a normal voice, I asked, "So who is taking care of Rafferty?" Her seventy-pound Airedale might be an exceptionally clever boy, but he certainly couldn't be living alone.

"Marie next door is taking him for walks and feeding him. She really likes him, but her yard isn't fenced, so she can't have a dog. This way, she has mine, at least temporarily." She reached for her juice again, but it took more effort this time. "Tell me about the Tea. How did today go?"

I gave her a quick overview, and she was pleased to hear about the high attendance and how much the vendors had been selling. Then I told her about Andrew, whom she'd only met once. I'd kept it from her yesterday, but now I had enough distance to talk about it without emotion. I also mentioned that Houston had almost landed in jail.

"Too bad they didn't keep him," she said.

"Isn't that the truth? Except my mother and my aunt Miranda were very upset, so I had to ask the police to let him go. Oh, and guess what I did then?" I told her about Lauren and getting the computers linked up, as well as our excursion to Houston's office. I was careful not to let anything slip about Houston's bid to take over the Manse. Tess would worry about it, and she didn't need worry — she needed rest and a little entertainment.

When I finished she looked tired, but she was smiling. "Too bad I'm stuck here."

"If you'd just get well, you could help me." I looked at my watch. "I better go. I have some things I need to do tonight."

My hand was resting on the edge of her bed, and she reached out to hold it. "Can't you stay a little longer?"

If it would make her feel better, I'd miss poker, dinner, and a night's sleep. "Sure, no problem," I said.

"Tell me your plans for tonight."

I started in about poker, making it as amusing as possible.

"Here's your juice. Would you like to sit up?"

"Where are the pills I asked you for?"

"I'm sorry, but the doctor hasn't authorized anything for anxiety. Maybe if you sipped your juice and then rested until dinner —"

"Maybe if you'd just give me the bed by the window, I wouldn't need to take any pills."

"I promise you, as soon as one is available, you'll have it —"

"I'm very sick, you know. Just hand me my purse. I'll bet I have some something in there."

"I can't do that. You might take a drug that would react badly with the medications your doctor has you on —"

"How would he know? He's stupid. Call him and tell him I need something to relax me."

"Yes, ma'am. I'll call right away." The footsteps almost raced out of the room.

I had done my best to talk over the woman and the nurse, but I kept losing my train of thought because it was so hard not to listen to their conversation.

"Wait," Tess said. "You're playing in a poker tournament? That's illegal."

"I can hear every word you girls are saying. If you're doing something illegal, I'll have to call the police. It's a sin to break laws, you know."

"It's just a fun tournament," I said to her. "There's no money involved."

"I hope you're telling me the truth."

"Yes, ma'am," I said.

Tess turned on her TV and aimed the bed speaker toward her roommate. Then she rolled closer to me, saying softly, "There." She was fading, and I wished I'd insisted on leaving earlier.

"You look tired," I said.

"Forget that. Kitzi, you could be arrested."

I kept my voice down. "Maybe. How else can I find out anything about Andrew's life?"

"And people will recognize you. Everyone does."

"I have a plan," I said, leaning over and whispering it in her ear.

She listened, and when I was finished there was a half smile on her face. "I've got to get well to protect you from yourself."

"You pick any reason — just get better," I said. "Now you need to rest. I'll see you tomorrow."

She pulled out one of the Red Vines. "Thanks, but go see Rafferty, instead; he needs the company."

I kissed her on the cheek. "I will."

"Stay safe."

A morale boost was what I needed. Something fun and funny. Maybe something that I could tell Tess about on my next visit. Goodwill is a great place for something unique, and I pulled into the one nearest my house. It wasn't ten minutes later that I was on the road again, grinning.

When I got home the Bead Tea was closed

and Lauren was eating soup in the kitchen. "Oh, hi," she said. "I hope you don't mind . . ." She gestured to the food in front of her.

"If you don't eat it, I'll end up throwing it out."

"Would you like some?"

"Sure. I'll take a bowl upstairs while I get ready."

She ladled it out, and I carried it carefully up the stairs, along with my sacks of goodies. This was going to be fun.

First I mixed the rinse for my hair and put it on, covering it carefully with plastic. While the color cured, I opened my purse and took out the few things I thought I'd need for the evening. They went into a small handbag with a picture of Marilyn Monroe on it. Next I ate my soup and put on fresh nail polish.

There was a tap on the door. "Kitzi?" It was Beth. It made me think of the candlestick. Damn, I wished I'd never seen that thing.

"I'm getting ready," I said. "Come on in."

"No, I'm busy, but I just wanted to know what you're going to wear."

I smiled. "I'm going incognito."

"What does that mean?"

"Don't dress up and don't look like yourself. Want some rinse for your hair?"

"Conditioner?"

"Nope. A color."

"Uh . . . no thanks. I'll just look like someone else who happens to have my color hair."

"If you change your mind," I said, "just let me know. Oh, and if you need some clothes, I've got plenty."

"Thanks."

By that time I'd overdone my hair, so I whipped into the bathroom to rinse it off. "Oh, my God." I'd definitely overdone it. I could only hope that tomorrow it would wash out.

I took my shower, and as I dried off, found the hair color streaking the towels. Funny, my hair didn't look like it was missing any.

Next I put on makeup, lots of makeup, and blew my hair dry. Only I bent over and blew it so that the hair was going up. Then I used the thickest gel I had to separate it and create what might be called whimsical spikes. When I was finished my hair looked like a cross between Meg Ryan's and Ronald McDonald's. Not great, but I sure didn't look like Kitzi Camden.

Next I put on my "new" crop pants from Goodwill and a sweater from my own closet that was just a little tight. I slipped on some flat shoes and long dangling earrings as well as the bracelet that matched. I took a last breath and stepped to the full-length mirror for inspection.

In front of me was a redheaded floozy wearing a lime green sweater; pants with lime green and hot pink circles; long, cheap hot pink earrings; and lime green shoes. And blue nail polish.

"Kitzi." Beth was back. "We probably need to go. Are you ready?"

"Sure." I picked up my purse and hurried out the door. Beth and Lauren were both in the hallway. "Well?" I said, opening my arms to give them the full view. "What do you think?"

There was shocked silence.

"You have to admit no one's going to know it's me," I said.

Beth started to laugh. "You look like La-Vern at the Laundromat, that character Cher used to play on her TV show."

I remembered her. "Too bad I don't have some of those things that go around your neck to hold your eyeglasses. She always wore those."

"That might be overkill," Beth said, still grinning.

"Oh, you think this is subtle?" I held out my purse and showed her my nails.

"Subtle isn't quite the word I'd use."

Lauren was stuttering. "I can't believe it. I mean, you look so, well, it's very, um, well, different, and uh . . ."

"She likes it," I said, patting my hairdo. "Now, shall we go? I have the directions and our money. My treat."

"Okay, Lupe," Beth said.

"No, no. You're Lupe. Lupe Muscadine. Like the grapes. I'm Katherine Zoelnick. Only you can call my by my nickname."

"Which is?"

"Acey."

Seventeen

"Turn down that road," Beth said, pointing to a country lane with barbed wire fencing on either side. "See, it says Pincher's Antique Auction."

I turned and went about five hundred yards when, just as the instructions said, there was a big, yellow metal building with cars parked all around it. As I pulled into the driveway, I said, "We're here."

"But do we want to be?"

"Yes." I found an empty space next to the building and parked in it. "Take your money out of my purse," I said. "And remember, your name is Lupe. Lupe Muscadine. And I'm Acey. Acey Zoelnick."

"How can I remember our names? I can't remember if a straight beats three of a kind." She counted out the bills and took her eighty dollars.

"It does," I said. "And a flush beats almost everything."

Before either of us could lose what little courage we had, I got out of the car and locked it with the remote. Unfortunately, Beth was still in the Land Rover and hadn't opened her door yet. When she did, the alarm went off and the lights started flashing. Nice inconspicuous start to the evening.

I finally hit the right button, and the car stopped its attention-getting routine.

Beth stepped out. "Way to go."

"Thank you. Could you reach my purse?"

She did, then slammed the door behind her. "I have to go to the bathroom."

"That's just nerves."

"No, it's tortilla soup." She looked at me and shook her head. "If this place does get raided, you're not only going to get arrested for illegal gambling, I'm betting they book you on prostitution, too."

"I'm a little too old for that. No, a lot too old for that." Then we were silent as we spotted the front door and a stream of men going in the building. A few were looking in our direction, probably because of the car alarm.

I don't know what I expected gamblers to look like, but at least half of these looked like college kids. There were also a couple of men in golf shirts and jeans, an older guy in western clothes with enough mud caked on his boots to convince me that he was a real cowboy, and a man in running shorts and tennis shoes. Across the front of his T-shirt it said, "I believe you have my stapler."

Beth and I looked at each other; it was clear neither of us understood that one.

The line split into two just inside the door, and within a minute we were in front of a card table with a metal money box on it. The woman behind it looked like my ninth-grade English teacher; she said in a smoker's voice, "Names?"

I told her, and she checked us off a computer list, then added, "That'll be eighty dollars a piece." As soon as we handed over the cash she held out a huge stack of playing cards. Some were the regulation type with red or blue backs while others had hunting dogs or wolves on the back side. "Pick a card and find the matching one at the tables. Red and blue are the tables on this side of the room; animals are on the other side. Aces deal."

We each pulled a card. Mine was a wolf back, and wouldn't you know, I pulled the ace of spades.

"Lucky," I said. Why didn't I feel that way?

Next, the woman delivered a spiel in a

monotone that made it obvious she'd said it lots of times before: "There are three thousand dollars in chips at each place; blinds are twenty-five and fifty dollars. They go up every half hour. Any questions or problems, you raise your hand and the tournament director will come around. Good luck."

"Thank you kindly," I said.

We were inside a barnlike building with high ceilings, a few windows around the outside, and bright lights. Eight round tables were spaced out on the concrete floor, and each had places for either eight or ten. About half the seats were already occupied, and as far as I could tell, they were all occupied by men.

"Well," I said to Beth, "at least there won't be a line at the ladies' room."

"We have to go to different tables." She held up the seven of hearts.

"That's a good thing," I said. "We'll learn twice as much. Now remember, ask about the other players. Tell them you knew Andrew; ask —"

"Kitzi, I'm here. That's about as much as you can expect of me at the moment."

"Are you about to have an anxiety attack?"

She rolled her eyes. "I'm about to have a heart attack. Damn, I wish I'd brought my beadwork. That would have calmed me down."

"Next time you'll know," I said. "Well, good luck."

"There won't be a next time. And same to you." She went off to find the hearts table.

In front of Beth I had remained cool, but the truth is I was shaking in my lime green shoes. Here's what I realized: I can play poker, I can speak to a room full of people, and I can have red hair, but I can't play poker in a room full of people when I have red hair and I'm wearing weird clothes. Or, maybe I can, but it seemed like a lot to ask.

I reminded myself that I was doing this primarily for Rebecca and secondarily because I'd thought it would be a hoot. I needed to get into character and start having some fun.

I found the spades table right away and took my spot where the ace was. "Evenin', gentlemen," I said, seating myself. I could feel myself falling into Texas-good-ol'-boy speak. In Texas it's a way for a woman to fit in when she otherwise wouldn't.

There were two college kids, one with frizzy black hair and a floppy beige fishing hat, and a second with red hair. Not as red as mine, but close. He was wearing a T-shirt from Las Vegas. I wondered if that impressed the other players.

"Hey," one of them said in response to my greeting. The red-haired one nodded.

There was a man about my age, nice looking, with salt-and-pepper hair and green-gold eyes. Cat's eyes. He was talking with a guy of about thirty who had a shaved head and a Texas Longhorns T-shirt. They looked up at me, nodded, and went back to their conversation.

The cowboy from outside walked up, turned one of the chairs around, and straddled it. "Howdy," he said to the table in general.

There were mumbled hellos before the guy with the stapler T-shirt sat down, followed by a mousy young woman. That was it. We had a full table, and no one had introduced themselves or shaken hands. I guess that's protocol when you might be arrested; that way you can't rat on anybody else.

The woman from the front door was suddenly at my elbow. "Deal 'em up."

Someone handed me a deck of cards, and the tournament started.

"Blinds," the young woman said, and the two college kids counted out a few of their chips.

I stood up to deal, because if I'm sitting

down I can't get the cards all the way across the table, and wouldn't you know, first thing, I flipped a card. "Shit."

The good-looking man said, "Make that your burn card for the next deal."

"Sure." I was handed back the card, and I placed it facedown in the middle of the table and finished the deal. By the time I looked at my own cards I was hoping for something really terrible so I could fold and concentrate on dealing. I got two aces. Pocket aces, as they're called, since no one else can see them.

The stapler guy said, "What are the denominations on the chips?"

I can't tell you how grateful I was that he asked so I didn't have to. Betting went around the table, and when it came to me I said, "I call." And put out my chips.

Time for the flop. I remembered to move the burn card, and then I dealt three cards facedown in the center and turned them over quickly. Two-king-ace. I now had three aces. I was going to end up winning this hand, and that had not been my intention.

This time I raised, half the table folded, and the cat's-eyes guy raised me back. I dealt one more card in the middle — a six. More betting. I was still raising, and everyone dropped out until it was just the good-looking cat's-eyes guy and me. One last card, a two of hearts, more bets, and a good third of my stack was on the table. If I didn't win, it would be a very short evening.

We showed our cards. I had a full house with aces and twos. The guy tossed his cards in, facedown.

"I guess you've played this game before," he said.

"Mostly with my grandkids," I admitted, collecting the chips.

Twenty minutes later I looked at the thirty-year-old with the shaved head. "You know, you're about the same age as a friend of mine. He plays here, too."

He grunted and put his gaze right back on his cards. Not much interest there. I picked up my two cards and found they were both kings. With this run of luck, I might have to go to the Bellagio in Las Vegas.

The flop, the three center cards, were put down: jack-king-ten. I could almost see the salivating around the table as everyone decided which cards they'd need to make a straight. I was looking at three kings and hoping they'd hold. The fourth card was a five, so we lost a raft of bidders. It was just the cat's-eyes man and me left.

"I bet," he said, putting out a stack of green chips, which were the next to the highest.

I nodded. "Okay, I raise." And I put out twice as many.

He raised again. "There you go."

I smiled sweetly. "Do you know who you're betting against?" I asked.

"Yes, and I'm quaking in my boots, but I can't back down now."

"In that case, I call."

The fifth card was dealt to the middle of the table and it was a seven. Cat's Eyes made a bet, and I raised it; I was pretty sure I had him. He called, and we both flipped our cards. My three kings won.

One of the college kids said to me, "Who are your grandkids, anyway? World Poker Tour champs?"

"Not yet," I said. "They're only five."

Eventually I started settling in, winning a few and losing a few. Two players from our table were already out of the tournament. One of the college kids — the one with the red hair — and the cowboy. At different times they'd gone all-in, betting their whole stack, and hadn't won the hand. I decided it was time to try asking about Andrew before any more went out.

I looked straight at the thirtyish guy with the shaved head. I used good-ol'-boy speak. "I didn't hear what you said last time. Did you say you knew my friend Andrew Lynch?"

Shave head shrugged. "Name doesn't ring a bell."

"About five-eleven, slender, dark-haired with some gray at the sides?" Most of the players were looking at their cards.

Under other circumstances I might have mentioned, politely, how rude it is not to answer when someone asks you a question. Especially when that someone happens to be your elder, but since I wasn't in familiar territory I wasn't sure the same rules applied. Maybe I was being rude by talking. I gave it one more try. "Andrew handles investments for a living." I was careful to keep it in the present tense.

This time the shrug showed even less interest. "I don't recall him, but I come to play cards, not to talk."

Which certainly put me in my place. No one else seemed to notice, except Cat's Eyes, who smiled and winked. We played the hand, and I was trying to figure my next move when suddenly people were being shifted around. Two of the tables were taken down because they no longer had players.

I gave myself a mental pat on the back. I had outlasted at least twenty of the men. Or sixteen if those were small tables; either way I was doing pretty darn well for my first tournament. I was looking around for Beth when I was tapped on the shoulder. It was the woman who'd been at the door. "If you'll move over there." She pointed two tables down, and I picked up my Marilyn Monroe purse and waved at the guys. "It's been a pleasure."

"Don't forget your chips," Cat's Eyes said.

"Good idea." I scooped them up and moved along. When I got to the new table I discovered that I would be sitting across from Beth.

"Oh, Ki— Katherine," she stumbled. "This is great. How are you doing?"

I set my chips on the table. "Not too bad."

"I guess. That stack is almost as tall as Trump Tower." She smiled at the men around the table. "Everyone, this is my friend Katherine Zoelnick, only we call her Acey. Acey, this is Gregg." She gestured to a big man with professionally smooth silver hair.

"Welcome," he said.

"Thank you. It's my pleasure," I said with something like stunned reverence for Beth's social skills.

Then she went around the table introducing every man there by name and occupation.

How could she do that? "Nice meeting all of you." No trace of my Texas twang.

"Oh, and K— Acey," Beth said, beaming at everyone as if she were the hostess at a quilting bee, "Gregg is a lawyer. He used to practice real estate law, but for the last eight years he's been involved in corporate law."

"No kidding," I said.

Beth was in go mode. "Yes, and he's got a kitten as rowdy as Sinatra. Only Gregg's kitten is orange and his name is Pippin."

"They're a handful, aren't they?" I said.

Gregg laughed. "Pippin thinks he rules the house. He's got the dog scared to death of him."

Cat's Eyes sauntered over to our table and took the seat next to Beth. "Seems I'm to join you good people."

"Welcome," Beth said. She introduced the entire group again. "And what was your name?" she asked him.

"Sandy." He nodded toward me. "And there's my arch rival."

"Acey?" Beth said. "Has she been taking your money?"

"More than I'd like. And I'd really hate to play against her grandkids."

Everyone looked a little surprised, but before I could explain, the call of "Deal 'em up" came. Gregg dealt.

Earlier that day I had told myself that I would be perfectly happy if could get a little information about Andrew at the tournament and if I didn't make a fool of myself. Problem was that once I started playing, and won a few hands, my old competitive spirit kicked in. I wanted to win the tournament. I wanted my blonde hair back, and I wanted to tell everyone my real name, too, just so they'd know who the champ was.

Since those last two things couldn't happen, I could at least win. During the first round of betting I started watching for tells, those little signs that showed a player was nervous. It wasn't easy to spot them because I didn't know these people. I didn't know who bet even when they didn't have a good hand, or who played conservatively. I would have to make best guesses and respond accordingly.

Luckily, I was dealt a jack and a four, and I didn't figure I needed to throw any chips away on a hand like that. It gave me a chance to watch. Beth played tight, very conservatively. Two others dropped out midway through the hand, and Gregg was the guy with the biggest stack and the biggest bets. He also won the pot.

During the deal I glanced at Beth. "Well?" I mouthed.

She gave me a disgusted look and mouthed back, "Okay." But she didn't say a word.

The next hand was dealt, and I folded long before we got to the second round of betting. Eventually Sandy won, and Beth said, "You know, Acey knows Andrew better than I do. Acey, Gregg said that Andrew is usually here twice a week, almost every week."

"Do the rest of you know Andrew, too?" I asked.

The men shook their heads no, except for Sandy, Mr. Cat's Eyes. He had his poker face on, and those green-gold eyes of his were staring right at me. I couldn't tell what was going on behind them.

I said, "Andrew's a pretty good player, isn't he?"

The man to my right chuckled. "He's good, but he can get caught up in the hand."

"Can't we all," Gregg said with a smile. "Making that bet just a few seconds too fast."

"Not you," someone said. "Never you."

"I'm not as bad as some," Gregg said.

"We've seen some real hair triggers around here."

Cards were being dealt again. That was the problem with trying to get information at a poker tournament: people insisted on playing poker. It was slowing down my questioning.

We finished out the hand, and Beth won. "Thank you, thank you. No applause please," she said, collecting her chips.

"Hey, Lupe," I said as she stacked them up, "did you know that Andrew worked for Houston Webber?"

Her expression said I was pushing things too far, but Gregg said, "He plays here, too, but not as often as Andrew. Isn't Houston a Camden?"

I tried to read something into his question, but his expression was bland, as if he were just looking for confirmation.

"He is," Beth said, and the cards were dealt and everyone got quiet.

"What kind of a player is Houston?" I asked.

We did some betting first, and finally Gregg said, "He's pretty cagey."

Sandy was staring at his cards, but he said, "I thought all the Camdens were cagey, until something gets their adrenaline running."

"Usually at the after games," Gregg said.

"What are those?" I asked.

"Oh, sometimes those of us who go out of the tournament early get together at someone's house and play," Gregg explained. "One night Andrew and Houston were there along with —"

"All in," Sandy said.

"Are you kidding me?" another man demanded. "I'm sure I have five aces."

"Then bet them," Gregg said.

I wanted to hear about that after party; specifically I wanted to know what had happened between Andrew and Houston and who else was there. I was waiting for the end of the hand to ask, when the two men flipped their cards over. Sandy lost and he was out of the tournament.

"Break," someone called from near the door. "Twenty minutes. Food is on the patio; if you're going to smoke, take it out to the end of the parking lot."

Beth came around the table, carrying her purse. "Come on, let's freshen up."

I hesitated, hoping I could get some more information, but the men had scattered.

"Sure." I picked up my purse, and we headed for the ladies room. Halfway there, I said, "This is ridiculous. Every time I get ready to ask a question it's time to play poker."

"Yes. And every time I start to play poker, you ask a question."

Inside the ladies room it was quiet, all the noise of the tournament filtered out. I looked in the mirror. "Oh, my God! I can't believe I'm out in public looking like this."

"It's not so bad," Beth said, going into a stall. "You just have to get used to it."

I straightened the lime green sweater and wiped mascara from under my eyes. "Nice hair," I said. I turned my head side to side to get a better look and the hot pink earrings swung around, catching me on the cheekbones. "Nice earrings, too."

"Yeah. I was thinking I'll have to borrow the whole outfit sometime."

I grinned. "But we are learning things," I said, taking out my lipstick. "I had no idea that Houston played Texas hold 'em! That's pretty amazing."

"You think he and Andrew came out here together?"

"I doubt if they rode together. Who wants to sit around for a couple of hours if you're out of the tournament and your ride is still playing? But they obviously did both go to the after game."

I wondered if Rebecca knew that Houston played poker. Surely she did. What would be the point of lying about it? The other thing I knew is that when Rebecca was going through her surgery and then the chemo, Houston had been very attentive to her. I doubted that he would leave her home alone so he could hang out in a metal building. It just wasn't his style.

As kids we had all played at the family gatherings. He was pretty good but not spectacular. He *was* cagey, though; I'd agree with that. Sometimes he'd get my brother, or more likely me, in competitive mode, pushing too hard, and then he'd trounce us.

What I wanted to know was how many times a week was Houston playing now? How much money did he spend on it? I did some math; if he played twice a week, it would run between six hundred and seven hundred dollars a month. And what was the cost of the after parties? I didn't see these guys playing for matchsticks like we used to.

If he were playing somewhere else, as well as this tournament, then the amount could be closer to a couple of thousand dollars a month. That added up pretty quickly, particularly on top of Rebecca's medical bills. I didn't think Houston was in the income bracket that would allow him to absorb those kinds of expenses easily.

Then there was the fact that he and Andrew were playing poker together. Somehow I'd always thought they had only a working relationship, although a very tight one. Did something happen out here that gave Andrew an advantage over Houston?

I needed to find out about that occasion Gregg had started to tell us about.

Beth came out of the stall, washed her hands, and dried them. "What are you thinking?" she asked.

"I'm trying to figure how we're going to get Gregg to tell us the story about Andrew and Houston."

Beth turned to look at me. "Do you think it matters?"

"You bet I do." While Beth put on lipstick, I tried to explain. "Houston is my cousin, and I love his wife. When I found out he was at the police station it didn't even occur to me that he could have killed Andrew. I was positive that he wouldn't do that kind of thing, but I didn't necessarily have a good reason for believing in him."

"No basis in fact?" she said. That had to be a law term she'd learned from her soon-to-be ex.

"I guess," I said. "Now I'm wondering if I wasn't a little hasty." I picked up my purse. "Gregg seems like a nice man. I'll try to track him down and ask him."

"That's what I wanted to tell you! Gregg is a legal shark. That's what one of the other guys called him. He could be the lawyer you're looking for."

"I just knew coming here tonight was important." I felt a tightness in my shoulders ease just a pinch. "Now if I can just win the tournament, the evening will be a total success."

"I love how you always think small," Beth said. "You could at least settle for second place."

We stepped out of the restroom. The metal building wasn't as big as it had originally seemed, and the men milling around were just regular men, not the hardened high rollers I'd expected. A few were drinking beers, and it was surprising how many were carrying around water bottles, just like the people in the chichi exercise clubs.

I wondered if Sandy had already left. I didn't see him inside, but then there was still a pretty good crowd to my right and I couldn't pick out everyone. I looked toward the windows to see if he was outside when Beth grabbed my arm.

"Oh, shit!" she said, pulling me backward. "Quick, get in the ladies' room."

"Beth. What's going on?" I was trying to

remain poised, but she was frantically jerking on me.

"There. Look outside the second window."

I glanced out, and I could clearly see two men walking purposefully toward the front door. I studied them, and my eyes widened. "Oh, hell!"

"We've got to get out of here!"

Eighteen

I practically flew back into the ladies' room. "How are we going to get out?"

Beth and I were frantically looking around. At the same time we spotted a small window up near the very high ceiling.

"Don't even think about it," Beth said.

"I wasn't."

"Is there a back door?" she asked.

"Yes. That double garage door in the corner."

"That's not going to work, either."

"How's this," I said. "We stay in here until the place closes and then we sneak out."

"Your brain has seized up. If they're raiding the tournament, I assume they'll look in the bathrooms."

"I'm going to check again." I stuck my head out. I could still see Sergeant Dwayne Granger walking on the outside of the building. He was two windows from the door. "He's getting closer. We've got to do something fast."

"Got a screwdriver?" she asked.

"Why?"

"It's a metal building — maybe we could take it apart."

"Beth! Think. We can't get trapped in here," I said. My brain felt like it was in overdrive. "Oh, wait. I've got it. We walk through the crowd and out the offices at the other end." I had one hand on the door ready to make my move.

"We better hope there's a door to the outside in that office. What if they start handcuffing people?"

I turned to her. "Then I expect you to keep us safe by offering Granger sexual favors. I'd do it, but you're more his type." I took a breath. "Okay, don't stay too close to me. I'm a tad conspicuous."

"No kidding." She grabbed my elbow. "And I'll have sex with him, but only once, and it has to be someplace comfortable. And if he comments on my weight then all bets are off."

"You'll never make it in the sleazy underbelly of crime."

I went first. I didn't see Granger or any other cops that I recognized, so as nonchalantly as possible, I moved toward my table, smiling at people as I went. My stack of chips was still in place, ready for me to start betting. Damn, I hated to leave them, but this was an emergency.

I kept on going, my eyes scanning the room like some kind of extraterrestrial robot. I still hadn't spotted Granger, but I did see Gregg at the far end of the room. I needed the man's name and his card. This was getting way too complicated for my nervous system.

The cowboy and one of the college kids were chatting at the first table I'd sat at, and I went toward them, as close to the wall as possible. Beth was taking a more middle route, but she seemed to be hiding behind a couple of men who were sauntering toward the door. That was an idea that might work. I slipped by the table, nodded at the cowboy and kept on going. That's when I saw Granger come in. He was scanning the room, too.

I froze, half behind the cowboy, half out in the open. Granger's gaze went right past me. Of course! He wouldn't recognize me like this, if I could just maintain some distance and keep my head turned away. I pretended great interest in the wall, where there was some light graffiti written in pencil: *Be alert; the world needs more lerts,* and *Gary is hott.*

While I was reading I kept my feet moving forward at a normal pace; the last thing I wanted to do was make a big move that would catch Granger's attention.

I was so intent on not being seen I almost smacked straight into Gregg.

"Excuse me," he said.

"My fault." I didn't dare look for Granger, but I had to know where he was. "Gregg, do you see a man of about five-eleven, average weight, brown hair, midfifties, with a thick mustache? He just came into the building."

I slipped behind Gregg while he looked. Luckily he was big enough to hide me almost completely. "No," he said. "No one of that description — wait. There he is. He's wearing a brown Windbreaker, and he's with another man. They're talking to the woman at the entrance."

Gregg didn't seem to find it unusual that I was standing in back of him while we talked, and he didn't question my request. "That's him," I said. "Please don't turn around."

"I wasn't planning to."

"Good. I have to get out of here before he sees me. And I'd like one of your cards. I need a lawyer."

"Don't start walking until I say to. I

suspect bumping into the man you mentioned could be a problem."

"Good suspecting."

The arrival of the police hadn't caused any ruckus at the poker tournament, at least from what I could see. The men were still casually talking, and no one seemed to take any special notice of the newcomers. Okay, so it wasn't a raid. Maybe they were just after us.

It was less than a minute later that Gregg said, "It's time. If you'll get on my left side, I'm going to start across the room. I might even point at some things by the office, so you can turn your head that way. He won't see your face." Next he pulled out his wallet as we began to move. I stayed just a half step behind Gregg so he was blocking my view completely.

"Where is he now?" I asked.

Gregg raised a finger to his lips, so I kept quiet. He didn't change his pace at all, and we moved slowly, easily toward the entrance. When we got there he stepped between me and the rest of the room, and the next thing I knew we were breathing fresh night air.

There were poker players sprinkled around the parking lot, some drinking, some smoking, and some eating. No one seemed to notice us.

"Here's my card." He handed it to me. "The cell number will reach me almost anytime."

"Thank you." I heaved a big breath. "And thank you for getting me out of there."

"Every man wants to rescue a damsel in distress at least once in his life."

"I suspect you've done it more than once."

He smiled. "I try."

"I'll be calling you tomorrow or Monday. Oh, and I'm Kitzi. Kitzi Camden."

"I know."

A hissing sound came from behind one of the parked cars. "Kitz." It was Beth. She was hiding behind a dark blue Mini Cooper. "Let's go!"

I waved to Gregg and hurried toward her. We ducked and ran using the vehicles as shields to keep us out of the sight of the windows. I didn't think Granger could spot us unless he was actually standing at a window looking out, but we weren't taking any chances. My slip-on shoes were giving me a problem, and I almost fell out of them.

"Grrr."

"Keep moving," Beth said.

As we ran I dug in my purse for the keys. When we were just two pickups from the Land Rover, I hit the remote; the lights started flashing and the horn blared.

"Shit!" It was Beth.

I was too busy punching buttons to cuss.

"The button on the left," someone called.

I pushed it and sure enough the alarm stopped. Within seconds Beth and I were in the car. "Go," she said.

"I'm going." I put it in gear and backed up carefully.

"Faster."

"It'll be noticeable if I run someone over. Trust me, it will slow up our exit by a bunch."

But it was safe now and we both knew it. Beth was sucking in huge amounts of air. "Granger doesn't have jurisdiction out here," she said between breaths. "We're in Williamson County, not Travis."

"He's police. He doesn't even have authority outside the city limits." I was on the narrow lane, still too close to the metal building for comfort. I knew I'd feel a whole lot better once we were on the highway doing seventy miles an hour away from here. At least it was night, which hid us a little, and my Land Rover was dark. "I figure he was out here looking for us."

"That's possible," she said. "But why make the trip? He knew where we'd be tomorrow. Unless it was urgent."

"Maybe he found out Andrew went to the

tournaments."

"And he was just following a lead?"

"I can't think why else he'd be there. Besides, I think I prefer that explanation." I turned right onto the highway and we were headed to Austin. Not a moment too soon, either. A car had pulled out of the parking lot right after us. It wasn't far behind. "Look back there," I said, gesturing.

I was driving a bit over the speed limit so I slowed down. I couldn't imagine that it was Granger on our tail, but on the off chance that he'd spotted us leaving and had followed, I didn't want to give him any excuse to stop us. I didn't think he knew my car, and I didn't think he'd recognize me with my floozy red hair, either.

"The car just turned this way," Beth said.

I have never wanted to speed so much in my life, but some instincts just can't be obeyed and I was pretty sure that was one of them. "What kind of car is it?"

"I don't know. It's big and black."

"SUV?"

"One of those monster ones."

"Like Nate's?" I asked.

Beth looked back again. "Who knows? It was too dark, and now all I can see are headlights."

We drove awhile in silence; all the while

my eyes were zigzagging from the side mirror to the rearview mirror. The lights stayed back there, pretty much keeping pace with us. We hadn't quite reached the city yet. The road was a bit narrow, despite the two lanes going in each direction, and I was surprised that on a Saturday night there were so few cars. Where were those crazy teenagers who were supposed to be driving too fast and going too far? What about the families, leaving grandma's house and headed for home? And where were all the highway lights? Didn't the Texas Department of Transportation have standards? I wasn't expecting chandeliers or automatic fog lights, but one or two plain old ordinary streetlights would have been nice.

We drove on another three or four miles before I turned to Beth. "You know," I said, "we're not being followed."

"We aren't?"

"No." I was beginning to see small businesses on the side of the highway. Not all together, and not many, but a few. "Someone else just left the tournament about the same time we did, and since they are headed to Austin, and we're going to Austin, we're on the same road."

"I believe you," Beth said, turning to face forward. "Are you buying it?"

"Yes, I think I am. That car back there has nothing to do with us."

"Good, then stop in that convenience store over there and let me get a cup of coffee."

I looked mirror to mirror and finally said, "We're not that far from the Manse. I'll make you a pot of coffee myself."

"You don't drink coffee, and the stuff you make is terrible. Besides, that was a test. I wanted to see if you really accepted the SUV as coincidence."

"I do," I said. "I have only a 10 percent reservation." I reached over and patted her leg. "But even a 10 percent risk is a big one when your best friend is taking it. I'd worry when you got out to get coffee, while I was safely locked in the car."

"You could have gotten out of the car and gone with me."

"Why, that never occurred to me."

And then I remembered that stupid candlestick hidden under Beth's bed. I know they say you can't take it with you, but if I'd known that those things were going to cause me so much grief, I'd have asked to bury them with my grandmother. Or maybe I could have forced them on Houston. They'd look good with the Mashad rug he had in his office.

"You didn't tell me what you did today," Beth said. "Did you visit Tess?"

"Only for about half an hour. She looked a lot better today," I said. "A lot." But it wasn't something I wanted to talk about right now. Every time I thought of Tess I felt a hole in my chest that went through my heart. I said, "I also went to visit the Yancys. Andrew's clients."

"The ones who were arguing with him on Thursday. It was Thursday, wasn't it?"

"It was. And I learned some interesting things." We were coming closer to Austin, and the road now had lights. Even stop-lights. There was a restaurant, families, and dozens of cars. Behind us, and in front, was a stream of vehicles all intent on getting someplace. I gestured toward them. "Where were all of these when we needed them?" I asked.

"Probably right here," she said. "So, what did you find out from the Yancys? And what were they like?"

I thought about that for a moment. "They were nice. They live near Balcones Country Club, and their home is lovely. A little dated, but what would have been termed *gracious living* in the seventies."

"How old are they?"

"Also seventies," I said. "But they both

seem pretty athletic. They can swing a golf club, so why couldn't they swing a candlestick? And both of them were at the party Thursday night —"

"Wait. What's this about a candlestick?"

I took a deep breath. "You can't tell a soul this, but that's what killed him."

"Someone clobbered him with a candlestick?"

I nodded. "It gets worse."

"How could it?"

"I found the other one under your bed."

"What?" The look of utter shock on her face was visible even in the faint light of the dashboard, and any doubts I might have had about my friend evaporated.

"Have you told the police?" she asked.

"Of course not," I said. "They'll wonder why it was there — and why I didn't mention it earlier."

"Well, what do we do now?" she said.

I changed lanes, in preparation for getting on the freeway. "I don't know. Try to figure out who put it there?" I glanced in the rearview mirror. "By the way, is our faithful follower still behind us?"

"Who can tell? What candlestick was it, by the way?"

"One of the two from the mantel."

"One of yours? Those big ones you don't like?"

"Yes," I said, my brain furiously putting together other associations. "The Yancys' grandson was killed in a car wreck when he was in college, and Andrew was also in the car," I said. "It would give them a motive for killing him, don't you think?"

"Yes, it would," she said. "But how did they get him into the Dumpster?"

I thought about that for a moment. Swinging a candlestick I could see. But the Dumpster Andrew had ended up in had six-foot sides, and I just couldn't see a seventy-year-old — even two seventy-year-olds — heaving a grown man into a Dumpster. Unless one of them drove a forklift. "You're right," I said. "That is a flaw in my theory."

"Do you know if the accident was Andrew's fault?" Beth asked.

"I don't know. There was at least one other young man in the car, and he was paralyzed from the accident. Donovan, the grandson, was several years older than Andrew, but that doesn't mean he was driving. It's one of the things I want to check out tomorrow."

"Did they say why they were having a disagreement with Andrew?" she asked.

"I assume it was because of the *High Jinx*."

I explained about the boat — or would that be considered a ship? — and how it was to be revamped and sold for a profit. "People do that with houses and cars all the time, so it sounds like a logical investment."

"If the resale market is good. Did they say anything about that?"

I shook my head. "One more thing to be checked out tomorrow. Maybe we could find the actual boat. It's supposed to be huge, so you know it has to be at the coast —"

"We have the Bead Tea, remember?"

"I remember." I had intended to enjoy tomorrow. The last day of any big event at the Manse is usually the most fun because everyone knows their jobs and there isn't much to be taken care of. I had planned to shop in the tent, have tea, and visit with people. Instead there were a whole lot of other things I needed to do.

"Is there anyone else on your list of suspects?" Beth asked.

Probably half the alumni of the University of Texas belonged on the list, and surely one or two of the poker players had disagreed with Andrew on something, but I didn't know those people so I could hardly suspect them. I'm not sure why, but learning that he and Houston had played poker together gave me an uneasy feeling. I'm a great believer in the subconscious — it sees all and hears all when the rest of our brain is busy worrying about something else entirely. I wondered if my subconscious had picked up something about that and I'd yet to move it to the upper regions of my brain where I could access it.

"What about Houston's clients?" Beth asked. "Lauren said that she handled them, and then she started helping with research. Since Rebecca's been sick, Houston hasn't been involved, and if Andrew was investing their money and lost it . . ." She paused. "Do you think any of them could have killed Andrew?"

Sometimes Beth and I still think alike; apparently this was one of those times, because that was something that had been bothering me, too. "I can't say anything about Houston's clients, but I have another idea. I know it's going to sound crazy at first, but hear me out, okay?"

"You rarely sound crazy," she said. "You do act crazy, but that's another story. In fact, sometimes that's kind of fun."

"Thank you, I think. Here's what I keep thinking about: what if Lauren was working with Houston's clients, handling everything while he took care of Rebecca, and she did something, say, illegal. Andrew could have discovered whatever it was and threatened to tell Houston or the police. To stop him, she killed him."

"She wasn't even at the party, was she?"

I thought about that. "I didn't see her particularly, but no one was checking. She could have been there."

"It's feasible, I think. I wondered about something, too," Beth said. "Does Houston actually take in cash? Money that she could have stolen?"

"Cash isn't something that shows up much these days for investments. I'm guessing, but it doesn't seem to be the norm." I thought some more, and a convoluted plan occurred to me. "Try this one," I said. "What if she had access to all the investment records, which I'm sure she did, and what if she created an affidavit requesting the transfer of something to her name? Money or stock — something of value that she now owns."

"Don't those affidavits have to be notarized?"

"Yes, and don't you think there are ways of faking that?"

"There's an awful lot of conjecture in this," Beth said.

"I'm just saying that Lauren ought to be

on the list, that's all," I said. "Guilty until proven innocent, that's my motto."

"That's not the American way."

"Oh, really?" I said. "Check with the IRS. Or any other federal enforcement agency. If they say you could have done it, you done it. At least until you prove otherwise."

"God, no wonder you left office."

I took the onramp to Loop One South, more often called Mopac. It runs along the Missouri-Pacific railroad line, which is where the name Mopac came from. "You know how most streets are named after people?" I asked. "Cesar Chavez? Martin Luther King Boulevard?"

"Congress Avenue?"

"That one was named after a lot of people."

"First Street? Second?" she suggested.

"You're not cooperating. I mean, why not name streets after everyday people? You know, with names like Mary," I said. "And Lamar. And Mopac."

"Mopac?"

"Fred and Ethyl Mopac. They used to hang out with Lady Bird and LBJ."

Beth barely smiled at what I thought was a pretty funny remark, but then I hadn't laughed, either.

"Who else is on your list?" she asked as

we drove through the night into Austin proper. The lights of the city were off to our left, and I still enjoyed seeing the capitol lit up. Like the one in Washington DC, it's a symbol of all that's right with people. It may not be successful all the time, but the government is still supposed to serve all the people. That deal of service to the people is what I believe in, and that's what the capitol stands for to me.

"The guard, Charlie. At the tent."

"He's security! Aren't they bonded and screened, or whatever they do?"

"Absolutely. They are also often from the military, and they know things about combat and such. Not only that," I went on, "he was outside and could have killed Andrew at any time. We don't know when that happened."

"And the candlestick?" Beth asked.

"Who would question a man in a security uniform if he walked into the house and picked one up?"

Beth was not convinced. "Let's not dwell on that. Who else is on your list of possibilities?"

I moved on. "Bruce. The owner of Accurate Construction. I like him, but he's certainly strong enough to use a candlestick as a weapon. Maybe even his wife, Delphine, could have done it. If Andrew took all their money —"

"But she's little. She's not even five feet tall, is she?"

I was nearing the Manse, which was a good thing. My brain was somewhere close to empty, and my body was in need of a recharge as well.

"She's little, but she's tough. You should have seen her out there the day that Bruce and his crew were tearing the roof off the house behind us. There were something like four layers of roofing, and they are heavy, but she was loading them in a trailer. Not only that, the woman is a black belt and she used to have her own dojo. What are those things they fight with? Pikes or something?"

"They use a lot of different weapons."

"Well, I'm betting that candlesticks could be one." I turned into the driveway, and I could feel myself mentally slumping. An awful lot had happened, and I wasn't up to all of it. I was grateful to be home.

The Manse was dark except for a light at the back door and a soft glow coming through the windows from the nightlights strategically placed around the house.

The big teal and white tent looked forlorn, like it had accidentally been forgotten when the circus left town. There was a slight wind, and the big trees behind it were moving gently. I pulled into the driveway and parked the car close to the garage, careful to lock it after Beth got out.

Maybe it had been all the emotional ups and downs of the day that had drained me. I didn't seem to have the energy to do much more than drag myself out of the Land Rover. The guard came out of the tent and waved before going back in again.

Beth was facing the street we'd just come from, and her expression went from tired to shocked.

"Kitzi! Look." She pointed, and I turned in time to see a large black SUV cruise very slowly by the entrance to the driveway.

Nineteen

We were both in our pajamas; Beth was on the rocker in my room, and I was sitting on the bed. Beth wore the expression of someone who was shell-shocked or beyond exhaustion. Since it was almost two in the morning, that was understandable.

"It had to have been the same one. He followed us all the way here," she said.

I shook my head for the umpteenth time. It seemed to be getting heavier. "We still don't know that. There must be thousands of big black SUVs in Austin, and to me, most of them look the same. And you still haven't answered the why. Why would someone follow us all the way home, and then not stop? If it was Gregg, making sure that we got home safely, he'd have pulled into the driveway, so we wouldn't worry. It couldn't have been Granger —"

"He drives some white cop-looking car."

"Which only supports my point. It was a

coincidence. Someone was lost. Or on their cell phone —"

"Which is why you checked three times to make sure the alarm was on. And why you asked the guard to be extra watchful tonight."

I rubbed my forehead. "I have a headache."

"I have a very bad feeling," she said. "If we wake up dead —"

I tried to shake my head, but I didn't have the strength. Luckily my mouth was still working just fine. "Only the good die young — I'll be here until I'm at least 112. So, if you wake up dead, come and tell me."

She stared at me for a good minute. I think it was just because she couldn't think of a comeback. Finally she said, "You're tired. Good night. I'll see you in the morning."

"See? We'll be fine. You just said so."

When I woke up, alive and well, there were voices coming from downstairs and the pounding of little feet. Sinatra, who sleeps on the foot of my bed, rolled over and looked at me, as if for protection.

"Too late," I said. "But you could hide under the bed." He let out a yowl and disappeared there only seconds before my three grandchildren burst into the room.

"Gran Kitzi!" said Gabrielle, our three-year-old mistress of all that is righteous. "You're still sleeping."

"No, she's not," Cliffie said. "She's wide awake. She's just in bed."

Shelby came to pat my hand. "Are you sick? Oh my gosh! Your hair!" She started giggling. "It's orange."

I reached up to touch it. I'd forgotten that little detail. "Yes, I'm sure it is," I said.

"Did it make you sick?" Gabrielle asked.

"No, honey," I said, climbing out of the bed and moving to the rocking chair. "I was up very late last night. You all look very nice. Where have you been?"

Shelby, who doesn't particularly like dresses, had on a short denim skirt, an orange knit top, and sandals with white flowers on the front. Her long blonde hair was pulled up into a ponytail that was braided. Little Gabrielle, who likes anything her mother likes, was wearing what used to be called a springtime frock in a print of pink and pale blue flowers. She was even wearing a hat and carrying a small pink purse that matched her ruffled socks.

Cliffie had on khaki pants, a white golf shirt, and semiclean athletic shoes. Quite a feat for a five-year-old boy.

"We went to church," Gabrielle said. "While you were sleeping."

"Yes," I said, "but I was out late last night, while you were sleeping."

Katie came into the room just as Shelby said, "Did you win the poker tournament last night?"

"The — what? Your —" Katie wasn't her usual articulate self.

Shelby spun around. "Mom! You shouldn't sneak in like that. It's not polite."

I've seen my all-too-perfect daughter nonplussed before, but this time she was actually spluttering. She had one finger pointed at me. "Your — your —"

I smiled at her. "Are you all right? It's just hair, Katie. I'll admit it's a little bright, but it is a rinse."

She swallowed hard. "It will come out? I mean, before the corporate meeting this week?"

"Well, I think so. If it doesn't you can just pretend you don't know me." I turned to look in the mirror, and I had to admit she had a point. Amazing how intense red hair can be in the daylight. It didn't help that most of it was now flowing upward in a way that suggested I was the victim of a wind tunnel gone bad. "I see what you mean. It is a bit, well, let's just make concessions since this is early morning."

"No, it's not," Shelby said, pointing to my clock. "It's almost —"

"Enough!" I put my hand over her mouth. "I have to take a shower and get dressed. Then I have a lot to do today, including some sport shopping in the tent for beads and a lot of research."

Cliffie came out of the bathroom holding the empty box that had contained my Spicey Nice rinse. "Is this what you put on your hair?" he asked.

"That's it."

"Look what it says." He read slowly but surely, " 'If this shade is darker than your nat . . . nat . . .' "

Katie grabbed the box. " 'Natural hair, it will not come out in twenty-eight shampoos.' "

Cliffie looked at me. "I guess that means you'll have orange hair for a long time," he said.

"Could be," I said.

"Kewl!" Shelby grinned. "Unless you wash your hair twenty-nine times."

"Yes, well, I don't think I'll do that today. Okay, everybody out and let me get dressed." I got up from the rocker to find I'd been sitting on the outfit I'd worn the night before, which didn't help its appearance. I shook out the sweater, then the pants.

Katie's eyes widened. "You wore those? Those lime green and hot pink . . . pants?"

"Yes, I did, but you're not seeing the best part." I went to the closet and put on the earrings and the lime shoes. I came out modeling them. "Well?"

The kids started laughing, while Katie turned pink, I assumed with embarrassment at her mother. She said, "Okay, kids, let's go downstairs and let Gran Kitzi get dressed. I'm sure it's going to take her a while to get ready."

"I could just throw those on," I said, pointing to the clothes on the rocker.

"Don't you dare."

I had no idea whether twenty-nine shampoos was the magic number to change me back to a blonde, but it wasn't two. By the time I was showered, dried off, and had my makeup on, I still had red hair. At least it was not quite as brilliant as it had been earlier, and the style was a lot better. It was my normal one: neck length with soft waves that sometimes broke into curls.

I chose black cotton slacks and a teal blouse. The teal looked wonderful with my hair. Not only that, I decided I had definitely lost a pound or two, since the slacks fit quite nicely. I finished the outfit with a teal-and-rose crystal necklace Beth had made me and went downstairs.

The volunteers were arriving and so were the guests. Beth was in the kitchen eating breakfast tacos out of white wrapping paper.

"See," I said, "you aren't dead. Oh, and those smell wonderful. There wouldn't be an extra one, would there?"

She moved just enough that I could see a plate that held at least half a dozen more. "There are several different kinds, and they're all great," she said.

I selected two and moved quickly out of the way of a couple of volunteers who were bringing in fresh strawberries. I was going to help, but not until I ate. "Where did these come from?" I asked. "Did Katie bring them? And where is Katie?"

"She took the kids and went down to your mother's. I think she considers me a bad influence. It might have been because I accompanied you to last night's poker tournament."

"Who told her that?" I asked, getting a plate for my tacos. "You want one of these?"

"No, thanks, I've had enough. It was Gabrielle. You have to do something about her before she turns into a government informer."

"Isn't that the truth. Oh, excuse me." I leaned around a young woman to fill a mug from the hot water tap on the sink so I could make some tea. "Where is the tea?" I asked.

"In the butler's pantry," she said, gesturing behind her.

"No, no. Sorry. I meant my tea." I opened a cupboard and found the canister. The back door opened, and I looked up in time to see a man walk in. With the sun behind him, for just a moment I wasn't sure who it was. Tall, dark-haired, slender, and then I knew. I intended to play hard to get, but a smile jumped up and engulfed my face. "Hi," I said.

Nate Wright was looking me up and down as his own one-sided smile started. "Are you the new maid?" he asked, coming over to me.

His eyes were crinkled with humor, and when he slid his arm around my waist I swear the sizzle was so powerful I thought I was going to shoot up like a rocket.

I smiled and spoke in a British accent. "Why, yes, sir. I am the new maid." I curtseyed. "Is there anything I can do for you?"

Nate used an Irish accent. “Ah, darlin’, there’s many a things a lass o’ the likes of you could do for a man like me. I’m partial to red hair, but, ah,” — he looked around at the volunteers and the caterers, some of whom were smiling, and one or two who were simply openmouthed — “now, might not be the time. If you’d be after accompanyin’ me this afternoon —”

Beth started applauding and the others joined in. When everyone went back to whatever they’d been doing, she said, “I thought I’d better break the mood before things got out of hand.”

I sat at the table with my tea and tacos. Nate joined me, asking, “Does that happen often around here? Things getting out of hand?”

“More than I’d like,” I said. Then I jumped up. “I have to get something.” I went to the library and came back with a pen and a tablet. “I have to make a list of the things to do today; if not, I’m going to forget half of them.”

“Which means you won’t be sailing on Lake Travis with me,” he said.

“Of course I will. It just won’t be this afternoon.”

“Well, that seems fair. Here.” He slid the tablet over in front of him. “I’ll write, you eat. Maybe I can even help you accomplish whatever it is you have to do. And I think I have an attorney for you."

"Really? That's wonderful, although I might have found one, too."

Beth's cell phone rang. "Hello," she said. "Shannan! How's San Francisco? Honey, of course, I didn't forget you. How could I forget my own daughter? I've just been a little busy." Beth looked at me and made a face. Then she listened for a minute. "Honey, it's the time difference; it's two hours later here. You think it's dinner time, and I'm already in bed." I crossed my eyes when she said that. She went on. "Well, I had my phone turned off last night. No, no. We didn't do anything special. What have you been doing? What kind of clothes did you buy? And where have you been eating?" Beth got up and started upstairs, listening as she went.

During her conversation, I had watched Nate, under cover of eating my tacos. He has the most expressive face; I've teased him that he looks like Clark Gable's son. As he turned the tablet to get a better angle, I noticed his hands. The fingers were long and square tipped, like an artist's hands. He claims to have no creative talent, just a few hobbies, and so far he hasn't even been willing to share those with me. I haven't yet seen his house, either, mainly because it's in Dallas and he'd been halfway around the world until recently. Although I was looking forward to it. You can tell a lot about a person from their home.

"Where would you like to start?" he asked. "On your list?"

I smiled at him, pretending I hadn't been staring. Or ogling. "I think we should start with the attorney," I said. "Gregg Jacques." I took a bite of taco.

Nate looked up, surprised. "That was the name I was going to give you. I've been told by three different people that if he can't help you, then you are beyond help."

"Really? Then my instincts were right — I met him last night."

"I thought Beth said you two were in bed early last night?"

I shook my head. "Not even close. We were at a poker tournament."

"Really? So, how'd you do?"

"I was intending to win, but about halfway through, which means I beat half the other players, something, well, happened. We had to make a hasty exit."

"You and Gregg?"

"No, Beth and I," I said. "Although I did hide behind Gregg to get out the door, which wasn't easy in my lime green slip-ons."

"I'm sorry I missed that." Nate wasn't quite laughing, but he was on the verge.

"We didn't take pictures, either," I said. "Which might have been a good thing. Katie wasn't too impressed with my outfit. Or the fact that I played in a poker tournament. You haven't met her yet, but —"

"Oh, but I have. I met her and your grandkids."

"When was that?" I asked.

"Earlier —"

"You're the one who brought the breakfast tacos! That was so nice of you. Thank you. They're great."

"There's orange juice in the refrigerator, too, if you'd like some."

"You," I said, "are wonderful."

Nate picked up the pen and held it out to me. "Could you say that a little louder? Or, just say it into my microph— or rather, my pen."

I pulled the pen toward me and said softly, "You are wonderful."

Nate tipped his head and said demurely, " 'Mutual, I'm sure.' "

It was a line from something, just the way he said it was the clue to that, but I couldn't quite place it. It had been said by a woman, not a man, which was throwing me off. She was a blonde, not bright, funny — "I've got it! It's from *White Christmas.*"

He seemed impressed, "You're good."

I batted my eyelashes. " 'Mutual, I'm sure.' "

I glanced up to find his dark eyes intent on me. The smile was gone, and in its place was a warmth and affection that I hadn't had directed toward me in a very long time. I could feel it all the way to my stomach and my toes. I wanted to say something, but for the life of me I couldn't think of what.

I reached out to touch him. He caught my hand and lifted it gently toward his lips, as if to kiss it.

"Kitzi!" Beth said loudly as she rolled into the kitchen. "Shannan and Ron have —" She stopped, and I dropped my hand back to my lap. "Bad timing," she said. "Sorry."

Nate gestured to the volunteers who were bustling around behind us. I'd forgotten all about them. "Not a problem," he said. "We didn't want an audience, anyway."

"Whew. Personal summer," I said, to explain the blush that I knew was creeping up my neck. "Here, sit," I said to Beth. "I'm going to warm up my tea while we make our list." I went to the sink and filled my cup with some additional hot water. "How is Shannan doing?"

"Oh, she's great. Having a wonderful time, but apparently she is finding her father a less than wonderful traveling companion. She says he does nothing but complain."

Which is just one of the many reasons that I have called the man Mo-Ron for many years. Not to his face, or to Beth's, but in my mind. Although Beth has heard me say it more than once. To avoid saying it now, I smiled. "Shannan's smart. She'll have him trained to enjoy himself in no time." I went back to the table. "Okay, it's list time. First, I have to call Gregg Jacques to see if he'll represent me."

"But your fax isn't working," Beth said. "He'll need copies of all the corporation documents."

Nate was writing the word *Jacques.* Then he looked up at me and smiled. I could feel his glance go through me.

Before I could blush again, I said, "No problem. I'll drop off the papers on my way to see Rafferty."

"Rafferty?" Nate asked.

"Tess's dog. She say's he needs some company, so I thought I'd visit him. I also thought about sneaking him into the hospital. Or maybe sneaking her out. Just for a short visit."

"I'm getting pretty good at clandestine activities," Nate said. "You can count me in." He wrote *Rafferty* and then *hospital* on the yellow tablet. "What else?"

"We have to check with Katie and see what she's found out. I asked her to call relatives to see how people were going to vote on the Manse." Nate wrote *Katie.*

It reminded me of why she might be so over the top with my poker playing. It wasn't the poker, or the outfit, or even the red hair. It was that Katie needed something from me, but I was never sure what. Maybe she needed me to *be* something. Staid? A more conventional mother, like my mother was? Ironic that the most noticeable personality traits skipped over a generation. My grandparents were wonderful, and sometimes flamboyant, while my parents were traditional. They approached life as if there were a book somewhere that told everyone how to be. Even worse, they acted as if everyone knew how we were measuring up against those rules. It isn't surprising they were sometimes appalled at the way my grandparents reveled in their life.

They'd found me a bit over the top, too, not that my father had even heard such phrasing when he was alive, and my mother simply wouldn't say it. She might recommend that I be more ladylike. Like Katie.

Then we had Shelby, who was becoming more and more becoming. I liked that. There was a rightness to it, so that everyone had someone they could point to as a model, and someone they could criticize as not doing "it", whatever "it" was, quite correctly.

"What are you smiling at?" Nate asked.

"Oh, just life in my lane. I think I like it."

"That's important. And by the way, it shows on you."

"Excuse me," Beth said. "We're making a list and checking it twice, remember? So keep up. Next, we need to find out whatever we can about the *High Jinx.*"

Nate looked up. "I was only gone one day, and I can't believe how much I've missed. I'll bite; what, or who is High Jinx?"

While Beth was explaining, and I was finishing a now-cold taco and drinking my tea, Lauren came in the back door with at least ten tiny sacks. I knew what she'd been doing. That's the problem with buying beads: you can spend hundreds of dollars and come away with a few bags so small they'll fit in your purse. It's not like spending hundreds of dollars on fabric or dog food. With those you can get some bulk.

Lauren did have one larger sack, and it banged as she set it on the table.

"Now, that doesn't have beads in it," I said.

She nodded. "I got some tools, too. You know, pliers and a crimping tool. But I'm not sure it's the best crimping tool for what I want to do."

Beth looked up. "What do you want to do?"

"I want to make jewelry, for sure," she said, taking a place at the table. "And then I want to try the peyote stitch for some amulet bags. They're wonderful. Beaded flowers would be fun to make, and I've got a book. Today I had a chance to talk with a woman who makes wire and bead dangles. I'm not sure what you call them, but they hang outside. You use large wire in the most amazing shapes, and you can put any kind of beads on them. You can use a few or a lot. They don't have a sound like chimes, but they pick up the light."

Beth was shaking her head. I said, "I tried to warn her last night, but she wouldn't listen."

"Nobody listens," Beth said. "It's kind of like playing the slot machines: 'Oh, I won't get hooked.' But then they are. I remember when you said to me, 'I'm only going to make a few bracelets.' What an understatement."

I nodded. "Last year I went through the Bead Show dragging my poor mother along, saying things like, 'Just one more booth. A few more beads. I need findings!' " I turned to Lauren. "You are now addicted."

"I am not. I just bought some beads."

I started counting out the sacks. "One, two, three, four, five —"

"I plan on making presents for people." She put the sacks resolutely on the floor. "I heard Beth talking about the *High Jinx* when I came in. Why were you talking about that?"

Now that surprised me. "You know about it?" I asked.

"Of course. It was one of Andrew's big investments. Except, I don't think it was working out."

This is exactly the kind of thing I wanted to know, and here was Lauren, staying at my house with a store of information in her head that would have taken me hours, maybe days to discover.

"What do you know about it?" I asked. "It's a boat, right?"

"Not really one boat," Lauren said. "Andrew formed an investment group that purchased five different yachts. They were in foreclosure, and the charter company that owned them was called High Jinx Charters."

Lauren really did have an amazing memory. She knew about all five of the yachts, size, condition, type of boat, and other details that were frankly fascinating.

The yacht that the company was named after, the *High Jinx,* was a seventy-two-foot Irwin ketch that had four staterooms, crew space, fourteen overhead hatches, and twenty portholes.

"How can you remember the number of portholes?" I asked.

"I like odd facts, and you have to admit, those are pretty odd."

She even knew the colors that were being used to redo the staterooms on each yacht, and some of the other repair needs. The ketch needed fiberglass repair, the teak stripped and restained, new sails including a spinnaker, all new fittings in the kitchen, a new dinghy, and a bottom job. That last one sounded to me like something that overly vain women have done by a plastic surgeon.

"Those aren't odd facts," Beth said. "How do you know all of that?"

"I made a lot of phone calls to the companies that were doing the work. Besides, I think I developed some kind of lust for the *High Jinx.* The pictures of her are amazing."

She let out a sigh. "I kept hoping all the investors would want to take her on a maiden cruise and I could come along."

Nate picked up the pad. "I assume Lauren can check out the *High Jinx.*"

"Really? Go to Galveston and see her? I'd love to," she said. "On my computer I might even have some of the information on her. What exactly do you want to know?"

While Lauren was thrilled, I was disappointed. I had wanted to take tomorrow off and drive to Galveston myself. Maybe take Nate along. Stop in Round Top and look at antiques. Spend the night in a hotel on the beach. Separate rooms, of course. Balconies overlooking the bay. Soft music coming from the hotel behind us. A soft wind blowing my hair. My red hair . . .

I let the fantasy go. It wasn't going to work no matter how much I wanted it to.

"We want to know what kind of an investment High Jinx Charters is turning into. Is it profitable? Marinas are busiest on weekends and so are yacht brokers, so you can probably get some good information. Anything you think might be connected to Andrew's murder."

"I can drive or fly, or whatever you want. I can go today. Now, if you like."

"Take a plane," I said. "And today is a

great time. I'll give you a credit card number. You can fly into Hobby and rent a car there. If you need more time, check into a hotel."

Lauren started picking up her sacks. "I'll get on the computer and see what I can find. Maybe I can even get a cheap ticket."

"I wouldn't count on that," I said. "Timing is the important thing. It's a good twenty to twenty-five-minute drive to the airport, even on Sunday without much traffic."

"Then I'd better hurry." She was gone before we could say good-bye.

"I can get someone to man my booth for a while," Beth said. "Then I'll check on that accident."

"Accident?" The list that Nate was writing was growing longer. "Is this an automobile accident? Recent vintage?"

"Years ago," I said. I would have explained, but my brother Stephen came flying in the back door. Brad Pitt looking distraught. "Stephen," I said, "are you okay?"

He stopped dead still. "Sure. Sure. I mean, well, I didn't expect to find you here."

"I live here," I reminded him. "You know everyone, don't you?"

"Oh, yeah. Hi." He vaguely looked around

at Nate and Beth. "Nice to see you." Then he focused on me. "Where's Katie? I need to talk to her."

I couldn't imagine that he was seeking advice from Katie on how to woo Debby. Talk about two people who were totally different; Katie and Debby hardly spoke the same language, and they certainly traveled to the beat of different drummers.

"She's down at the gatehouse with your mother," Beth said.

"Great. Talk with you all later —" And he all but ran out the door.

I looked around the table. "He's going to be so disappointed," I said.

Nate frowned. "Why is that?"

"Because he obviously didn't want to talk to me, but I'm going to the gatehouse anyway. Whatever he wants to see Katie about is bound to be interesting. I can't wait to find out what it is. Nate, do you want to come with me?"

TWENTY

"There you are!" Stephen snapped. I could hear his voice while I was still walking up to the gatehouse.

"I was in the bathroom," Katie was saying. "Are you upset about something?"

"Yes, I am! I want to know what in the hell you were doing, calling up all of the relatives," Stephen was demanding.

Hearing his tone, I was glad Nate decided to tour the tent instead of coming with me. No woman wants her family having a yelling match in front of a new male friend.

Katie sounded stunned. "I was finding out how they are voting on the upcoming corporation vote. And I don't understand —"

"I know that. You don't understand anything. Don't you think it's a little rude? Who do you think you are to demand —"

I stepped in through the glass doors. "I'll tell you who she is," I said in my senatorial voice. "She is Katherine Camden, my daughter. Since the upcoming vote might end up putting me out of house and home, I think it's damned nice of Katie to get involved."

"Well, I think it's disgusting," he said, dismissing my opinion. "Next she'll be on *The Jerry Springer Show.* This isn't a political election, Kitzi; it's a family corporation, and she shouldn't be doing that."

I had never noticed before what a snob Stephen is. He certainly has no reason to be one, since he doesn't have a whole lot going for him except a pretty face. Still, people get the oddest notions about their place in the world. Apparently he is one of those. I know several others, politicians, both at the state and national level.

Katie was standing tall and rigid. "Well, at least I'm doing something," she said. "When was the last time you did something of value, Stephen? Or anything at all?"

She was no longer calling him "Uncle Stephen," and if the two of them kept at it, they might both do something that would qualify for the Springer show. I glanced around looking for my mother, who wasn't anywhere in sight, and for my grandchildren, who were also missing. I was glad on both counts.

"Wait a minute," I said, holding up both

hands. "I appreciate that we have some differences of opinion, so why don't we sit down and talk about them. There may be something going on here that we're not all aware of."

"I'm willing," Katie said. "Obviously I'm not aware of much of anything, since I just came out of the bathroom and he was here accusing me of things."

At that point Stephen made what was nearly a fatal blunder: he raised his index finger and shook it less than a foot away from Katie's face. "You have a lot of growing up to do, and a lot to learn about how our family operates —"

"And you, Stephen," I said, "are full of it. Not only that, you are the one who has a lot of growing up to do. How are you going to like it when Houston kicks Mother out of this house? Can she come live with you? Will you take care of her? Will Debby cook for her? See, it's not quite as simple as you thought, is it?"

In retrospect it's obvious that Katie and I both slammed Stephen pretty hard, but he did have a chance to end the hostilities peacefully and he chose not to.

Stephen's handsome face flushed a dangerous red. "I don't know why I bothered even trying to talk to you. You have no idea what's appropriate for the Camden family — or for the Manse."

My internal radar started blipping. "What do you mean, what's appropriate for the Manse? You can't mean the Bead Tea . . ."

Katie put her hands on her hips. "Do you have something to do with Houston's little scheme to put Mother and Grandmother — your own mother, Stephen — out of her family home?"

He opened and closed his mouth a few times. "What? Where did you hear that?"

"So you don't?" Katie folded her arms and stared him down like a schoolmistress. "I'm glad to hear it. Because if you do, I can't think of any snake with its belly lower to the ground than yours."

Stephen took a step back. "I don't know why I even bothered to come here. Obviously neither of you has any interest in maintaining a reasonable level of . . . of *decorum,* and then you start bandying about insults . . ." He stared at me. "You seem to think this is some kind of Senate game, where you can buy off the votes. Well, this is the Camden family, not some bunch of sleazy politicians."

"I'm sure Grandfather would be delighted to hear your characterization of politicians," I said coolly.

He stood staring at both of us for a moment. "You're . . . you're both *impossible!*" he spluttered. Then he stormed out of the gatehouse, slamming the door behind him.

As his retreating back disappeared behind the house, I turned to Katie. "What do you think that was all about?"

Katie bit her lip. "I don't know. But I think we should probably step up the search for an attorney."

By the time I got back to the kitchen, Stephen was long gone. Beth eyed me over a laptop as I pulled a pitcher of iced tea from the refrigerator and poured myself a big glass. I would have preferred a glass of Muscovito, but it was a little early to crack open a bottle of booze.

"How did it go?" she asked.

"You don't want to know," I said. "I don't care if it *is* Sunday — I'm calling Gregg Jacques right now."

Beth's eyes widened. "You don't think Stephen's —"

"Gone to the other side?" I took a big swig of iced tea. It wasn't Muscovito, but it helped. "I'm not sure," I said. "He told me I had no idea what was right for the Manse, which makes me suspicious. And did I tell you he asked to borrow money from me the other day?"

"What for?"

"He didn't say."

"Do you think he got mixed up in Andrew's little investment club?"

I sighed. "I know he's trying to win back Debby."

Beth rolled her eyes. "The material girl?"

"Exactly. So if Andrew promised a big return, I can imagine Stephen might go for it."

"But what does that have to do with the Manse?"

"I don't know. I've got a bad feeling about all of this, which is why I'm going to see if I can engage the services of a big-gun attorney right now. Whatever happens, I'm going to be ready."

"On Sunday?"

"On Sunday."

"Well, before you go charging off, I need a little info from you."

I suddenly realized that Beth was scheduled to be at her booth right now. "I forgot to ask: did you get someone to watch the booth for you?"

"My friend Delta was happy to do it. I figured I'd take an hour or two and see what I could turn up." She nodded toward the small computer on the table in front of her.

My eyebrows went up. "When did you get a laptop?"

"Lauren let me borrow hers. Now, when did the accident happen? The one that killed the Yancys' grandson."

"Let's see . . . Andrew was in college, and he's — he *was* thirty-one, so I guess that would put it at ten to fifteen years ago."

"What was the boy's name?"

"The one who died? Donovan. I don't know if his last name was Yancy, but the first name is unusual."

"How about the other one, the one who ended up in a wheelchair?"

Another good question. "That's one of the things I was hoping to find out."

"Anything else that might help?"

At that moment, a woman with a big tray of mini quiches staggered into the kitchen. "Is there room in the fridge for these?"

"Sure," I said. "Just scoot things out of the way if you need to."

"Would you like one?"

Even though I had just polished off two breakfast tacos, I couldn't turn down quiche. Besides, after my run-in with Stephen, I needed some caloric support. "Would I ever." I snagged two and turned to Beth. "Want one?"

"I'm dieting, remember?"

I shrugged. “You don’t know what you’re missing.”

“Don’t tempt me. I’ve got forty-five more pounds to go. But on the accident, is there anything else?”

I sighed. “Sorry, Beth. I’m afraid that’s all I’ve got.” I popped the second quiche into my mouth and helped the young woman with the tray rearrange the bottom shelf. Then I retreated to my office to call Gregg. I’d feel better knowing my affairs were in the hands of a talented attorney. Besides, if I was lucky, I might even get him to share the rest of the story he started at the Texas hold ’em tournament.

I wasn’t lucky. Gregg’s voice mail picked up, both at his office and on his cell phone. Which wasn’t surprising, since it was Sunday. I guessed it made sense; even high-powered lawyers need a day off from time to time.

I left a message and hung up. A moment later, I made one more phone call.

“Jacqueline? It’s Kitzi Camden.”

“Kitzi! How the heck are you? It’s been ages.” When I was in the Senate, Jacqueline Pacitti had been my best researcher; if I wanted to know something, whether it was the governor’s favorite brand of boots or the voting record of one of the other senators, all I had to do was call her, and she'd find everything I needed — and then some.

"I know. I hate to bother you, but I wondered if you could look something up for me? I'd do it myself, but I'm stumped."

"Shoot."

I told her everything I knew about High Jinx Charters. "But please, don't say anything to anyone about it."

"How fast do you need it?"

"As fast as you can get it."

"Well, it's Sunday, so most of my contacts won't be in, but I know of a few databases that might help."

"Thanks, Jackie. Why don't you and Eric plan on coming over to dinner soon? It's been too long."

"That would be wonderful. We can talk about old times!"

I gave her my home number and my cell number, and Sinatra leaped into my lap as I set down the phone. Beth was looking up the accident, Lauren was headed to Galveston, Jacqueline was researching High Jinx Charters, and I was at loose ends. I was about to go down to the kitchen and forage for another mini quiche when Nate appeared in the doorway. My heart rate picked up a few notches at his lazy smile.

"Beth said I'd find you here. How'd things

go with your brother?" he asked.

I sighed. "I was just on the phone trying to get through to Gregg."

"That bad, huh?"

"Something is rotten in the state of Denmark."

"Heaven will direct it," he said. I was impressed; it's not often you find a man who not only recognizes a quote from *Hamlet* but who can also come back with the next line. Then he grinned. "But I suspect in this case, heaven will get a little help."

I sighed. "He said something about my not knowing what was best for the Manse that made me suspicious."

Nate's eyes darkened. "You think he's involved with Houston on this?"

I reached down and scratched Sinatra's chin. "I don't know. But right now, I'm at an impasse. Beth's looking up the accident, Lauren's chasing down the *High Jinx,* and I'm spinning my wheels."

Nate crossed the room and rounded the desk. I swear I could hear the sparks crackle as he put his hands on my shoulders and began to rub. My tense muscles softened into butter under his strong fingers.

"There must be something we can do," he said.

"You're already doing it," I purred. My

hand stopped scratching. Sinatra huffed and jumped off my lap, stalking out of the office.

I leaned back into the chair, enjoying Nate's closeness, thinking maybe I should just let things go for the day, when he said, "Have you looked at the guest list yet?"

"The guest list?"

"Didn't Granger ask for it? It might give us at least a few leads."

I sighed again. "I already went through it with Granger, but there's a chance I might have missed something."

"I'll bet Judy has a copy."

"You're right! Let's head down to the tent." I wasn't convinced we'd learn anything, but it was better than sitting around doing nothing. Our bodies brushed as I slipped past him to the door, and a zing went through me. Even if we didn't find anything on the guest list, I could think of worse things than spending an hour or so in close quarters with Nate.

Judy was helping arrange a display of Swarovski crystal necklaces and matching earrings when we found her. The crystals shimmered in the morning light, and I regretted not bringing my purse. "How are sales going?" I asked.

She beamed at me. "Wonderfully. Thank

you so much for letting us use the Manse; we've been so busy this weekend. By the end of the event we'll probably have at least a hundred thousand dollars to contribute to the Ovarian Cancer Organization. And tickets for the necklace are still selling!"

"I'm planning to buy a few more myself," I said, thinking of Stephen's comment about what was right for the Manse. My thoughts turned to Tess and Houston's wife Rebecca, both wonderful women, both struggling with this terrible disease. If helping to find a cure for suffering wasn't the best possible use for the Manse, what was?

"I was hoping you could help us out," I said.

Judy smiled. "What can I do for you?"

"Do you have an extra copy of the guest list for the reception Thursday night?"

Her face clouded. "The police asked for it, too. For their investigation into that young man's . . ."

"Yes," Nate said. "Do you have a spare copy?"

"I'm sure I have one here somewhere." She turned and flipped through a couple of binders. "Here it is. I think this is the only printout I've got, but it's saved on the computer, so you can have it."

"Thanks, Judy. I'll get it back to you this

afternoon."

"Take your time," she said. "And by the way, I like your hair!"

I raised my hand to my hair and blushed slightly. "Thank you. It's not permanent."

"Maybe it should be," Nate murmured as we walked away from the booth.

"You like it red?"

"It certainly suits your temperament."

I laughed. "I think I'll stick with blonde. Where shall we go? My office?"

"We need two chairs. How about the balcony?"

"Great idea. Let's get a pitcher of iced tea and head upstairs."

Ten minutes later, we settled ourselves in on the wrought-iron love seat, our thighs touching as Nate pulled out the list. Beth hadn't found anything out yet on the accident but promised to come up and tell us if she did. I took a sip of iced tea and leaned toward Nate. The morning was already hot, but it wasn't all due to the sun. I swear that man emanated heat.

"Now, let's see here. What are we looking for?" Nate said.

I flipped a notebook open to a blank page and poised my pen as he ran his finger down the list. "Anything familiar," I said. "Or odd."

"Okay. I guess we can cross off Andrew."

Despite the heat, I shivered a bit. "We know Houston and Rebecca," I said. "And Bruce and Delphine. They were outside the night Andrew died." I blushed, remembering what they had broken up. "And the Yancys."

"Just the two of them?"

"Louise and Earl. Stephen was there, and Lauren, of course."

He turned to look at me. "Do you think Lauren could have done it?"

"I don't know. She's been so helpful, and she just doesn't seem like the type."

"They say Ted Bundy didn't, either," Nate said.

I sighed. "I know, I know." Suddenly a thought occurred to me. "Wait. Is there someone named Sandy on there?" I didn't think I would have missed Cat's Eyes at the party, but I couldn't be sure.

"Who's Sandy?"

"Someone I met at the poker tournament last night." I took a sip of tea and scanned the page with him.

"Let's find out," he said.

We were moving through the second page when my eyes skidded to a stop. "Wait a moment."

"What?"

"That name. Linder. Marian and John Linder."

"What about it?"

"I've seen it somewhere before. I just can't place it." I thought for a moment. Where had I seen it? It was on a folder somewhere, in a desk . . . "Hang on. I remember it now. That was the name on the client file I found in Houston's office."

"Do you think it's connected?"

"I don't know. I guess it's possible." As we turned to the third page, the door to the house squeaked, and I looked up to see Beth.

"Am I interrupting something?"

Well, yes, but I didn't mind. "No, no," I said. "We were just going over the guest list from Friday night. What did you find out?"

"Not much, I'm afraid. Andrew was driving, it seems, and he was the only one to make it out without major injuries. I found an old newspaper article. According to the papers, Donovan and the other boy weren't wearing seat belts."

I sucked in my breath. "God, what a tragedy."

"Anyway," she said, "I found out the other boy's name. The one who ended up in the wheelchair."

"And?"
"His name was Keith Linder."

Twenty-One

"Keith *Linder?*" I said. "Are you sure?"

Beth's brow creased. "Why? Do you know him?"

"No," Nate said, "but I'm guessing his parents were at the reception Thursday night."

Her eyes widened. "Do you think . . ."

"I don't know," I said. "The file I saw said they lived in Pflugerville. Unless they have an unlisted number, their address should be in the phone book. Anyone up for a short drive?"

"I'd love to," Beth said. "But I have to get back to my booth. Delta said she'd cover it for an hour, and I've only got ten minutes left."

I turned to Nate. "Are you up for it?"

His face split into a broad grin. "I'm always up for another adventure with my favorite redhead."

Beth rolled her eyes. "I think I'm glad I'm

not coming. I hate feeling like a third wheel."

An hour later, we turned onto Cuthbert Cove, a cul-de-sac in a housing development that, based on the size of the trees, had been built within the last few years. Although I was excited to uncover another lead, I didn't want the ride to end; Nate was fabulous company, and we'd sung to the Beatles and laughed the whole way. "Paperback Writer" was still streaming from the speakers as Nate's SUV slowed to a stop in front of 2305, a brick one-story ranch with two small crape myrtles and a *For Sale* sign in the front yard.

"Well, this is it," he said. "What do we say when we knock on the door?"

"That Andrew was Houston's partner, and we're hoping they can give us some information that will shed light on what happened."

Nate grinned. "And that they're suspects?"

"I think we'd probably be better off keeping that under our hats for now. I wonder why they're selling the house."

"Let's go find out."

As we headed up the front walk, I noticed a ramp next to the steps. Did Keith still live with his parents? Then Nate's hand brushed mine, and I stopped thinking about everything. Well, not *quite* everything . . .

"Ready?" He squeezed my hand, sending an electric current through my body.

"Here goes nothing." I reached out and pushed the doorbell.

The woman who answered the door must have been twenty years younger than Mrs. Yancy, but she looked old beyond her years. Streaks of white peppered her springy black hair, and both her face and frame looked worn, as if she'd carried some heavy burden.

"Can I help you?" she asked in a thin voice. "If you're interested in the house, I guess you can take a look."

I realized she thought Nate and I were a couple out house hunting on a Sunday afternoon, and I felt my face heat up. "Oh, no," I said. "We're not looking for a house. Are you Mrs. Linder?"

She nodded.

"I don't believe we've met, but you were at my house the other night, for the Bead Tea reception." I proffered my hand. "I'm Kitzi Camden, and this is my friend, Nate Wright."

Nate dipped his head, and if he'd had a hat, he would have doffed it. "Pleased to meet you, Mrs. Linder."

Mrs. Linder looked confused. "But . . .

your hair . . ."

My hand rose to my head, which I now remembered was orange, and I smiled. "I guess I needed a change. We were wondering if we could ask you a few questions about Thursday night."

"Of course. Do come in." Nate and I followed her into her small, dark living room. The house smelled faintly of boiled cabbage, and the surfaces were crowded with porcelain and crystal animals, the kind you see on the Shopping Channel. The shades were down, and despite the newness of the house, the sagging couches and fifties side tables mirrored Mrs. Linder's weariness. She was a meticulous housekeeper, though; there wasn't a speck of dust anywhere.

"What lovely figurines," I said.

"Thank you." Her lips twitched into a sweet smile that lifted years from her face. "The agent told me I should clear them up while the house was on the market, but I couldn't do it." She caressed a crystal dolphin's back. "They make me feel at home." She looked up and realized Nate and I were still standing by the front hall. "Please, sit down. Can I get you something to drink?"

"Oh, no thanks," I said, sitting down on a worn blue-plaid couch. I was disappointed when Nate sat down at the other end.

"You have a lovely house," Nate said when Mrs. Linder had settled herself on the love seat opposite us. "May I ask why you're moving?"

Her face sagged again. "We had some investments we thought were doing really well, and we were going to move into a bigger place. But now . . ."

I leaned forward. "Were you working with Andrew Lynch?"

Her thin eyebrows rose in surprise. "How did you know?"

"Several people were," I said. "He was my cousin's business partner. I understand things weren't going as well as they could with some of his investment strategies."

She sighed. "We thought they were, but then Earl and Louise called and told me things weren't going so well. John and I talked with Andrew last week, and we couldn't get a straight answer." She slumped into the couch. "And now, with Andrew gone, I don't know what to do about it. We put everything we had into it, everything we'd been building since Keith finished his therapy . . ."

"Is Keith your son?"

She nodded. "Our only child. We wanted another one, but it wasn't in God's plan, I suppose. Keith was in an accident many years ago — with Andrew, and with another young man, named Donovan. The Yancys' grandson." She twisted her thin lips. "It was awful. Poor Donovan didn't make it, and Keith was paralyzed from the waist down. He had years of therapy. Eventually, the insurance money ran out, and we put every penny we had into making him well again." She shrugged in sadness and resignation. "He's better, but he'll never be quite the same."

It was sad, I thought, how one split second can shatter a life. If Andrew and his friends had decided to see a movie instead of hitting Sixth Street, or if someone else had driven, or if they'd left just five minutes later, maybe the Yancys would still have their grandson and Keith Linder would be able to walk. I gazed at Marian Linder's tired frame. She and her son had suffered because of Andrew's poor judgment in the past. Had the loss of their money been enough to make her snap? "It sounds like you did everything you could to help him through it," I said. "He's a lucky young man. Does he live here with you?"

Her eyes flickered to the line of photos on the mantel. Framed snapshots of a young, dark-haired man. Smiling. "He works part-time at the local bank. We keep encouraging him to do more, but after the accident, he never quite got his confidence back."

I ran my eyes over the photos, realizing that none of them included a wheelchair. It appeared that Keith wasn't the only one who hadn't come to terms with his handicap. "How did you meet Andrew?" I asked.

"We knew him before the accident; he and Keith were friends at UT. The three of them were coming back from Sixth Street when it happened. They never made it."

Nate and I sat silent as she relived a moment long past. I could only imagine what it would be like to have the police arrive at your door, to tell you that your son was paralyzed, or worse . . .

Finally, she continued. "Then we lost touch with him for years, until he called us up about six months ago and said he'd discovered an investment plan with huge returns. A sure bet. We were still scrambling to catch up on savings, and the Yancys said they were having great results, so we decided to give it a shot."

"Did the Yancys tell you about the Bead Tea?"

"No, it was your cousin, Houston." She shook her head. "It's a shame about his wife's cancer — she's so lovely, and friendly, too. The last time we were in the office, he asked us to come and support the cause. I knew the Yancys would be there, and I've always wanted to see the Manse . . ." She flushed slightly.

"Any time you want a personal tour, you let me know."

Her face lit up. "Really?"

I smiled and fished a card from my purse. "Just give me a call, and we'll set up a time."

She smiled. "Oh, that would be wonderful! Maybe Keith could come, too. He really enjoyed the reception on Thursday — he spent a lot of time touring the house." I didn't remember seeing a wheelchair, but there were so many people there, I might have missed it. "He always wanted to be an architect, you know," she added.

"Maybe he still could be. Has he taken any classes?"

She shook her head. "Like I said, since the accident . . ."

"He's still young," I said. "Lots of people make career changes. Even Nate here has changed course a couple of times."

"Really?" she said.

"Yup. And your son's got plenty of time," he said. "One thing confuses me, though; if Keith was there, why wasn't his name on the guest list?"

"Oh, he wasn't supposed to be, but Ellie Lawler and her husband couldn't go, so she gave us the extra tickets. I was kind of surprised Keith was interested; I guess he wanted to see the inside of the Manse."

"Did you run into Andrew while you were there?" Nate asked.

"We tried to, but every time we spotted him, he disappeared before we could get to him. We did talk with your cousin Houston for a while. A charming man. And his wife . . ." She shook her head. "Life can be so unfair sometimes, can't it?"

My heart twinged. The Yancys had lost their grandson, and Mrs. Linder's only child had been paralyzed by an accident. And then there was Rebecca — even though she was in remission, ovarian cancer could be tricky. And Tess, lying in her hospital bed, next to that awful woman. I sighed. Life *was* unfair. And there wasn't much we could do about it. Maybe Nate could help me smuggle Rafferty into the hospital this afternoon.

"Is there anything else I can help you with?" Mrs. Linder's voice pulled me back to the living room.

I blinked. "I don't think so. Except for one thing — if you don't mind me asking, what was Andrew investing your money in?"

"A yacht called the *High Jinx.*"

I suppressed a grimace. "That's what I thought." I stood up. "Thank you so much for your time, Mrs. Linder. I hope your investments work out better than you hoped. And any time you and your son want to see the Manse, just give me a call."

As we stood to go, the front door opened. "That must be Keith," Mrs. Linder said. A moment later, a dark-haired man in a wheelchair rolled into the living room. His eyes widened when he saw me, and the chair wheeled to an abrupt halt.

Mrs. Linder smiled. "Sweetheart, this is Kitzi Camden and her friend Nate. Remember Kitzi? She's the lady who owns the Manse." Something about her tone reminded me of Katie reprimanding Gabrielle. Mrs. Linder sounded like she was addressing a three-year-old, not a man in his thirties.

"Oh, where the Bead Tea reception was." I studied Keith's face. His cheeks were drawn, and much of the vigor I could see in the photos on the mantel had faded, but his brown eyes stared at me with intensity. They looked familiar somehow, but I couldn't place them. "Nice house," he said.

"I'm glad you liked it. I was just telling your mother that you're welcome to a private tour whenever you'd like."

"Great. Thanks. I've got to go get ready for work." He wheeled past us. "Nice to meet you."

As her son disappeared down a dark hallway, Mrs. Linder turned to Nate and me. "Thank you so much for visiting. I'm afraid I wasn't much help, though."

Nate smiled at her. "You've been a big help. Can we get in touch with you if we have any more questions?"

Her eyes brightened as Nate touched her shoulder, and I shook my head in wonder. No woman was immune to the man's animal magnetism. "Of course," she said, her voice suddenly chipper. "Let me get you my number." She hurried to the kitchen and returned with a scrap of paper, beaming at Nate. "Call me anytime."

"And if you want a tour, just let me know. I'd love to spend more time visiting with Keith."

Her brightness faded a little at the mention of her son. "Of course. That would be lovely."

"So, do you think we can put Mrs. Linder on the suspect list?" Nate asked as he bit into a turkey sandwich. On the way back to the Manse, we had stopped at Schlotzky's, an Austin-based chain that makes — in my opinion, anyway — the best turkey sandwiches in town. We sat across from each other at a small table by the window, our knees almost touching.

I swallowed a bite of cheese and turkey bliss, complete with olives — I had opted for the high-calorie Turkey Original — and took a sip of Diet Coke. At least the drink was low-cal. "I don't know. She doesn't seem the type, but I could be wrong. Her son sure did look surprised to see us, though, didn't he?"

"Maybe they don't get many visitors."

"Maybe it was my orange hair," I joked. "But I wonder what bank he works at. None of the ones I know about are open Sunday afternoons."

Nate nodded. "Keith was at the party Thursday night. Maybe he killed Andrew over his parents' investments."

"But how could a man in a wheelchair hit someone over the head and then get him into a six-foot-tall Dumpster?"

"Good point. Maybe he had help."

"It's possible. I can't imagine Mrs. Linder being involved, but we haven't met her husband."

"Maybe the Yancys helped him."

"Still, I just don't see it happening. He

hands the candlestick to Mr. Yancy and says, 'Would you mind braining our investment counselor? And I could use a little help getting the body out to the Dumpster when you're done.' "

Nate laughed, a deep belly laugh that sent a current of warmth through me. "No, I can't quite see it. Maybe we need to take a closer look at Mr. Yancy, though."

"Or Bruce, the contractor next door. He and his wife were investing, too. Or maybe there's another angle we haven't even looked at. Lauren said he wasn't seeing anyone, but maybe he was. For all we know, it could have been a crime of passion."

He took a last swig of his Coke and glanced at his watch. "It's almost two o'clock. What shall we do next?"

I glanced at my half-eaten sandwich. "Let me finish eating, and we'll talk."

As we climbed back into the car fifteen minutes later, the CD switched to "Eleanor Rigby," the violins dipping into a minor key and singing of death. Tears pricked my eyes, and I swallowed hard. "Nate, what do you say to picking up Rafferty and going to visit Tess?"

He glanced at me. "I know I agreed to this earlier, but isn't Rafferty an Airedale?"

I nodded.

"And isn't Tess in the hospital?"

I nodded again, and my heart squeezed. I didn't know how many days she had left, and if I didn't do something soon, she might never see Rafferty again.

He reached over and took my hand. "You don't let anything get in your way, do you?"

We had just turned south onto I-35 when my cell phone rang.

"Kitzi?"

It was Jacqueline. "How's it going? Did you make any headway?"

"I don't know if it helps, but I just looked up the registration records on the boats registered to High Jinx Charters. They haven't changed ownership in five years."

"So?"

"So the foreclosure sale you told me about never happened."

"What does that mean?"

She took a deep breath. "It means your friend's investment firm never bought the boats."

Twenty-Two

My pulse quickened. "Did you find out who owns the company?"

"Something called A.C. Investments in Corpus Christi. The owner of record is a guy named Alexander Corcoran."

Well, that explained the A.C. "Is there a business phone number?"

"I called it. It goes to an answering machine."

"I guess we can try it tomorrow. Anything else?"

"That's it for now."

"Thanks, Jacqueline. You're a wonder."

"Any time," she said. "I'll probably have more info tomorrow."

"I'll talk to you later in the week, and we'll set up dinner."

"I'm looking forward to it!" she said.

I hung up and told Nate what Jacqueline had found out. "So I'm guessing that all the money Andrew's clients contributed didn't get them squat," I said.

"But what about the renovations Lauren was talking about?"

"I'm betting Andrew used his clients' cash to refurbish the boats so that whoever owned them could resell them," I said.

"Or reopen the charter service. So who owns the boats now?"

"A company called A.C. Investments run by an Alexander Corcoran."

Nate sighed. "Sounds like Andrew was getting into some pretty dirty business. Should we call Lauren?"

I hesitated. "I think I'd rather wait."

Nate's brow creased. "You think Lauren's involved?"

"I don't know. I'm just curious to see what kind of information she calls with."

"Maybe we should go down and join her."

I stifled images of Nate and me, out on the beach, the sun sparkling on the waves, strawberry margaritas in our hands . . . "I just wish we didn't have the Bead Tea still going on."

"On the plus side," he said, "we have another lead to follow. Now, where is Rafferty?"

A half hour later we pulled up outside of Tess's neighbor's house. Marie greeted us at the front door, with Rafferty bounding up behind her. She grabbed his collar and pushed a lock of blonde hair from her pink face. "How are you going to get him in?"

"We're still working on that," Nate said.

I bent down and stroked Rafferty's fuzzy head, and he looked up at me with wet brown eyes. "Ready, Raff?" He licked my hand, and I smiled at Marie. "Thank you so much for taking care of him. We'll have him back in an hour or two."

"Good luck getting him in," she said. "Too bad Raff's not a toy poodle!"

Nate grinned at her as we stepped out the front door. "Or a chihuahua." A moment later, as we loaded Rafferty into the back-seat of Nate's Navigator, he said, "So, Miss Kitzi. How exactly *are* we getting this dog up to Tess's room?"

"Do you have a spare blanket in the back?"

"What do we need a blanket for?"

"Trust me," I said.

Nate laughed. "Do I have a choice?"

By the time we pulled into the parking lot at Seton Hospital, Rafferty was stretched out on my lap, nose glued to the window. "I'll bet you can't wait to see Tess, can you, big boy?" At the sound of his mistress's name, his ears perked up. I turned to Nate.

"Would you mind pulling up near the emergency room?"

"The emergency room?"

I nodded, and he cruised to a stop near the sliding double doors. I untangled myself from Rafferty and turned to Nate. "Please park in the parking garage, and meet me on the first floor by the elevator. And bring the blanket."

"Aye aye, captain." I slid out of the car and shut the door, careful not to close it on Rafferty. As Nate piloted the Navigator to the parking garage, I slipped through the sliding glass doors into the waiting area for the emergency room. Only a few of the chairs were occupied, and the triage nurse, a slight redheaded woman, looked up as I approached. "Can I help you?"

"I hate to bother you, but I'm taking an old friend to visit a patient, and I don't know if he'll be able to walk up there." I hadn't told a lie — just exercised the sin of omission a bit. "Is there a spare wheelchair I could borrow?"

She glanced at the waiting area and said, "Sure. Things are pretty slow right now. Can you get it back in an hour?"

"No problem. Thank you so much. My friend will be so happy for the visit."

The nurse smiled, and her face lit up like

sunshine. I felt a little twinge at having misled her — but then again, she *was* bringing joy into a sick woman's life. Even if she wasn't aware of the number of hospital regulations I was about to break. Ignorance is bliss, or so they say.

Nate and Rafferty were waiting for me just inside the garage entrance. Nate's eyebrows leapt up as I wheeled the chair up next to the elevator and patted the seat. "Hop in, Raff." As the Airedale jumped up onto the vinyl seat, I turned to Nate. "Blanket, please."

"You're planning on taking Rafferty up in a *wheelchair?*" He shook his head in wonder and handed me an orange fleece blanket.

"Well, it was easier to get than a gurney." Rafferty shifted, and his tags jingled. "I should probably get rid of the collar, though."

"Probably. Too bad his legs are too short to reach the footrests."

"We'll say he's an amputee." With Nate's help, I removed the collar and arranged the blanket until the only thing visible was Rafferty's wet black nose.

Nate stepped back to look at Rafferty's nose protruding from the blanket. "And maybe the victim of plastic surgery gone wrong? I admire your initiative, Kitz, but I don't think the nurses are going to fall for it . . ."

"Don't worry," I said. "I've got a plan for that."

His mouth twitched into a grin, and I had to resist the urge to kiss him. "Well, that's a relief. Let's have it, then."

I told him what I needed him to do, and he nodded. "I'll follow you in five minutes," I said.

"I'll do my best. Good luck." He leaned down and kissed the top of my head. The tingle shot all the way down to my toes, and a delicious warmth rippled through me as I watched his long, lean body striding toward the emergency room doors.

Five minutes later, I arranged Rafferty's blanket, gave him a few reassuring pats, and pointed the wheelchair toward the hospital. Within moments, the doors slid open, and a cool, antiseptic breeze enveloped us.

We were in.

I put my head down and walked briskly, heading for the elevator bank. Rafferty sat remarkably still for an Airedale, only his wet nose protruding from the blanket. So far, so good. We powered past the stuffed animals and balloons on display at the gift shop without running into anyone, and I hoped our luck would hold.

I turned the last corner jabbed at the elevator's Up button, murmuring soothing words to Rafferty as we waited. One minute, two minutes . . . my body tensed at the sound of approaching footsteps. Just before they rounded the corner, the elevator dinged, and a woman with two small children spilled out of the furthest door.

As they passed the wheelchair, the younger child, a girl around Shelby's age, peered at Rafferty. "Mommy, who's in that wheelchair?"

"Someone who has a hard time walking, dear," her mother replied. I smiled at the girl and pushed the chair into the elevator, pushing the Door Close button, praying it would work before whoever was coming down the hall turned up.

"But Mommy," I heard her say as the door began its slow slide closed. "It didn't *look* like a person. It looked like a . . ." Before she could finish, the door snicked shut, and I let out a long, slow breath. Close call. I stroked Rafferty's head and told him we were almost there.

A moment later, the elevator door opened a mere ten feet away from the nurses' station. Fortunately, Nate was in position, draped over the counter and entertaining the nurses. As I hustled past the station toward Tess's room, the sound of women's laughter followed me.

It was only when I reached Tess's door that I remembered she had a roommate. I hesitated for a moment. Should I check first, to see if she was there? Maybe she would be asleep. If not, I could always disable the Call Nurse button.

After a moment of indecision, I pushed open the door and wheeled Rafferty through it. I needn't have worried about Tess's roommate, whose eyes hardly flickered from the program blaring from the television in the corner as I pushed the wheelchair past her bed. Instead of whining and complaining, she was listening to the television at top volume. Poor Tess. On the plus side, Tess's roommate did look better today. Maybe she would be checking out soon.

As I rounded the curtain to Tess's bed, my step light with relief, all the breath whooshed out of me, and the wheelchair shuddered to a stop.

Tess was hardly recognizable. In the twenty-four hours since my last visit, her eyes had sunken, and her pale skin looked stretched over the bones of her face. The IV was filled with red again — another transfusion — but it didn't seem to be helping. I watched her shallow breathing for a moment, then pulled the blanket off of Rafferty, who leaped from the wheelchair to Tess's bedside, propping his paws up on the edge of the bed and nuzzling his mistress's face.

Her eyelids fluttered, and she lifted her head, staring at Rafferty in disbelief. A radiant smile transformed her hollow features, and for a few glorious seconds, I saw the woman I once knew and loved. Then her head dropped to the pillow in exhaustion and her face clouded with pain. My heart wrenched.

"Kitzi," she said, her voice barely above a whisper. "I can't believe it. You brought him here." She patted the bed next to her. "Come here, boy." Rafferty hopped up and lay down next to her, licking Tess's gaunt hand and gazing at her with shiny brown eyes. "I've missed you so much, Raff."

As he snuggled into her, the door opened again, and Nate walked around the curtain. "Hi, Tess," he said, smiling at her. "I'm glad to meet you; I've heard so many wonderful things about you. I'm Nate Wright, Kitzi's partner in crime."

Tess smiled. "It's hard to keep up with Kitzi, isn't it? I did it for years, and it just about wore me out." Nate's eyes darkened with worry as Tess laughed and then struggled to catch her breath.

"How are you doing?" I asked Tess, moving to the other side of the bed and squeezing her hand. My eyes drifted to her bedside table, where the Red Vines I had brought lay virtually untouched.

"Not so hot." She stroked Rafferty's head. The television droned in the corner, a woman wailing over a lost lover.

"I can imagine, having to listen to that all the time," I murmured, jerking my head toward the television.

"Don't they have rules about that?" Nate asked in a hushed voice. "Can we get her a headset?"

"Oh, that doesn't bother me. It's better than listening to complaining. Besides, I can sleep through anything these days." She gave me a weak smile. "The trouble is staying awake."

I eyed her gaunt frame. "Do they have you on new medication?"

She shook her head. "They're doing everything they can," she said. "But you know how this disease is. The test results didn't come in too well."

"What's wrong?"

She looked away from me, out the window. "It's spreading, Kitzi." She swallowed hard. "And it's inoperable."

My heart felt like it was splintering in my chest. I squeezed back tears.

Tess took a shuddery, shallow breath and looked back at me. I could see the pain in her eyes, and more than anything, I wanted to do something to take it away, give her some hope, some peace. I couldn't believe this once-vibrant woman was dying right in front of me. It wasn't fair.

"There isn't a whole lot anyone can do," she said. "At this point, it's mainly the painkillers that are keeping me going."

I willed the tears away. "Oh, Tess. Can you get a second opinion?"

She sighed. "Three doctors looked at the tests. They're pretty conclusive."

I swallowed down the lump that had formed in my throat. "Is there anything else I can do for you?"

Tess hugged Rafferty. "You've already done it, Kitzi. You've already done it."

We stayed for almost an hour, until Tess finally slumped back against the pillow and dozed off again, exhausted. Rafferty licked her face, but she didn't stir. I coaxed him back into the wheelchair, arranged the blanket, and headed past the curtain to the door. As we passed the older woman's bed, her sharp eyes flicked to Rafferty's nose, which poked out from under the blanket.

"You brought a dog?"

I was about get down on my knees and beg her not to tell anyone when her hard face broke out into a sad smile. "I wish you'd told me. I haven't seen my poodle Chamois for almost two weeks now."

Nate smiled back at her. "I don't think he can sit still long enough for another visit, but next time we bring him, we'll make sure to include you."

"Oh, I'm checking out the day after tomorrow," she said, "so if you don't come back soon, I won't be here."

As we hustled Rafferty back to the elevator, the awful thought occurred to me that Tess might not be there, either.

The nurses' station was empty, and we slipped into the elevator without anyone noticing. Except for a touch-and-go moment when Raff spotted a stuffed squirrel in the gift-shop window, the rest of the ride to the parking garage went smoothly, and as Nate took Rafferty up the stairs to his car, I returned the wheelchair to the redheaded nurse.

"Did your visit go okay?" she asked.

I smiled. "Yes, it really cheered her up. Thanks so much for your help." I turned and left the hospital, with its smell of cleansers and sickness and death, and walked out into the hot June air. It wasn't until I closed the door of Nate's Navigator behind me that the tears came.

Nate's warm arms encircled me as I sobbed, my chest heaving. "It's just not fair," I snuffled into his soft shirt. "She's so young, so vibrant. And there's nothing anyone can do for her." He held me tight as the waves of grief washed over me, until finally the tears stopped coming. After a long time, I sat up and wiped my eyes. "Sorry about that. Our parking fee is probably in the triple digits now."

"That's the least of my worries," Nate said, kissing the top of my head.

I snuggled into him. "Thanks so much for your help, Nate. I couldn't have made it past the nurses' station without you."

"Anytime, Kitzi. Anytime."

I reached for a tissue. "I hate this disease."

"I know," he said softly. "Me too." I remembered that he'd been through this before. He had lost his mother to ovarian cancer.

As I wiped my eyes, Nate glanced back at Rafferty, who had started doing minilaps in the back of the SUV. As much as he'd enjoyed his visit with Tess, the strain of having to stay still for so long was catching up with him. "I think we'd better get this dog home. What do you say?"

I nodded and reached for a tissue. "Other-wise your leather seats are toast."

As we pulled out of the parking garage, my cell phone rang. I pulled it out of my purse and glanced at the number on the display. It was Gregg Jacques.

Twenty-Three

I hit Talk. "Hello?"

"Kitzi?"

"Hi. Gregg?"

"The very same. I didn't expect to be hearing from you so soon after our little rendezvous at the Texas hold 'em tournament the other night."

"Thanks for helping me get out of there."

"It's not every day that I get a chance to help a damsel in distress. So, are you calling for poker tips? Although as I recall, you seemed to be holding your own just fine."

"Actually, no. I'm calling for legal advice."

Gregg's voice turned serious. "What can I help you with?"

As Nate drove toward Tess's house, I laid out the situation with Houston, and his plan to take over the Manse.

"Why do you think he wants control? Is he interested in selling the place and splitting up the profits?"

I blinked. "You know, I hadn't thought of that, but you could be right."

"I think I have an appointment open Tuesday at ten thirty. Can you get all the paperwork together by then?"

I thought of the papers I filched from Houston's office. Should I bring them, too? "I think so. Before you go, though, I want to ask you one more thing."

"Shoot."

"Last night, you were starting to tell a story about Houston and Andrew getting together with someone after one of the tournaments. I was curious to hear the rest of it."

"Oh, yeah. It was a few months ago. There was a party after the tournament — out at Rob Roy, on Lake Austin. Andrew and Houston brought a few investors in from the coast, and they were playing high stakes — I mean *really* high stakes."

"What happened?"

"I pulled out early, but Houston and Andrew kept going until they were the only two left. Houston bet everything, and I mean everything. It must have been twenty, thirty thousand dollars on the table."

"What happened?"

"All he had was a pair of tens. He was bluffing, and Andrew took it all home with a full house."

"Is that how Houston always plays? Betting everything?"

"I don't know. I haven't played with him that often — I only go to those tournaments once in a while — but he's not a cautious player, I can tell you that."

Twenty or thirty thousand dollars. That was a lot of money. Where were they getting it? "The man at the table with us — Sandy — was he there that night?"

"Sandy Corcoran? I think so, actually. Why?"

The skin on my arms prickled. "Do you happen to know what kind of car he drives?"

"I think I've seen him in an Expedition."

"What color?"

"Navy blue, I think. But what does this have to do with Houston and the Manse?"

I thought of the dark-colored SUV that followed me home from the Texas hold 'em game Saturday night. It looked black, but it could have been dark blue. "I'm not sure," I said. "But I plan to find out."

When I hung up and told Nate what I had found out, his eyebrows shot up. "So you think this cat-eyed guy is Andrew's silent partner?"

"Sandy is a nickname for Alexander, isn't

it? Too much of a coincidence." I dialed another number on my cell phone. "Maybe Beth can help me find out."

She picked up on the second ring. "Kitzi! Did you find out anything about the kid in the accident?"

"I'll tell you all about it later. Beth, do you think you could ask Granger — Dwayne — to look something up for me?"

"Sure. What is it?"

"Ask him to run a check on Alexander Corcoran. He runs a company called A.C. Investments, based in Corpus Christi."

"Is this related to the *High Jinx*?"

"That's what I'm guessing. I think he was Andrew's silent partner in the investment scheme."

She drew in her breath. "Do you think he might have killed Andrew?"

"I don't know, but I'm pretty sure he's the one who followed us home from the Texas Hold 'em tournament. Come to think of it, while you're sweet-talking him, could you find out why Granger was there?"

"How exactly am I supposed to do that? He doesn't know we were there."

"I'm sure you'll think of something. Use those feminine wiles."

She groaned. "When are you planning on

coming home? The final banquet starts at six."

I glanced at my watch. It was coming up on four o'clock already. "I forgot all about it. We'll drop Rafferty off, and then we'll head back to the Manse."

"Tess's dog?"

"We snuck him into the hospital for a visit."

"You took an Airedale into the hospital? How did you manage that? Or do I want to know?"

"We stuck him in a wheelchair and covered him with a blanket. Our cover story was to say he was an amputee with a bad nose job."

She laughed. "Only you, Kitzi. Only you."

"So you'll call Dwayne?"

"As soon as I get off the phone with you," she said. I could tell from the brightness in her voice that she was looking forward to it. I wasn't overly fond of Dwayne, but if he helped my friend get over Ron, maybe it wasn't such a bad thing.

When Nate and I pulled into the driveway of the Manse forty minutes later, preparations for the banquet were in full swing. White-jacketed caterers were lugging foil-covered trays into the kitchen, and a young woman staggered under the weight of a huge arrangement of gladiolus, lilies, and roses.

"I've got to go home and change, but may I escort you to the banquet tonight?" Nate asked as he pulled up by the front door.

I gazed into his dark eyes. "I can't think of anything I'd like better," I said. "Thanks so much for all your help today."

"Glad I could be of service, ma'am. I'll be back in an hour or so. Do you think you can keep out of trouble till then?"

I thought of the phone call I planned to make the moment I got inside. Would that be considered trouble? "I'll do my best," I said. He leaned over and gave me a last, lingering kiss before I slipped out of the Navigator and headed up the front walk. I paused at the door to watch his car as it pulled out of the driveway and headed up the street.

When I walked into the kitchen, the caterers were bustling around, and the heavenly smell of sautéed garlic filled the vanilla-colored space. Beth was already dressed, in a rose-colored chiffon dress that showed off her new curves. "You look fantastic," I said.

"And you'd better get cracking." As we retreated from the bustle of the kitchen to the living room, she took in my rumpled capri pants and linen top with a sweep of her eyes. "How did your meeting with the Linders go?"

"Another family taken in by Andrew's little scheme, I'm afraid. Apparently they were here the night of the reception, but I didn't recognize them."

"Do you think they could have killed Andrew?"

"I only met Mrs. Linder, and she seemed somehow too . . . too weak. And her son was in a wheelchair, so there's no way he could have gotten Andrew into that Dumpster."

"Another dead end, then." Beth sighed and looked at her watch. "You need to start getting ready. It's almost five."

"I will. I just have one more phone call to make. Did you get in touch with Dwayne?"

"He promised to run Corcoran through the computer this evening. If he finds something out, he said he'll swing by. I haven't said anything about the Texas hold 'em game yet, though."

"Thanks. Let me know what he finds out."

"And who are you calling?"

I grimaced. "Stephen. I'd rather talk to him in person, but he's not coming to the banquet tonight, and I need to have a discussion with him before I see Houston."

Her eyes narrowed. "I thought Gregg was going to do that."

"If I play my cards right, I might not need Gregg," I said.

When I told her what I suspected, she let out a long, low whistle. "I hope you're right. Then again, I hope you're *not* right."

"Me too."

I was about to head upstairs when Mother walked in, looking elegant in a cream satin dress and a string of delicate pearls interspersed with teal-colored tourmaline. "Kitzi, why aren't you dressed? And have you looked at what's going on in the conservatory? The flowers haven't arrived yet, the caterers forgot to chill the wine, and the banquet is set to begin in less than an hour."

"I just saw the florist on my way in, Mother. I'm sure Judy has it under control."

Beth gently took her elbow and steered her toward the kitchen. "Why don't I go check it out with you? That way Kitzi can go get ready."

Mother glanced at my head on the way out the door. "I hope you can find something to wear with that hair color," she said.

"Kitzi will look beautiful, as always," Beth said. "Now, let's go see what we can do about the wine."

I shot Beth a smile of gratitude as she

shepherded Mother to the kitchen. Then I climbed the stairs to my office, slid behind the desk, and dialed my brother's number. It was only when the phone was ringing at the other end that I realized I didn't know what I was going to say.

I'd done it again. Ready, fire, aim.

Debby answered on the third ring.

"Hi, Debby, it's Kitzi. Is Stephen there?"

"Hang on a moment." She put the phone down with a clunk, and I could hear Lily's voice in the background for a minute or two before Stephen picked up.

"Kitzi?" My brother's voice was guarded.

Suddenly I knew just what to say. To heck with the niceties. I was mad, and besides, I needed time for beautification before Nate turned up again. "Tell me, Stephen. How much was Houston planning on getting for the Manse?"

He was silent. I stared at the teal and white striped tents outside, and the people milling around on the grass, admiring the pink begonias. He was planning on selling all of this — our family history — for quick cash. Finally, he croaked, "What?"

I focused on the framed picture of my grandfather on the wall by the door. "And how much were you getting? Enough to get back together with Debby?"

"I don't know what you're talking about," he stuttered.

"Cut the crap, Stephen." Before he could criticize my inappropriate language, I added, "There's no point in lying about it. How much?"

He sighed. "We only had a preliminary market analysis done — we couldn't do a full appraisal without involving you — but it would have been enough for me to put my family back together again. It was all for Lily . . . She needs her daddy."

I rolled my eyes. They'd be one big happy family, all right. Right up until the day Stephen ran out of money again.

"If you had so much cash coming to you from the proceeds of the Manse, why did you ask me for a loan the other day?"

"I didn't know how long the sale would take, and Andrew had a great investment opportunity."

"But Andrew was dead when you asked to borrow money."

"Houston was picking up the reins."

I snorted. "That was big of him."

"Kitzi," he said, "I hope you understand . . . It was the best plan for everyone."

"I understand, Stephen. I understand all too well. Thank you for being honest with me." I hung up the phone and turned to look out the window. The sun was dipping low in the sky, gilding the leaves of the pecan trees. Everything looked so peaceful, so deceptively serene.

A long sigh escaped me. Money could be a blessing. It could also tear families apart.

I turned from the window and headed to my bedroom to get dressed. I still had a big night in front of me.

Thirty minutes isn't much time to primp, but I did the best I could with a bottle of hairspray. I picked an emerald green, off-the-shoulder gown from my short row of formal dresses. Since I was a redhead for the night, I figured I might as well make the most of it. I finished my makeup, slipped on the matching heels, and frowned at my reflection in the mirror. Those early morning walks hadn't been working as well as I'd hoped. Then again, I reflected, walking doesn't require a lot of effort on the part of your upper arms. I grabbed a wrap from the closet and looked again. Much better. Just as long as I didn't get carried away and start throwing my arms around.

I added a malachite necklace and earrings Beth had made for me — dark green beads interspersed with black crystals and held together with a delicate silver chain — and gave myself a final once-over in the mirror. Not bad. I touched up my lipstick and swept out the door to meet Nate.

When I headed downstairs to the conservatory a few minutes later, I felt as though I were stepping into the ballroom at Cinderella's castle. Candles flickered on white-linen-clad tablecloths, waiters bearing trays of wine and hors d'oeuvres wove through the guests already in attendance, and a swing band played Sinatra's "Yellow Moon" from the corner. The tourmaline necklace, displayed on the fireplace where the candlesticks once resided, sparkled in the warm light.

Judy O'Bannon stopped me as I headed across the room toward Mother, who stood with Beth by the door to the living room. "Kitzi, I just wanted to thank you," she said, eyes crinkling into a warm smile. "Everything is beautiful, and we sold so many tickets for the necklace that we've raised several thousand dollars more than we'd hoped."

"I'm so glad to hear it," I said. And I was. I was all for anything that would help Tess — and Rebecca — gain some ground.

"How's your friend Tess?" she asked.

"Not so good. I'm afraid there's not much anyone can do for her now."

The glow in Judy's eyes dimmed. "I'm so sorry to hear that. It's so often the case these days. I'm hoping that will change."

"So am I," I said, and an image of Tess's gaunt face passed through my mind. I took a deep breath and focused on the conservatory. "Whoever did the flowers did a marvelous job," I said.

"I know, aren't they beautiful? Everything is wonderful. Thank you again for letting us use the Manse."

"Anytime, Judy."

She glanced at her watch. "I hate to run, but I have to check on the caterers."

"I'll see you later, then." As she bustled toward the kitchen doors, I started toward Mother again. I hadn't taken two steps before someone slipped an arm around my waist.

Startled, I turned to face Nate, who had exchanged his jeans for a tuxedo that looked like it had been custom-made for him. Prince Charming in Cinderella's castle.

"You look lovely," he said. "May I get you a drink?"

"You bet," I said as he steered me toward the nearest bar.

"Two Muscovitos," he said to the bartender.

"But they don't have Muscovito," I

pointed out. "The caterers told me it's just chardonnay and pinot noir."

"For you they do." He squeezed my hand as the bartender flipped open a cooler and pulled out a bottle of my favorite wine. "After a day like today, a lady needs a glass or two of her favorite wine."

I laughed. "You know the way to a woman's heart, Nate Wright."

He bent down to kiss my hand. "I'm counting on it."

A flush of red that I'm sure clashed with my hair crept up to my cheeks. "By the way, you look great in a tux. Like Roger Moore, only cuter."

He sipped his wine, eyes glinting. "Maybe I should have ordered a martini."

"Shaken . . ."

"Not stirred," he finished. "Now, shall we mingle? Or would you prefer to find a quiet corner for two?"

My eyes scanned the room, stopping at a perfect platinum blonde in a pale blue dress. Rebecca. Next to her stood Houston, a protective arm around her thin frame.

"I think I'll opt for the quiet corner," I said, "but first I have talk to my cousin for a moment. Do you think you can keep Rebecca occupied for a minute or two?"

"Houston's wife?" He cocked a dark

eyebrow. "What are you up to, Miss Kitzi?"

I told him some of the truth, but not all of it. "There's something I need to discuss with Houston, and I'd prefer Rebecca wasn't there to hear it."

"Isn't that why you hired Gregg?" He was beginning to sound like Beth.

"I just need five minutes," I said.

"As my lady commands," he said, and followed me through the crowd to Houston and Rebecca.

My cousin's mouth tightened when he saw me headed toward him, and he bent down to whisper something to Rebecca. She nodded, and the two of them glided away, but I picked up the pace and cut them off.

"Rebecca," I said, "you look lovely. Blonde really does suit you!"

She laughed, and I was relieved to see a warmth in her cheeks that came from more than makeup. Maybe she was on the upswing.

"We've exchanged hair colors! You look great as a redhead."

"I guess everyone needs a change of pace sometimes."

"I just got word back from the doctor today — my numbers are down."

"That's great!" I said. That meant the treatment was working.

"I knew we'd beat it." She beamed.

Relief poured through me, and I gave her a quick hug. "I am so glad — I can't tell you how glad."

"No kidding," she said. "I'll be back to red hair in no time!"

I gave her shoulder a last squeeze and put my hand on my cousin's arm. "Rebecca, could you spare Houston for a moment? I have something I want to show him."

Before Houston could protest, I entwined my arm with his and guided him toward the door.

Twenty-Four

"What can I help you with, Kitzi?" Houston asked when I closed the living-room door behind us. My eyes slid to the empty sofa table where the candlesticks once stood.

"Houston," I said quietly, "how much were you planning on getting for the Manse?"

"What?" His eyes skittered around the room. He looked like a trapped animal. "What are you talking about?"

"I know all about the plan to sell the house and turn it into a museum." He stared at me, speechless. To tell the truth, it was kind of weird seeing him without anything to say. "How much money do you owe, Houston? And what did Sandy Corcoran promise you if you picked up Andrew's investment scheme?"

The blood drained out of my cousin's handsome face, and he swept a nervous hand over his silver hair. "How did you find all this out?" Suddenly his eyes narrowed. "The flashlight in my office . . ." He shook his index finger at me. "You broke in. While I was with the police, you broke in. That's illegal, you know."

Well, maybe it was, but I decided that was beside the point. "It doesn't matter. I talked with Stephen today, and he confirmed it."

Houston's mouth was a thin line, and he looked pale under his tennis-court tan.

"You were awfully nervous Thursday night. Jumpy." Houston started to say something, but I interrupted him. "Some of the people you owe money to were here, weren't they? They were starting to put pressure on you."

He put his hands up. He had regained his composure and with it the tone of voice that had convinced his clients to entrust all their money to him. "All right, all right. I had a couple of bad nights, and a few people loaned me some money. They knew I was good for it."

"Did they?"

"Of course. I always pay them back . . ."

I raised my eyebrows. "This has happened before?"

He said nothing.

"Houston, what was the deal Sandy offered you? How much?"

He sighed, and somehow the air escaping him seemed to deflate him. He turned away from me. "Okay, okay. He offered me fifty thousand if I took it over. When Andrew got involved, I didn't like it — something didn't seem kosher — but I had so much going on with Rebecca, his clients were doing really well . . ."

"Like the Yancys? And the Linders?"

He swung around. "What about them?"

"They lost a lot of money on Andrew and Sandy's little yacht venture."

"What?" he croaked.

"Sandy Corcoran was running a scam. He never sold the investors the boats — I think he just used their money to fix them up. I'm guessing he goosed their returns by funneling some of the new investors' money into existing accounts." I remembered the discrepancy in the Yancys' account. "And when that ran out, Andrew started playing with the numbers on the statements. Moving money around, making balances look bigger than they were."

Houston sank into a chair. "No . . ."

"Houston, I have an important question to ask you."

He looked up at me, suddenly haggard. He seemed to have aged ten years in the last five minutes.

"Do you know who killed Andrew?" I said.

His face turned gray with horror. "No . . . I have no idea."

"I didn't think so. I just had to ask." I walked toward him and sat down on the chair opposite him. "Look. I know things haven't always been great between us, but I want to help you."

"You're kidding me, right?"

I sighed. "How much do you owe?"

He looked away. "About $170,000."

"Gambling debts?"

He nodded. "If I can sell Rebecca's Cinder Sage, it should cover most of it. But I'll still be short about eighty thousand."

He must have been desperate if he was planning to sell the horse that never lost. Too bad he played cards instead of sticking to the track. "If you call off the vote on the house, I'll help you pay the loans — even do what I can to get your business back on track. I don't know how much damage Andrew did, and whether we can recoup your clients' money, but we'll do what we can to fix it."

He looked up. "You'd do that for me?"

"But there's a catch."

His eyes turned wary. "I figured there had to be."

I held his gaze. "You have to go into a

program for gambling addiction." He stared at me for a moment, then started to get up. I grabbed his arm. "Houston, you have a problem. You need to deal with it. For your sake — and for Rebecca's."

He drooped into the chair again. "With the illness . . . it's just been so hard lately."

I thought of Rebecca's shining eyes, and of Tess, alone in her hospital bed. "I know. Get some help, Houston. For her sake. Get this behind you so that you can focus on your wife. She's getting better, but she still needs you."

He was silent for a long moment, looking at the floor. Then his eyes cut to me. "I'll think about it."

He walked to the door and disappeared into the crowded conservatory. When the door shut behind him, I sat there for a long time, staring at the empty spot on the sofa table where the candlesticks had stood, until the door opened and Nate came in.

"What happened?"

I reached for my wineglass and stood up. "I think I may have just averted a family crisis," I said.

"You talked Houston out of it?"

I took his arm. "We'll see. I'm hoping it'll work out, but I'm not counting my chickens just yet."

As we exited into the conservatory, Mother caught up with me. "I saw Houston coming out of the living room a few minutes ago. Is everything okay?"

There was no need to tell her that her nephew was planning to kick her out of the Manse so he could sell it, and that her own son was planning to join him. Or that he had a gambling problem, for that matter. "We just had a little talk about the Manse. And Rebecca. Everything's fine."

She nodded approvingly. "And no more trouble with the police. Miranda will be very happy to hear that."

The band wound up "Blue Skies," and I moved closer to Nate, thinking that despite the magical atmosphere and the handsome man at my side, the sky felt more gray than blue. A moment later, Judy picked up a microphone from the podium in front of the fireplace and invited everyone to be seated.

"Are you at table three?" I asked Mother.

"No. For some reason, I'm at table two," she said.

I gave her a quick hug, inhaling the scent of her Youth Dew perfume. "I'll see you after dinner, then."

Nate had arranged to sit next to me, and as he pushed my chair in for me and settled himself at my left side, Beth took the seat to my right. "Did Granger find anything out?" I whispered to her as the waiter set a plate of Caesar salad in front of me.

"Nothing yet." She patted her beaded purse, a new acquisition from the tents outside. "I've got my cell phone set to vibrate, just in case." She gave Nate a meaningful glance. "You seem to be having an interesting evening."

"You don't know the half of it," I said, thinking of Houston.

Her eyebrows arched up. "I'm all ears."

"I'll tell you later," I hissed as a young, fashionably dressed couple found their seats at our table and introduced themselves. "But I do have some good news."

"What?"

"Rebecca seems to be in remission."

Beth's eyes grew round. "You're kidding me! That's wonderful!"

"I know. Fingers crossed that it stays that way."

"Toes, too," Beth said.

The food was delicious — crusty bread and a luscious chicken Cordon Bleu followed the salad — and Nate's presence beside me made my whole body hum. Despite the lively conversation and the good food, though, my mind kept straying to

Andrew's murder. Something kept niggling at me, something someone had said, but I couldn't put my finger on it. Finally, the waiters did the rounds with plates of chocolate torte and pots of coffee, and Judy stood up at the podium again.

After thanking everybody who had helped make the Tea a success and reading the names of loved ones lost to ovarian cancer in the past year — a list to which I was afraid at least one woman I loved would soon be added — an assistant brought the box of raffle tickets to her. She plunged her hand in and pulled out a slip of paper.

"And the winner of the tourmaline necklace is . . . Beth Fairfield!"

I squealed as Beth stood up, mouth open in surprise.

"Woo-hoo, Beth!" I shouted over the applause. She beamed, and Nate and I clapped as hard as we could as she went up to receive the necklace. After what she'd been through with Mo-Ron, she deserved every bit of happiness that came her way. It was only when she walked back to the table, her face flushed above the glittering necklace, that I remembered the candlestick under her bed, and a wave of uneasiness swept through me. I hadn't gotten to the bottom of things yet.

■ ■ ■ ■

I came down for breakfast late the next morning, my head aching from an overdose of sweet white wine. After the banquet, Nate and I had gone up to the balcony and finished a second bottle of Muscovito together under a blanket of stars. Just before midnight, he swept away in his Lincoln Navigator, promising to be back the next day. It was probably a good thing, too; with all the excitement of the last week, I was short on sleep.

The caterers had cleaned everything up the night before, and for the first time in three days, the kitchen was quiet, the countertops clear. Beth looked up from a plate of scrambled egg whites when I walked in. "Guess what?" she said, eyes bright.

"What? And where's the tea?"

"What do you mean, where's the tea? Isn't this your kitchen?"

"Not for the last few days it hasn't been."

Beth gestured toward the counter with a fork. "I just made a pot."

"Did you use the hot-water dispenser?"

"No, I did it the old-fashioned way." She grinned. "Like civilized folks. Anyway, you were right about Mr. Cat's Eyes. Dwayne ran a check on him. Turns out he's a con man — usually operates under the name Anderson Crawford."

I poured myself a cup of tea, added a spoonful of sugar, and used the first warm sip to wash down a Tylenol. "Have they talked to him yet?"

"They went out there last night, once they figured out who he was. They got a search warrant and found Andrew's computer in his house."

"So that's who powered down the computer while Lauren was hooked up to it."

Beth nodded. "When Dwayne found it, he thought Sandy might have killed Andrew — but it turns out he was in L.A. the night Andrew died."

I sat down across from her. "So we were right. It was a Ponzi scheme."

Beth nodded. "Seems he's pulled this kind of thing before: he buys businesses in trouble, finds a respectable partner to hawk them to clients, and then uses the funds coming in to upgrade them and resell them. Then Sandy, or Alexander, or whatever he goes by, disappears, leaving his innocent partner to tell his clients that the investment tanked. In the meantime, Sandy sells up and walks away with the cash."

"Nice," I said. "It's a good thing we

caught him. Maybe if they sell *High Jinx,* Bruce and everyone else will get their money back."

Beth scooped up a forkful of eggs and took a sip of tea. "That's the hope, anyway. And did I mention he works with a partner?"

"A partner? Other than Andrew?"

Beth looked up at me. "A young woman. Her name is Leila Ketchum."

My stomach lurched. "Lauren."

Beth nodded. "They've done it once or twice before. She takes a job as an assistant of some sort and then sees if she can find a way to hook Sandy up with one of the decision makers."

"But she's been helping us!" Somehow, even though on some level I knew it was true, my mind couldn't wrap itself around this new information. Maybe it was because I hadn't had my morning tea yet.

"She's been following our progress and probably reporting back to her boss. Trying to keep the blame on Andrew, so she and Sandy could slip away."

I thought about Lauren — her excitement when I told her she could stay at the Manse, her eagerness to help us find out more about Andrew's investment scheme . . . "Are you sure? After all, she did get us into

Andrew's computer. And Houston's office."

"For all we know, before she did it she sent an e-mail to Sandy to let him know what was up. Which might be why the computer was gone when we got there. And remember how nervous she was? She was afraid of getting caught, all right. Caught by us."

"I can't believe it," I said. Although in truth, I could. The BMW, the nice house in Hyde Park . . . still, I was disappointed. I had trusted her. "Have the cops found her?"

"We sent her to Galveston, remember? She should still be there; at least I hope she's still there. Unless Sandy got a chance to warn her." Beth's eyes widened. "Kitzi, you gave her your credit card. Shouldn't you call the company and cancel it?"

I grimaced. "If I did, it might tip her off. Shoot." I took a swig of tea. "Does Granger think one of them might have killed Andrew?" I asked.

"As I mentioned, they thought it might have been Sandy, but he was in L.A."

"But Lauren wasn't."

Beth shook her head. "Nope. She was here at the Manse the whole time."

"And if Andrew was starting to make trouble," I said, "Lauren could have decided to take care of the problem herself. She's young, she's in shape . . ."

"Dwayne will call us as soon as he knows anything. In the meantime, if she gets in touch, we find out where she's staying and pretend nothing new has happened. Although I don't know why she bothered to do the 'research' when she already knew it all."

"If she didn't, she'd blow her cover," Beth said. "Like you said, though, we can't let her know that we know."

Beth was right. If we knew where Lauren was, the police could find her in Galveston. But if we called her and tried to get her to come back, she might get nervous and call Sandy, and when Sandy didn't answer, she might do a disappearing act. I shivered to think that I might have harbored a murderer under my roof. "Got it."

"So that's my news," Beth said. "What happened with Stephen last night?"

"It's not nearly as exciting as what you found out, but at least I made some progress," I said, and told her about my phone call to my brother and my conversation with Houston.

"Wow," she said. "So they were planning to sell the Manse? And now he's considering backing down on the corporate takeover?"

"I told him I'd cover his debts and help get his business on track if he backed down and went into a program. I'm hoping he bites." If he didn't, I didn't want to think about what it would do to Rebecca when she found everything out.

"I had no idea he was addicted to gambling," Beth said. "Does Rebecca know about it?"

"No, she doesn't. He's been protecting her. And please don't tell anyone else, either — I don't want Mother to worry."

Beth sucked at her lip. "Do you think Houston might have killed Andrew?"

I shook my head gingerly; the Tylenol hadn't kicked in yet. "I asked him, in a roundabout way, and I believe his answer."

"Well, then, at least we're pretty sure your cousin isn't a murderer."

The thing that had been niggling at the back of my mind twitched again, but at that moment, the door opened and Mother walked in.

I shooed all thoughts of Houston and Lauren and Sandy Corcoran from my head and put on a smile. "Hello, Mother."

"Good morning, Kitzi darling. Did you sleep all right?"

"Fine, thanks. How about you?" Actually, she looked remarkably refreshed. I had walked down to the gatehouse with her right after the dinner ended to make sure she got to bed early; the weekend had been exhausting for her. I was happy to see that there was no sign of fatigue this morning, and I was glad we had managed to keep most of the upsetting news — the takeover of the Manse, the details of Andrew's murder, and Houston's gambling problem — from reaching her ears.

"The cleanup seems to be going quite well, and everyone I talked to seems to think the Tea was a big success."

"That's what Judy said. She told me they raised even more than they'd expected to." I smiled at Beth. "And Ms. Fairfield here walked away with the grand prize."

Beth smiled and stood up. "Speaking of prizes, Ron and Shannan are coming back into town. I promised I'd pick them up at the airport."

"Weren't they supposed to be gone a week?" I asked.

"Yeah. I don't know what happened, but I suspect I'll hear all about it from Shannan this afternoon." She looked at me. "I'll call you if I hear anything."

Beth stowed her plate in the dishwasher and headed for the door.

"What did she mean by that?" asked

Mother.

"Oh, she was talking about the bead sales," I said, and changed the subject. "How is it coming out there?"

"It was fine a few minutes ago, but I'd better make sure none of the trucks end up in the begonia beds again." A moment later, she followed Beth out the door, and I sat in the relative peace of the kitchen — disturbed only by the occasional growl of a diesel engine outside. I sipped my tea and toasted myself a bagel, trying to make sense of things.

Lauren had betrayed us, and might even have killed Andrew with the candlestick from the conservatory. The candlestick whose twin I had found under Beth's bed.

I sighed. The whole thing felt like a scenario from Clue. Next thing I knew, someone would turn up shot by a revolver in the library. It was too bad we didn't have Colonel Mustard pottering around the Manse; I could just pin the murder on him.

I was about to take the first bite of bagel when the thing that had been niggling at the back of my brain for the last twenty-four hours broke free.

Thirty minutes later, I pulled up outside the Yancys' house. A dark blue minivan I didn't remember seeing during my previous visit was parked in the driveway, and as I passed it on my way up the front walk, I noticed it had handicap plates.

Mrs. Yancy opened the door almost immediately, surprise in her gray eyes. Her hand flew up to her crepey neck.

"Miss Camden . . . Kitzi. What a surprise."

"May I come in, Mrs. Yancy?"

"Of course. I have a visitor. I hope you don't mind."

As I stepped into the living room, the dark eyes of Keith Linder rose to meet mine. He wasn't the company I was expecting — I was thinking it might be one of Mrs. Yancy's golf partners — and I wondered why neither of them had mentioned they were in contact with one another.

"Hello, Keith," I said.

He nodded.

I turned to Mrs. Yancy. "I didn't know you two were friends."

Mrs. Yancy's eyes flicked nervously to the young man in the wheelchair. "Ever since the accident, we've been very close. Keith comes to visit a couple of times a week." That was strange, I thought. Last time I was here, she referred to him only as "the other boy" in the accident. She turned to me. "Won't you sit down? Can I get you something to drink?"

I sat down on the nearest sofa. "No, thanks, I'm fine. Is Mr. Yancy here?"

"Oh, he has a standing golf game on Mondays."

"How nice." I leaned forward. "Mrs. Yancy, I have a few questions about the investment plan Andrew put together for you, but I'm afraid this isn't a good time . . ." I looked at Keith.

"Oh, it's fine. Besides, Keith's family is involved, too."

This wasn't how I pictured this conversation happening, but I went ahead anyway. "How much did you invest with Andrew?"

She shook her head. "About a hundred thousand, unfortunately."

"That's a lot of money."

"Oh, yes. When we got the statement, Earl was furious. Andrew tried to tell us it was an accounting error, but it didn't make sense."

"And you?"

"Oh, I was angry, of course, but what can you do?" She raised her hands in a gesture of resignation.

I glanced at Keith, then back at the older woman. "Mrs. Yancy, how did you know Andrew was hit over the head with a candlestick?"

Her eyes widened, and her hand flew to her throat again. "What? Why, it was on the news, of course."

"No," I said. "No, it wasn't. The police never released that information."

"What are you trying to say?" Keith growled.

The skin of my arms prickled, but I pressed on. "What I'm trying to figure out is how you got him into the Dumpster."

The room was silent for a moment, as if everything were in suspended animation. Then Keith's voice exploded from the wheelchair.

"It was me, all right?" His eyes blazed. "I did it. When he told me how much money he'd lost for us, I blew up. I whacked him over the head and used the wheelchair lift to get him into the Dumpster. So leave Mrs. Yancy alone."

Mrs. Yancy's face paled, and she shook her head violently, her pageboy swinging. "Keith, no . . ."

"You killed Andrew?" I hadn't considered that possibility, since he was in a wheelchair. But if Andrew had been sitting down, it would have been easy. I glanced at Keith's upper arms. He certainly had the strength; his biceps swelled from years of propelling his body in the chair.

"The dear boy is trying to take the blame for my actions," Mrs. Yancy said, her voice wobbling. "But the responsibility is mine. When Andrew told me how much money we had lost — and how much the Linders were losing — I just couldn't take it. He got the greatest gift of all — he walked away from that accident with hardly a bump or a bruise — and we lost everything. *Everything.*" Her eyes shot to Donovan's picture, smiling from atop the television. "And then, to turn around and ruin our lives *again* . . ." She took a deep, shuddery breath. "When he turned to leave, I grabbed the nearest thing and just hit him with it. I didn't mean to kill him . . . I was just so *angry* . . . and that's when Keith came in."

"No." Keith's voice was low and cold. "Stop."

I ignored him and focused on Mrs. Yancy. "So he helped you get rid of the body," I said.

She nodded. "His van has a wheelchair lift." She shuddered. "Keith draped him over his lap and wheeled him out into the back. We hid him behind a bush. I waited with . . . with the body until Keith got back with the van."

Keith's voice was low and menacing. "Mrs. Y . . ."

I pressed on. "How did he do it without anyone noticing?"

"He kept the lights off, and since the van is dark blue, you can't see it. I don't know how he did it, but Keith pulled Andrew up onto the chair with him, then he used the wheelchair lift to tip him into the Dumpster." Her face was pale, and her voice shook slightly. "We figured he would be safe there, that no one would find him there . . ."

"What about the second candlestick? The one under my friend's bed?"

Mrs. Yancy nodded at Keith, who had gone rigid in his chair. "That was Keith's idea. I didn't know whose room it was; I just ran upstairs and shoved it under the first bed I found. If one candlestick was missing, it might look suspicious. We were hoping that with two gone, it would take longer to figure out what had happened."

"Does your husband know?" I asked.

She sighed. "I think he suspects something, but I don't think he has any idea how bad things are."

I shook my head. "What a mess. This must have been an awful couple of days for you." I could imagine her rage at Andrew, the impulse that drove her to strike at him. It was yet another tragedy, piled on top of the others — Donovan's death, Keith's paralysis. I reached into my purse and flipped open my cell phone. “I think we need to explain what happened to the police. Considering the circumstances, they might go easy on you.”

Mrs. Yancy blinked at me. At the same moment, Keith’s wheelchair barreled across the room, and he smacked the cell phone out of my hand. I watched it skitter across the beige carpet.

“Who else knows?” he demanded. His dark eyes turned my stomach to ice.

I croaked, “Why does it matter?” A lump formed in my throat. Why hadn’t I told someone where I was going? I had done it again. Ready, fire, aim.

“Because I am not going to let you put Mrs. Yancy in jail,” he said.

“We have no idea how this is going to turn out,” I said. “She could just be charged with manslaughter. She didn’t plan to do it.”

“I’m not willing to take that risk,” he said.

I gauged the distance to the door. If I sprinted, I could make it. In one swift motion, I pushed myself to my feet and ran.

Three steps later, I tripped over an end table and tumbled to the floor, skidding to a halt on Mrs. Yancy’s living-room carpet.

Twenty-Five

"Get up." Keith's voice was hard and cold. I got to my knees, brushed myself off, and looked up to face the dark void of a gun barrel.

"Keith." Mrs. Yancy's voice quavered. "This isn't necessary."

"I was afraid this would happen," he said. He was talking to Mrs. Yancy, but his dark eyes never left mine. "Ever since she showed up at our place, I've been waiting."

"Is that why you've been by so much since . . . since the accident at the Manse?" she asked.

"I didn't want to worry you, but I wanted to be around. Just in case."

"Keith, I'm not sure this is the right thing to do . . ."

His eyes flickered to her. "We'll do what we have to."

My stomach did a flip-flop. Mrs. Yancy sucked in a breath and nodded toward the gun. "Is that really necessary?"

"I refuse to let you go to jail because that rat bastard screwed us over."

"Keith!"

"Sorry about the language, Mrs. Y." In my opinion, it seemed a bit much for him to be apologizing for his language when he was holding a gun on an innocent woman, but unfortunately, Mrs. Yancy didn't object. Keith glanced at his watch. "We only have a half hour," he said. "Earl will be back at eleven thirty."

Mrs. Yancy's voice wobbled. "What . . . what are you going to do?"

"Take care of the problem."

My eyes skittered around the room, looking for something to defend myself with. Hummel figurines, gold drapes, blue couches . . . nothing I could lay my hands on. "Get up," he said.

My knees shook as I rose to my feet.

"Go that way," he said, waving the gun toward the kitchen. My brain struggled to kick into gear. The kitchen wasn't a bad place. Kitchens have knives. As I moved in that direction, I dragged my feet a bit. If I stalled, maybe Earl would get home in time to save me. A butcher's knife was better than nothing, but I wouldn't want to lay odds on it against a revolver.

Or whatever it was Keith was pointing at me. "Get going," he said. "We don't have all day."

I didn't have a chance to pick up a knife. Mrs. Yancy didn't even have any on the counter, and the only thing small enough to pick up was a plastic banana from the fake fruit display on the kitchen table. There was no time even to grab that; he rolled up right behind me, herding me through the utility room and into the garage.

"Keith, I don't know about this," Mrs. Yancy was saying as I stepped into the cluttered garage. Lumber, rope, garden hose, dented metal toolboxes. Nothing, nothing, nothing. Damn.

"I'm not crazy about it either, but what choice do we have?" I glanced back at him. His face was pale, but his eyes were hard little stones. "Lie down," he barked.

I sent a last desperate glance around the garage before I did what he asked. Out of the corner of my eye, I spotted a pair of hedge clippers, just a few feet to my left.

As soon as my body touched the concrete, I tucked myself into a ball and rolled to the left. At the same time, a thud sounded behind me, and Mrs. Yancy shrieked, "No!" My hand groped for the clippers. A shot ricocheted past me. I whirled around to face

Keith, and something clattered to the concrete.

Keith slumped in the wheelchair, his head lolling to the side, the gun on the floor beside him. Above him stood Mrs. Yancy, a yellowed two-by-four clutched in her hand.

"I'm sorry," she whispered. "I had no idea it would come to this."

I dropped the hedge clippers, and my whole body started to shake.

Two hours later I was back in the Manse kitchen, nursing an iced tea while Nate rubbed my shoulders. I had called him right after dialing 911, and he had driven to the Yancys' as fast as his Navigator could go.

The police cruisers had been first to arrive, and Granger appeared fifteen minutes later. As men and women in blue suits swarmed the living room and garage, I pulled the sergeant into the kitchen. I didn't know how much the Camden influence would sway him, but I did the best I could. "I hope you'll be easy on her," I said. "I don't think she meant to kill him, and she saved my life."

He smiled grimly. "I can't make any promises, but I'll see what I can do."

I tilted my head to one side. "By the way, why were you at that Texas hold 'em tournament the other night?"

He narrowed his eyes at me. "How did you know that?"

"A friend told me."

"I was following a lead," he said gruffly, and stalked out of the kitchen.

I walked back into the living room as Mr. Yancy burst through the door, demanding to know what was going on. When one of the officers explained the situation, his ruddy face turned deeper red. "Nonsense! I'll have my attorneys hang you out to dry!" he roared.

"Earl," Mrs. Yancy said to him. "Enough."

He turned to face her, and his whole body sagged. "Is it true?" he whispered.

She nodded briefly and turned away.

Now Earl Yancy sat in a chair in the corner, his head in his hands, rocking from side to side as they snapped handcuffs onto his wife's wrists.

Before they took Mrs. Yancy to the police car, I squeezed her arm. "Thanks for saving my life. If I can help you with finding an attorney, or anything at all, please call me."

Her face was bleached white, and she looked very old, but she straightened her shoulders and said, "Thank you, Miss Camden."

As she shuffled out the door, flanked by

policemen, my eyes turned to her husband. He had raised his head and watched her go, his shoulders sagging, eyes forlorn. I walked over and put a hand on his shoulder. "Do you have someone to stay with?" I asked gently.

He looked up at me, his face haggard. "I'm staying here. She'll be back soon."

"I hope you're right," I said. I gave him my phone number to call if he needed me. He wadded it up and stuck it into his pants pocket without looking at me.

A minute later, Nate showed up, and after I gave the police my statement, he escorted me home.

Now, in the Manse kitchen, Nate moved his hands up to rub my neck as I sipped my iced tea. It was a relief to be back at the Manse, and Nate's gentle neck massage felt like heaven. "So it was the Yancys after all," he said.

"Not both of them. Just her." I shook my head. "And then Keith covered it up for her."

"And was prepared to kill you to do it."

I shivered under his warm hands. "Yesterday I was convinced it was Sandy Corcoran. And for a while, I even thought it might be Bruce." I thought of Delphine's fabulous cooking and Bruce's warm smile, and was relieved I had been wrong. As I told Nate what Granger had discovered about Andrew's business partner, the phone rang. It was Katie.

"How are you holding up?" she asked.

"Much better now," I said, and filled her in on the details. I didn't tell her everything about Houston, just that he was innocent of murder and that he'd decided to drop the push to transfer the Manse. At least I hoped he had — he still hadn't responded to my offer.

"Thank God they caught the murderer," she said.

"I know. And we won't have a custody battle over the Manse, either." Hopefully not, anyway. "By the way, Rebecca's in remission."

Katie gasped. "That's wonderful news! So the chemo worked?"

"Looks like it," I said, looking at the tourmaline beads Beth had left on the counter. At least one victim had escaped. The phone beeped in my ear. "I've got another call — can I ring you back?"

"Of course," she said. "So glad everything's working out."

"Give the kids my love," I said, and clicked over.

"Kitzi?" It was Houston.

"Houston." I sat up and straightened my back.

"I thought about your proposition last night, and I think . . . I think I'll take you up on it, if it's still open."

Relief washed through me. I'd thrown him a lifeline, and he'd taken it. "It is. We're going to have some work to do, though." I told him about Mrs. Yancy, and then gave him the rundown on what Granger had discovered about Corcoran, who was already in custody. The police were on their way to intercept Lauren at the Holiday Inn in Galveston.

He sucked in his breath. "God. I had no idea."

"Neither did Andrew's clients. Look, why don't I call Gregg Jacques and see what he can do? You may have some fraud charges in the wake of all of this, and he'll be able to help you out."

"What about Harrington?"

I remembered the pompous lawyer who had called me just before the Bead Tea began. I was willing to help out, but not if it meant dealing with Harrington. "If we're going to do this, I want to go with Gregg."

He was silent for a moment, and when he spoke, his voice was resigned. "All right."

"I have an appointment with him at ten

thirty tomorrow. Why don't you meet me there?"

"I'll plan on it."

When I hung up, Nate eyed me quizzically, but I didn't mention Houston's gambling problem. It was hard enough for Houston that I knew. Instead I changed the subject. "Did you know Lauren was involved, too?"

"With the murder?"

"No. She was Corcoran's partner." I told him what the police had discovered about Corcoran's true identity, and the scams that he and Lauren, a.k.a. Leila, had run in the past.

"So we were right," he said. "It was a Ponzi scheme." He shook his head. "It's a shame about Lauren. I liked her."

"Me, too. For a few minutes, I thought she might be the murderer, but it just didn't feel right." I sighed. "I'm just hoping Andrew's clients can get their money back. The Yancys are going to need it to pay lawyers' fees."

"Ah, yes. The Yancys. Why the heck didn't you tell anyone where you were going?" he asked.

"I just didn't think, I guess."

"Well, it's lucky for you Mrs. Yancy has a conscience."

"Hey, I could have taken him down with the hedge clippers."

"Miss Kitzi, the next time you decide to play Nancy Drew, at least make sure Ned knows where you're going."

I turned and batted my eyelashes at him. "Are you applying for the job?"

"If you'll have me, ma'am."

I smiled. "I'd be delighted."

"That's a good thing," he said, "because on my way over to pick you up, I called my travel agent."

I sat upright. "Why? Are you going on a trip?"

"I hope so. How does South Padre sound?"

"What do you mean?"

"Well, with the Bead Tea, your cousin trying to take over the house, Andrew's death, and everything else that's been going on around here, you need a vacation."

"But what about Tess? And Beth? I still don't know what happened with Shannan and Ron . . ."

He stroked my forehead. "Relax, Kitzi. We'll visit Tess before we go, and then again when we get back. And Beth knows your cell phone number, doesn't she?"

He was right. I closed my eyes as his strong hands massaged my neck. Long walks on sandy beaches, cold margaritas, the wind through my red hair . . . "Nate," I murmured, "you're incredible."

He leaned down to kiss me. Just before our lips touched, he whispered, "So are you."

MAKE YOUR OWN CELL PHONE DANGLE

Looped Cell Phone Dangle

Materials

4 2mm facet tourmaline rondelles
2 4mm crystals (one pink, one green)
1 foot 26-gauge sterling wire
8 inches black waxed linen

Tools

Chain nose pliers
Round nose pliers
Craft glue

Instructions

1. String 2 inches of faceted rondelles onto the sterling wire.
2. Mold wire into an oval and cross ends of wire into a V at the top of the oval.
3. Take one end of wire and wrap it around the other end of wire three times to form a coil. Clip excess wire from coil. Flatten

end with chain nose pliers to make smooth.

4. String one crystal onto remaining end of wire.
5. Use round nose pliers to form a loop at the top of the crystal by turning the wire away from you with your right hand while pulling the wire around the round nose pliers with your left hand. Wrap the excess wire around the bottom of the loop three times. Clip off excess wire and flatten end with chain nose pliers to make smooth.
6. Repeat steps 1–5 for second oval.
7. String waxed linen through one loop and tie a knot at the end. Add a little glue to secure it.
8. String opposite end of waxed linen through second loop and tie a knot at the end. Add a little glue to secure it.

Straight Cell Phone Dangle

Materials

2 4–6 mm facet tourmaline teardrops
4 4mm crystals (two pink, two brown)
10 4–6 mm facet tourmaline rondelles
1 foot 26-gauge sterling silver wire
8 inches black waxed linen

Tools

Round nose pliers
Chain nose pliers
Craft glue

Instructions

1. String one teardrop onto wire. Bend wire into a V at point of teardrop.
2. Bend one end of wire straight up and the other at a 90-degree angle (perpendicular) to the first wire.
3. Wrap bent wire around straight wire three times to form a coil. clip excess wire from coil and flatten end with chain nose pliers to make smooth.
4. String beads onto straightened wire in a 2 rondelles, crystal, 1 rondelle, crystal, 2 rondelles pattern.
5. Make a loop at the top of the beads using the round nose pliers by turning the wire away from you with your right hand while pulling the wire around the round nose pliers with your left hand.
6. Twist remaining wire around base of loop three times to form a coil. Clip excess wire from coil and flatten with chain nose pliers to make smooth.
7. Repeat steps 1–6 for second drop.
8. Thread waxed linen through one loop of a drop and tie in a knot at end of cord.

Add a little glue to secure knot.

9. Thread waxed linen through second loop of a drop and tie in a knot at end of cord. Add a little glue to secure knot.

Patterns courtesy of Beadz! in Austin, Texas.

Dear Reader,

It saddens me to say that *Beads of Doubt* is the last work written by Barbara Burnett Smith, a talented writer whose bubbly personality shone through on every page she wrote. As I'm sure you already know, Barbara was an amazing writer. But she was also a friend and mentor to countless people, including me.

On February 19, 2005, Barbara was killed in a car accident in San Antonio, Texas. She left behind not just a huge circle of family and friends, but an unfinished manuscript. *Beads of Doubt,* the second book in the Kitzi Camden beading mystery series.

When Barbara's husband Gary Petry asked me to finish the book, I was honored by the request. Although I will never be Barbara, I have done my best to finish *Beads of Doubt* as Barbara would have wanted.

As you read *Beads of Doubt,* you'll notice

that ovarian cancer figures prominently in the storyline. The reason for this is deeply personal: Barbara's sister Carol died of the disease only a few months before Barbara's tragic death. *Beads of Doubt* was, on some levels, Barbara's tribute to her sister — and her way of spreading the word about this dreadful disease, which often goes undetected until it is too late.

Although ovarian cancer is a fairly common disease, there's still a lot of research to be done — both on finding a good method for early detection and on new ways to treat the disease. Please consider making a contribution to the Ovarian Cancer Research Foundation. Every penny counts toward finding a screening test that can catch this deadly disease early enough to stop its spread.

And as for Barbara? I miss her every day. She was a fabulous writer, a warm and loving friend, and an incredible person with an unquenchable enthusiasm for life. I am honored to have helped *Beads of Doubt* shine a little more of her light, even though she herself is gone.

All best,
Karen MacInerney

The National Ovarian Cancer Coalition (NOCC) is the leading nonprofit organization whose mission is to raise awareness and provide ovarian cancer education and support to women and their families across the country.

Ovarian cancer ranks fifth as the cause of cancer death among women and is the number one killer among women's reproductive cancers. Due to the subtle symptoms and lack of a screening test, 75 percent of women with ovarian cancer are diagnosed in the late stages when the prognosis is poor. If detected in the early stages, the five-year survival rate is 90 percent.

To improve these grim statistics, NOCC recently launched the "Break the Silence" campaign to jumpstart public dialogue and awareness of the symptoms of and risk factors for ovarian cancer, and to ultimately improve survival rates. To facilitate physician discussions, a downloadable "Conversation Starter" is available at www.ovarian.org to help women effectively prepare questions. Committed volunteers continue to advance NOCC's mission through a toll-free helpline, comprehensive website, peer support, professional education, and the promotion of research and educational programs that facilitate greater awareness and dialogue about ovarian cancer.

For more information or to make a donation, contact the National Ovarian Cancer Coalition by visiting www.ovarian.org or calling 1-888-OVARIAN.

BARBARA BURNETT SMITH MENTORING AUTHORS FOUNDATION 2007

Barbara's passing in 2005 was deeply felt by many. In her memory, the Barbara Burnett Smith Mentoring Authors Foundation will allow countless others to benefit from her spirit and inspiration. The Barbara Burnett Smith Mentoring Authors Foundation is dedicated to the support and growth of a mentoring community for writers. It is our goal to see her spirit live on and change the lives of others as Barbara changed all of ours.

The foundation has applied for 501(c)3 nonprofit status. We expect your contributions to be tax deductible. Through your giving, the foundation can continue its mission of supporting published authors that mentor aspiring writers, thereby, assisting in creating new literary works of art. Your generous contributions will be deeply appreciated.

Contact

Barbara Burnett Smith Mentoring Au-

thors Foundation
Email: Info@Purplesagetexas.com
Website: www.Purplesagetexas.com
Phone: (512) 285-1185 or (281) 704-0180

The employees of Thorndike Press hope you have enjoyed this Large Print book. All our Thorndike and Wheeler Large Print titles are designed for easy reading, and all our books are made to last. Other Thorndike Press Large Print books are available at your library, through selected bookstores, or directly from us.

For information about titles, please call:

(800) 223-1244

or visit our Web site at:

www.gale.com/thorndike
www.gale.com/wheeler

To share your comments, please write:

Publisher
Thorndike Press
295 Kennedy Memorial Drive
Waterville, ME 04901